Tranquility Point

Pamela S. Meyers

He who dwells in the shelter of the Most High
will abide in the shadow of the Almighty.
I will say to the Lord, "My refuge and my fortress,
my God, in whom I trust."
—Psalm 91: 1-2 (ESV)

ACKNOWLEDGMENTS

No book is written in a vacuum, and *Tranquility Point* is no exception.

A big thank you goes to my friend and critique partner, Yvonne Anderson, who edited my first draft. More than that, I had no idea she had such a strong knowledge of farming. She set me straight on quite a few things. Like Yvonne did with *Shelter Bay*, she stuck with this story from start to finish, and I have been truly blessed by her expertise.

I am also grateful, as always, for the Lake Geneva Public Library and their provision of microfilms of Lake Geneva's local weekly paper from the time of World War I. The papers gave me a snapshot of what life was like in Lake Geneva from 1916-1918. Also, a huge thank you to the Geneva Lake Museum for their contributions of photos and written materials about home-front Lake Geneva during World War I.

I cannot leave out the many books written about Wisconsin's contributions to the war effort. I learned a lot about my home state that I hadn't known before, such as the neutral stance of Senator LaFollette and how he fought for a long while to try to keep our country out of the fray.

Thanks also to my life group: Judy, Fran, and Betty, as well as my dear friends, Cathi and Ane. I covet the prayers you said for me and your encouragement as I persevered through the writing process.

Thanks to my publisher, Kathy Cretsinger, who consistently shows great faith in me to put out a good story. I love working with Mantle Rock Publishing!

And last but never least, I'm very grateful to my Lord and Savior, Jesus Christ for His providing me with the desire to write and the ability to tell a story that portrays how people of faith deal with life's conflicts and trials.

June 2, 1916

"Hannah Maureen Murphy, what are you doing out here almost naked?"

Hannah continued to dry off her arms. "Oh, Pop, if a woman wants to swim and not just splash around, she can't wear one of those silly dresses. Could you swim in one of those?"

Her father stepped onto the dock and approached her. "No, but that's beside the point." He scooped up her robe from where she'd tossed it and dropped it over her wet body. He reached over and dragged the fabric over a bare shoulder he'd failed to cover.

She had half a mind to shrug off the robe and dive back into the water. Instead, she worked her arms into the sleeves.

By now, his face was as red as a tomato. She lifted her chin. "You can't get me to change my mind."

"Does your mother know you're wearing such a scanty…" He paused as if searching for the right word.

"Yes, I do know, Nate. It's called a swimsuit, and stop being such a fuddy-duddy." Mama came across the dock, her ankle-length skirt lifting in the breeze. "You seem to forget that back when we were courting how I said the very same thing." She smiled at Hannah. "Did you have a nice swim?"

Hannah couldn't stop grinning. "Yes. You can't imagine the freedom of movement. You should get one of these swimsuits, Mama."

"I'm tempted, but you'd best limit your wearing it to our pier only. I'm sure in time, the style will take hold, but at the moment, there are probably more neighbors who agree with your father than us."

Hannah opened her mouth then shut it. Now wasn't the time to debate the issue. But she wasn't a child. She was twenty-two years old, a recent college graduate, and fully grown up. This was 1916, not the 1890s, when her mother had defied her parents and worn bloomers to accommodate her bicycle riding. She'd only heard that story about a hundred times.

She grabbed up her towel from where she'd tossed it on a bench and began working it through her bobbed hair. "I need to get dressed. Charley McGrath and I are meeting Elly Hansen and George Muller for dinner."

"It's nice you're keeping up with the people you've gone to school with all your life," Mama said. "Charley seems like a nice fellow."

"I'm going because the only way I can see Elly these days is if I see George too. To even things out, Elly invited Charley." She stepped past her parents and padded across the dock to the shore. Another no-no she bucked last year. What was wrong with women being barefoot in summer? The only thing better than a swim in Geneva Lake was having the grass tickle your feet on the way to the house.

She circled the spring house. Made to look like a gazebo with pretty flowered pots, it was a comfortable spot where one could sit on a hot summer day and catch a breeze off the lake.

The spring house must have been where Mama had been watching her swim.

Ahead, at the top of the short hill, sat the Queen Anne home her great-grandfather built after the great fire in Chicago. Moderate in size when compared to some of the other homes built on the lakeshore, he called the estate Safe Refuge because the land was precisely that for the family. Instead of heading up the steps to the veranda, she circled to her right and came to a flagstone path that led to the two-story cottage she now called home.

Hannah stepped inside and went directly to the living room window that gave a clear view of the dock and her parents. Her father's stiff posture indicated Mama hadn't yet softened his anger. They rarely argued, and when they did disagree, Pop usually came around to seeing things from her mother's more flexible point of view.

She glanced around the small, cozy room, taking in its casual arts and crafts style, and breathed in the scent of the last of the purple hyacinths Mama had picked that morning and placed on the hearth. Their sweet fragrance would disappear by tomorrow. If only she had time to linger and enjoy the room and the novel she'd recently begun reading, but she had that dinner date.

Thankfully, she and Charley were not dining alone. Otherwise, she'd be bored listening to him go on and on about the way the Socialist party in Wisconsin was growing stronger and needed to be stopped. She agreed with most of what he said, but that didn't mean it was all she wanted to talk about over dinner.

A few hours later, Hannah, wearing a soft yellow, linen dress she'd updated with a wide Roman-style belt, and Charley, looking dapper in a navy, pin-striped suit, stepped into the Geneva Café, a small eatery on Main Street, and joined Elly and George at their table.

Ellie grinned, "I love your hair, Hannah. I wish I had the nerve to bob mine." She patted her dark blond up-do.

"You should do it, El. You won't go back to waist-long hair again."

Charley's gaze swept around the table. "Now that we've all graduated from college, what's next on your agendas? I know Hannah is heading to law school at the university in the fall, and I'm starting my new job in a few weeks. What about you, George? You graduated before the rest of us. What have you been up to?"

George shook his head. "I had to drop out for a couple of years. I graduated two weeks ago and have a new job at a bank in Milwaukee."

Elly grinned. "I've been hired to teach third grade at a grammar school in Milwaukee." She smiled lovingly at George. "Why don't you tell them our news, dear?"

Hannah frowned. Dear? Our news?

George grinned as if he'd just won a million dollars. "I asked Elly to marry me, and we'll be getting married over Thanksgiving."

Elly pulled a glove off her left hand and held it up. A small diamond glittered from her ring finger. "He asked me the day I graduated from teacher's college."

Hannah forced a smile as a sense of loss washed over her. What happened to those talks she and Elly had about their futures? Elly hoped to become a teacher then possibly a school principal while Hannah's job as a lawyer would lead to perhaps becoming a district attorney. They had no time for marriage and children until they reached their goals. She took Elly's hand and pulled it closer to study the gem. "I'm so happy for you both, but I had no idea..."

"That we were a couple?" George asked. "We ran into each other over Christmas break and started going out. Much of our courting was done through letters except for a couple of times when we were both home for the weekend. We can't wait to set up housekeeping in Milwaukee. That is unless the U.S. decides to join the fighting over in Europe. I couldn't believe how much grief I received during my interview for my bank job."

Charley frowned. "Grief? How so?"

"My German last name. Was I sympathetic to the Kaiser? Do I have thoughts about joining the German army? I've never been to Germany in my life. My grandparents immigrated and settled in Chicago, and my parents moved to Lake Geneva when Dad got a job with the bank."

"But the U.S. is neutral, so why the fuss?" Hannah asked.

George shrugged. "Many Germans who immigrated to the U.S. in the past decade or so have returned to Germany to join up. Thankfully, the bosses at the bank believed me, and I start in two weeks. I'm currently looking for a flat or small house to rent for us." He took Elly's hand and smiled at her.

Charley leaned back in his chair. "Better make sure the rental agreement has a clause that if the U.S. joins the war and you're drafted, you can break the lease. I did that before I rented my apartment in Chicago after Crane hired me."

George stared at him. "Crane? As in the same Crane that owns Jerseyhurst on the lakeshore?"

"One and the same."

As the men talked, Hannah's thoughts of spending the summer with her town friends disintegrated. Between marriage, jobs, and the war that was so far away, it seemed nothing would ever be the same again. Would it be any different tomorrow when she got together with her lakeshore friends?

CHAPTER TWO

A loud *ahooga* sounded from the circular driveway, and Hannah gathered up her teacup from the kitchen table. "There are the girls. Don't wait dinner on me, Mama. I have no idea when I'll be back, and there should be plenty to eat at the Bauers'."

Mama laughed. "I don't know why you bother to sleep in the cottage when you're here for all your meals."

"I'd be existing on peanut butter sandwiches if I didn't eat here. I did enough of that during college. Besides, I'd miss my family if I stayed over there all the time." She came to her mother and hugged her from behind with one arm as she set her cup next to the sink. The horn sounded again and she hurried to the outside door and waved at the three women sitting in the Studebaker convertible. "I'll be right out."

"That's a nice automobile. Where did Bertie get the money to pay for that?"

Hannah startled and faced her mother, who'd managed to come up behind her without making a sound. "You know most of my lakeshore friends' parents have several cars nowadays for their older children to use. That way, they don't have to be always driving them to town from the other side of the lake."

"Well, you and your sisters are fortunate you've always lived in or near town and don't need to depend on others to drive you places. From here, you can walk the shore path or bicycle."

"Bicycle like you did when you were my age and wore those bloomers?" She tried unsuccessfully to stifle a snicker.

"Don't start teasing me about my bloomers. I was the first woman in Lake Geneva to wear them."

Hannah grinned. "And like you, I'm the first woman to wear a practical swimsuit." She stepped over to the hall tree and picked up a cloth tote.

Her mother eyed the bag. "You don't have that new swimsuit in there, do you?"

"What made you say that? Pop ordered me not to wear it anywhere but here, didn't he?"

"Yes. But I know you too well, my darling daughter." She reached for the bag, but Hannah stepped back with a grin before Mama could grab hold of it.

"Can't keep them waiting." She opened the door and scurried toward the convertible. As she climbed in the back seat next to Janie Benson, her mother's shouted answer was lost in the wind. "Let's go, ladies. It's going to be a beautiful day."

They pulled out onto the state road and headed west. Hannah leaned her head back as the wind whipped her hair around. A year ago, she would have worn a hat and held it on her head with her hand to keep her up-do in place. This was freedom, and she loved it. Janie Oliver leaned over and peeked in Hannah's tote. "Did you bring it?"

Hannah scowled and pulled her bag away from Janie's snooping eyes. "Bring what?"

"You know. The swimsuit."

"Of course, I brought it. We're going to swim today, aren't

we? I had to hide it at the bottom of my bag and hope Mama didn't decide to peek."

Suzanne Wilson turned in the front passenger seat and peered over the seatback. "You brought the suit, but that doesn't mean you'll wear it in mixed company."

Hannah raised her chin. "Who says? Everything that should be covered is covered. Wait until you get one of your own. Wear it once, and you'll never go back to those swim dresses."

"I bet you'll chicken out." Suzanne faced the front of the car again.

"I bet I won't." Hannah crossed her arms and stared out at the passing landscape. She'd thrown the suit into her tote but hadn't yet made up her mind if she would put it on. The men invited to the gathering had never seen her bare legs. Maybe she should have brought the swim dress.

Bertie made a turn toward Williams Bay followed by another turn down a tree-lined road toward the lake and Tranquility Point, the Bauers' estate on the eastern shore of Williams Bay. Hannah had been to the large, white frame home several times but had always approached it by boat.

"I wonder what Ted Bauer looks like these days. Have any of you seen him since he went off to boarding school?" Bertie asked.

"He's probably overweight," Suzanne said. "College food is fattening, and I imagine boarding school food is as well."

Janie sighed. "And here I am skinny Minnie. I could use a few pounds."

Suzanne chuckled. "If I could, I'd give you mine."

They stared at her. Suzanne was anything but overweight.

"We're here." Bertie guided the car between a pair of stone pillars and down a gravel drive past flowerbeds of beautiful pink and white petunias and a lush, green lawn. She pulled up behind a shiny blue Buick roadster parked in front of a stone path that led to the home's door. "We're not the first to arrive. I don't recognize the car, do you?"

Hannah craned her neck from the back seat. "I don't either, but with people returning to the lake, I'm sure we'll be seeing a lot of new vehicles around."

The roadster's driver door opened, and a tall, dark blond, broad-shouldered man climbed out, wearing golf knickers and an open-collared shirt that did little to disguise his muscular arms. He leaned into the backseat and lifted out a golf bag, then faced the Studebaker and narrowed his gaze. He slung the bag of clubs over his shoulder and stepped toward them.

Hannah let out the breath she was holding. "Oh, my word, it's Ted Bauer. And he's anything but overweight."

CHAPTER THREE

*T*ed Bauer approached the red convertible. Seeing the carful of his childhood friends all grown up, he immediately regretted his decision to spend his summers out east with Yale's rowing team. When he'd left for boarding school in ninth grade, his lake friends had all been kids, but not anymore. He let his gaze settle first on the blond behind the wheel. The only blond he remembered was Bertie Drummond, but she had a face full of freckles back then, not the creamy complexion he saw now.

The brunette in the front passenger seat he didn't recognize but wouldn't mind getting more acquainted. The curly-haired gal in the back seat had to be Janie Oliver, but he'd refrain calling her by name until he could be sure. He let his gaze travel to the last of the girls. Her dark reddish-brown hair cut in a stylish bob like women wore these days could only belong to Hannah Murphy. His eighth-grade crush. She was cute when she was in sixth grade but now was positively stunning.

He grinned. "You must be Hannah."

She startled. "How did you know? I don't look anything like the girl you knew when you were last in Lake Geneva."

He chuckled. "You're the only girl I've ever known with green eyes like yours and hair the color of mahogany. Good to see you again."

"Good to see you too." She ran her gaze over his frame. "You look like all that schooling wasn't spent behind a desk."

"Four years on the Yale rowing team are to blame." He pulled his gaze away, suddenly feeling as tongue-tied as he'd been when he was thirteen and wanting in the worst way to invite her over for a swim. He ran his gaze over their faces. "Thanks for coming, ladies. I hope you brought swimwear. The water is perfect." He caught Hannah's gaze in his own. "That's where I'm headed next. There's a changing room inside the walkout on the lower level. You can reach it by going around at the front of the house." He turned and headed toward the back door. When his mother suggested he invite his former summer gang over for a gathering, he thought no one would come. Was he ever wrong.

THE WOMEN FOLLOWED the flagstone pathway around the house. As with most of the homes on the lakeshore, the front of the house faced the lake. Hannah hugged her tote bag to her chest as she walked. With one look into Ted Bauer's dark-brown eyes, her confidence about wearing her new swimsuit disintegrated. The last she wanted was for him or any man she was interested in to think her brazen.

"Hannah, you'd better hurry. After the way Ted invited you to swim, you better get changed."

Hannah snapped out of her reverie. She hadn't realized the girls were several paces ahead. "He invited all of us."

"Not the way I saw it," Janie said. "He only had eyes for you."

She looked at Janie. "I'm not sure I'm going to swim today."

"Of course, you are." Janie looped arms with Hannah and pulled her along to the door.

The door to the changing room closed behind them, and Bertie drew her swim dress from her bag and began to slip out of her skirt.

Hannah dropped into a chair. "It was much easier to wear the suit on my own dock when it was only me. If one of you had one similar, I'd feel much better."

Suzanne tossed her bag into a chair and faced Hannah, her arms akimbo on her hips. "Where did your courage go, Miss Murphy? You were the first to bob your hair and one of the first women to apply to the university law school. Don't stop now."

She shrugged. "I don't know."

"My guess is your courage disappeared as soon as Mr. Brown Eyes took notice of you, and you realized he still has that school-boy crush on you. Why don't you put the suit on and let us be the judge? If you're showing too much skin, we'll tell you."

She quirked her head. "What do you mean, school-boy crush?"

Bertie laughed. "You don't remember how he followed you around that summer before he went off to boarding school? He was gangly and pimply, and you were cute and athletic."

Memories of winning the girls' tennis tournament that year flowed into her thoughts, and she laughed. I had forgotten. But he was older and already going into high school. I didn't notice anything that indicated he feels that way now."

"Oh, it was nothing like that today," Janie said. "But, he did have a funny expression when he looked at you."

Hannah waved her hand. "He was only trying to decide who I was. Your offer to judge how I look in the suit sounds reasonable. But I don't know."

"I think it's a great idea," Janie chimed in. She darted to the door and turned the lock. "We'll be the only ones to see it unless you decide to be brave."

Suzanne picked up Hannah's bag and pulled out the navy-blue garment. She held it up. "Looks modest enough for me. Come on, show us how it looks."

Hannah began unbuttoning her blouse. The only people who'd seen her in it were her parents, and Pop made it clear what he thought. She really needed the opinion of her friends. She grabbed the suit out of Suzanne's hand and slipped behind a folding screen.

On the other side of the partition, rustling noises indicated the others were changing into their swim costumes. She quickly removed her clothes, stepped into the suit, and tugged it up.

After arranging the straps on her shoulders to assure the fabric was exactly where it belonged, she called out, "Okay, girls. I'm ready." Without waiting for an answer, she stepped around the screen and spun. "What do you think?" She looked from Janie, who wore a one-piece black dress and long black stockings to Suzanne, whose swim dress was several inches shorter than Janie's, but accessorized by the same dark stockings. Over in the corner, with her back to the others, Bertie struggled at pulling on her stockings.

After several moments of silence, Hannah let out a sigh. "You all hate it."

Suzanne rushed over. "No, we don't. At least I don't. I love it and am jealous I don't have one myself."

"I love it too." Janie gripped her skirt. "I wish I had a pair of scissors. I'd cut off at least six inches off this thing."

By then, Bertie had given up on pulling up her stockings. "What I love is that you aren't wearing these infuriating things. She worked the legwear off her ankles and stuffed it all into her bag. I'm going without."

"Good idea." Suzanne began peeling hers off. "At least we can show support for you, Hannah, by going barelegged."

Janie removed one of her stockings and started on the other. "I heard one of the razor companies is designing a razor for women."

"To shave what?" Hannah carried her bag over to a table and set it down. "Last I looked, none of us have beards."

"Underarms and legs. They're saying it's for a smooth look. But the ads don't say legs as if it's off-color to mention the fact that women do have them."

Hannah frowned. "What do we call them then?"

Janie shrugged. "I don't know. Silly, isn't it?"

Hannah grabbed one of the large towels set out for guests and draped it over her shoulders. "I should've thought to bring something to wear over my suit until I get to the dock. I guess this towel will do."

Suzanne waved a hand. "You look fine."

Loud pounding came at the door. "Hey, there are people out here who need to change too. No time for a gabfest in there."

At the male voice, they looked at each other. Janie went to the door and opened it. Several of the men they'd grown up with during summers at the lake stood hands on hips and glaring at them until their gazes landed on Hannah. One of them let out a low whistle.

"Why, Hannah Murphy, you have legs!"

Her face heated, but she didn't shrink back. "I sure do, and so does every one of us." She stepped aside, and the others each stuck out a bare leg.

Loud laughter erupted as the men stepped back to let the women pass by. Outside, the girls burst into giggles. Hannah glanced across the lawn toward the dock, and her giggles faded. Instead of the usual man's swim shirt with short sleeves, Ted Bauer's scoop-necked, royal blue sleeveless top accentuated every inch of his muscular shoulders and arms.

He turned his head before she could look away and waved. "Come on down. The water is perfect."

Behind her, Janie whispered, "He's not the wimpy kid who went off to boarding school. I think that's the Yale school colors he's wearing."

Hannah clutched her towel, where it met under her chin. "Seems I'm not the only fashion setter today." She started across the grass, loving the feel of the freshly mowed lawn against her bare feet.

A wide grin split Ted's handsome face as she approached. "It looks like you intend to do some serious swimming."

She nodded. "I decided if I wanted to swim for exercise, I needed to wear what the athletes wear." She glanced at his muscular arms and quickly pulled her gaze away. "Is that the same reason for no sleeves for you?"

"Pretty much. This is the uniform I wore on the Yale rowing team. Sleeves get in the way when you're rowing. It works well for swimming too." He glanced past her shoulder. "Looks like you've started a trend with your friends."

She quirked her head. "I don't understand."

"They've all ditched their stockings."

"We couldn't let Hannah get all the fun." Suzanne came up next to Hannah and ran her gaze over Ted from his head to his feet. "Nor you either." Her words came out sounding like a purr.

Hannah fought the urge to push her off the pier. Not a very nice thought, since Suzanne didn't know how to swim. Behind them, men's voices sounded, and soon the guys they'd had to vacate the changing room for walked up, all but one wearing short-sleeved shirts. The one who dared to wear a shirt like Ted's looked woefully lacking in muscles. There was something to be said about the older style suits.

She tossed her towel onto a bench, moved to the edge of the pier and dove. The cool, spring-fed water had a bite to it, but as soon as she began to glide through the water, using the crawl, the chill dissolved into something refreshing. She switched to the breaststroke, bringing her legs up to her body then down. A stroke she could never do well with skirt fabric trying to wrap itself around her legs.

Off to her left, Ted glided past, doing the same stroke. He

paused and treaded water while waiting for her to catch up. "Want to race back to the dock?"

She laughed and began treading water several feet from him, noticing for the first time how the sun illuminated the gold flecks in his otherwise dark brown eyes. "I think you already beat me. How long did it take you to catch up?"

"Not long. Don't feel bad. I've been swimming laps at the university pool."

"That's what I need to start doing. Why don't we ease our way back to the others and talk along the way? You were ahead of me in school. I assume you graduated from Yale two years ago. What are you doing now?"

He began a side stroke toward the dock. "I just finished my second year of law school at Northwestern. I'm living in Chicago a few blocks from Northwestern's law school building. What are you doing with your life?"

"I graduated from the University of Wisconsin last month and am starting law school at UW in the fall."

He stopped swimming and grinned. "Really? It sounds like we have more in common than Geneva Lake. How would you like to have dinner with me tomorrow night?"

Butterflies she hadn't felt since her last semi-serious relationship two years ago erupted in her stomach. "I'd like that. I'm working in my father's office from one to five tomorrow, but I'm available any time after six."

He grinned and flicked his fingers in the water, sending a splash her direction. "Sounds good. I'll pick you up at Safe Refuge at six-thirty. That is where you're living now. Right?"

"Yes, we moved from our house on Main Street two years ago after my grandfather died." She returned his splash. "Bet you can't catch me." She dove underwater and swam toward the dock until he grabbed her feet and pulled her in a circle through the water. He let go and placed his hands on her waist and lifted her out of the water.

He laughed. "Looks like I caught me a fish. Best I throw her back in. As much as I'd like to keep her." He tossed her several feet away, and she dropped into the lake.

She hadn't had this much fun since she was little when Pop would toss her around. She popped her head out of the water and giggled. "What if the fish doesn't want to be thrown back in?"

His eyes rounded, and he swam over and grabbed her by the feet and pulled her toward him. "Then he'll have to keep her."

She wanted to say she would like that, but she held her tongue. She hardly knew the man, but he was already working himself into her heart. It was happening too fast. They had all summer to get to know each other before they'd be heading off to different schools. Did she want a long-distance romance as Elly had?

Shouts and laughter from the dock rode the wind, and she glanced over. Janie waved. "They're setting out food for us on the porch."

She glanced at Ted. "Sounds like playtime is over." She dove under the water and swam toward the dock, not popping up until she was only feet from the ladder. Ted came up beside her. "I like a girl that isn't afraid to be athletic. Save me a seat next to you on the porch."

"Okay." She scooted up the ladder and quickly towel-dried her hair, grateful she was born with wavy hair and not straight like Pop's or curly like Mama's. The bob would soon dry in place. No fuss. She draped the damp towel over her shoulders and joined Bertie as they walked up the lawn toward the house.

"A word to the wise," Bertie whispered.

Hannah frowned at her friend. "What do you mean?"

"Miss Suzanne is aiming to horn in on whatever you've started out there with Ted. She's already scheming how she's going to get a new swimsuit like yours and invite him to her house for a swim."

Hannah rolled her eyes. "I don't have a hold on him, but we have a date for tomorrow night. Bertie, something clicked between us out there. I'm not sure if I imagined it or if he felt the same."

"Well, he asked you for a date. Something must have happened."

"Agreed." She had no time for childish games. If Ted turned out to be the man God had for her, it would happen, and no one, including Suzanne, could stop it.

After changing out of her wet swimsuit into the cotton skirt and white blouse she wore from home, she stepped out onto the lawn and scanned the crowd. Ted Bauer's height made him easy to spot, and Suzanne's flouncy hat with its flowered adornment couldn't be missed either. The girl had obviously made up her mind to fish before the newest addition in the pond could be hooked by someone else.

She drew in a deep breath and strode across the grass toward the pair, grateful she'd worn her flat shoes rather than the heels she preferred. So much easier for walking on grass if she had to wear shoes.

A wide grin filled Ted's face as she approached. "There's the girl I've been looking for. Did you save us a couple of seats?"

Hannah shook her head. "I just finished changing and didn't have a chance." He ran his gaze over her frame with a look of appreciation then glanced at Suzanne. "Nice to meet you, Suzanne. I need to finish a conversation Hannah and I began earlier."

Before Suzanne could close her dropped jaw, Ted offered Hannah his elbow. "Let's claim seats on the veranda before heading to the buffet."

After Ted laid his jacket across two cushions on a small rattan sofa, they filled their plates then returned to the sofa where they sat side by side.

Ted bit into a fried chicken leg. He chewed, and swallowed. then grinned at Hannah.

She resisted the urge to wipe a drizzle from his chin and laughed. "By the look on your face it appears I'm going to enjoy this meal."

He wiped his chin with his napkin. "It's no secret I love a plate of good fried chicken. I'm impressed you want to become a lawyer, but what made you decide on the University of Wisconsin law school?"

She shrugged and nibbled at a chicken leg. "Familiarity, mostly. UW's law school also seemed to be the most open to accepting women. Not all law schools are created equal."

He nodded. "I get that, but did you know Northwestern already has several women enrolled? It's an excellent school. Why don't you apply? There are still open slots for the fall."

The man was moving fast. Normally she'd run the other way, but with Ted she liked it. She laughed. "That's a new way to woo a girl."

"Me? Woo a girl?" He waved a raw carrot stick in the air like a baton, "Never happen." He munched on the carrot. "But I am enjoying your company, and if we were attending the same school, it would mean not having to go our separate ways at the end of summer. I only have one more year before I graduate, but what with the way things are happening in Europe these days, who knows what the next year will bring."

"Do you think the U.S. will join the war? Wilson seems set on keeping us out of it."

"He does, but the government has an eye on my father's company. It used to be a part of a larger one that is in Germany, and business has slowed down a lot since the Brits got into the mess. My father has never become a naturalized citizen, and I've noticed some discrimination around here, but not like it is in the city. Before I left school for the summer, they asked if I intend to go overseas and fight with the Germans since that's my home country. I tell them again, and again I'm an American, born and raised, and I do not support the Kaiser."

"I had no idea it was so bad. What about your mother, Ted?"

"She was born in Chicago. Her mother came here as a child, and when her parents became citizens, she automatically did too."

Ted took a bite of baked beans. "Enough of this war talk. I'm feeling bad about how we gave Suzanne the slip. What do you say we find her and make sure she's okay?"

A warm feeling washed over her. The man's concern for her friend ratcheted up his appeal a few more notches. The summer was definitely looking up.

CHAPTER FOUR

Two Months Later

A knock came at the cottage door as Hannah slipped on her favorite cardigan sweater, a light-weight summer knit. She wasn't to meet Ted at the Safe Refuge dock for another ten minutes. It must be Mama. She opened the door, laughing. "Yes, we'll be careful on the boat at …" She lifted her gaze a couple of feet higher.

Ted grinned down at her, his mesmerizing dark eyes leaving her almost speechless. "I apologize for being early. My parents are using the boat to visit a friend on the south shore, so I drove over in my father's new Overland. It's a dream to drive, so I hope you don't mind."

Grateful she'd managed to gather herself, she offered him a smile. "I was looking forward to one of our glorious sunsets out on the water, but we can do the same in a convertible. Right?"

He answered with another grin and a kiss on her cheek. "There's a girl after my own heart."

She snagged a hat from the hall tree and tilted her head. "Are you saying I haven't been in your heart until now?"

He leaned down and kissed her on the mouth. "Only a figure of speech. You know you've been in my heart all summer long."

"As you have been in mine. Take me to this car you're so excited about." She stepped through the door and came to a stop. "Uh, oh."

He came up beside her and chuckled. "Looks like our transportation has garnered some attention."

"You can interpret their taking liberties as a compliment. To them, you are a member of the family, and what's yours is theirs. They know better than to get into vehicles that don't belong to us."

They walked up on Hannah's little sisters, who were so involved in their pretend ride they hadn't noticed they were no longer alone. Hannah tugged on the younger one's braids.

Annie stopped mid-laugh and stared up at her big sister. "Margie, you're in trouble now."

Margie turned and stared up at Ted. "Hi, Ted. We knew it was your car because we saw you drive in."

He crossed his arms and affected a stern expression. "I did drive it here, but it's not my car, and if my father knew two little girls were playing with his expensive automobile, he wouldn't be happy. Next time ask first."

The girls nodded and looked down as if on cue. "I'm sorry," Margie said. "It was my idea. Annie just came along like always. Right, Annie?"

Annie raised her head. "Right about what? Being sorry or always coming along?"

Hannah swallowed a laugh and looked at Ted. "What do you think? Are you ready to forgive them?"

"I think so. Maybe next time, I'll take you two for a ride."

"Not today?" Annie asked.

Hannah rolled her eyes. "No, because we have dinner plans."

The girl's lower lip pushed out like a tiny shelf. "Not even a little ride?"

"Not even." Hannah waved them away. If she didn't soon let Ted know about her surprise, she'd burst, and she wanted to tell him in private. "Now, get in the house, both of you."

Ted pulled out his pocket watch and checked it. "I think we have time for a short ride. Go on. Get in the car."

The girls giggled and scrambled into the back seat while he leaned toward Hannah and whispered. "The look on your face says I overstepped."

"No. I'm just not used to my men friends paying my kid sisters any mind."

"Glad I'm the first one." He winked and waited for her to slide onto the front passenger seat and shut the door, then whispered in her ear. "And I hope I'm the last."

Butterflies erupted in her stomach. If they'd been alone, she'd have hugged him right there. Maybe even kissed him.

Ted made his way around the front of the car to his door and slid behind the wheel. He glanced over his shoulder. "Now you hold on tight back there. I don't want you flying out when we take the curves. I'd hate to have you fall into the grass where the snakes are."

"Snakes?" Margie screeched the word.

"Why do you think they call it Snake Road?"

"Because of all the curves?" Annie's voice quivered.

"That's what they want us to believe, but I know better." Ted glanced at Hannah and winked.

"I think Mama will be calling us in for dinner any minute." Margie opened the car door. "Let's go, Annie."

The girls climbed out, slamming the door behind them, and ran toward the big house.

Hannah burst out laughing. "That was brilliant. Sometimes little sisters can be a pain."

He started the car and put it in gear. "And I have the opposite problem being the youngest."

She frowned as he pressed on the gas and drove down the

lane to the exit. "I don't understand. Annie is spoiled rotten by my parents."

"Maybe it's different with boys. I was often left out of Peter's fun—or so it seemed. I guess you wouldn't know that with only girls in your family."

She sighed. "I had a younger brother named Rory."

He glanced at her. "Had? You never told me about him before."

"I don't mention him often. He was born three years after me, but came early and died before he'd lived a day. I was too young to understand, but I remember being confused at how he could appear so perfect and not live. My father explained because he was premature, his lungs weren't developed enough. But being a doctor, he still took it hard that he couldn't prevent him from passing."

"That must have been a difficult time. I'm sorry." He turned onto Snake Road and soon they were inside Lake Geneva's city limits and driving past the lake. A lone sailboat skimmed across the water, and she stifled a sigh. If she didn't tell him her surprise soon, it would have to wait until later.

"Summer is quickly coming to an end, and soon the boats will be gone," Ted said. "Are you sad to see the warm weather end?"

"Yes and no. This has been one of my best summers, thanks to you." She reached over and squeezed his hand as it rested on the gearshift.

"He turned his hand over and wove their fingers together. "I agree. It's been a bright spot in an otherwise difficult time for my family."

She frowned. "Because of the war? I thought things had calmed for your father."

He let go of her hand and gripped the wheel so hard his knuckles turned white. "There's chatter that if the U.S. gets into the war, the German immigrants who were never naturalized will be deported. As I told you before, my dad never became a U.S. citizen. The harassment toward those like him is heating up."

"I'd better read the news more often. I had no idea."

"It's not talked about much." At the town's main intersection, he turned right on Broad Street then into a parking space in front of the Geneva Hotel. "Let's talk about something more pleasant." He cut the motor and angled in his seat to face her. I'm glad we're finally going to eat here. We've been saying all summer we wanted to."

She gave herself a moment to redirect her thoughts. "My parents ate here a few weeks ago and said it's quite nice. But we have at least a month before school begins. Why the hurry?"

He shrugged. "It seemed like a good time." He leaned over and kissed her. "You are very special, Hannah Murphy." He drew in a breath and let it out. "I'd better put the top up before we go inside." He climbed out of the vehicle and began fiddling with something behind the back seat. The folded top popped up, and he maneuvered the canvas covering into a position where it met the top of the windshield and snapped it in place.

Pushing away her sense of something being wrong, she noted what he did and snapped the covering in place on her side. "Is there anything else to be done?"

He grinned his approval. "Only to roll up your windows, and I'll do the same over here." His task finished, he came around and held out his hand. "Ready?"

He kept hold of her hand after she exited the car and wove their fingers together. "Have you noticed how well our hands fit together? It must be a good sign."

"I was thinking the same thing."

"As you said, this summer has been beyond wonderful. I wish it hadn't gone so fast."

Her stomach dipped. They'd seen each other almost every night since the swimming party. Despite her mother's strong cautionary warnings that summer romances often faded with the autumn leaves, she was falling in love.

They reached the door to the hotel, went down some steps, and followed an arrow that indicated the way to the dining room. As they walked through an open-air gallery, Ted gestured toward the view. "Frank Lloyd Wright was very wise to design this so the lagoon over there is visible. And you can also see the lake off to the right. There is no more stunning view of Geneva Lake than from right here. Why would anyone want to live anywhere else?"

Surprised at the emotion in his voice, she couldn't help but sense something was up. "You're certainly melancholy this evening. Is everything okay?"

"How could it not be with my girl beside me and a beautiful evening ahead. I'm a blessed man." He squeezed her hand and bent to kiss her cheek.

They came to what was called the lower lobby, and Hannah let go of Ted's hand and strode toward the massive fireplace, its design shaped like the setting sun.

He came up beside her. "Unique, isn't it?"

"Yes. It's very fitting for this room."

"Agreed. I think the dining room is over there." Ted pointed to a door off to the side of the fireplace and offered her his elbow. "Shall we?"

They stepped into a spacious, dimly-lit room filled with cloth-covered tables and cushioned rattan chairs. Ted announced their arrival to the maître d', who led them to a corner table near several tall potted palms, giving a sense of privacy. The host moved a chair away from the table and nodded at Hannah. She sat as Ted sat in the chair at a right angle to her.

After the man left, she chuckled. "I think you upset his plan by you not sitting across from me."

"I don't care. I don't want to have to talk to you across the table."

She glanced around at what she was able to see of the spacious dining room and noted several tables of couples and a few larger groups. "The town needed something like this."

"I don't know why we waited so long to come here. Would you like to order drinks before we look at the menu?"

She nodded. "Iced tea would be perfect."

A waiter arrived and handed Ted their menus. He ordered two iced teas then gave Hannah the night's bill-of-fare. "I've heard the fried chicken is wonderful. You know me and fried chicken, but feel free to order whatever you want."

She set the menu down. "You're not the only one who loves fried chicken.

The waiter returned with their teas, and Ted ordered two chicken dinners. After the waiter left, she took a deep breath. There was no time like the present to spring her surprise on him.

"Hannah, I've heard several stories about how Safe Refuge got its name. Is it bad manners to ask you which is correct?"

"Why would it be bad manners? I've always thought it was because the Great Fire destroyed my great grandfather's properties, but something my Aunt Katie said once led me to think it was something else. When I asked for more details though, she clammed up."

He pursed his lips. "Hmmm. Nothing more intriguing than a family secret."

"I know, and I have a feeling Safe Refuge has a lot of them. Do you know of any Bauer family secrets?"

He looked off. "I'm sure there are plenty, but I've often wondered why my father never became a U.S. citizen, even after he bought Bauer Pharmaceuticals from the German parent company."

"That sounds intriguing. Change of subject. There's something—"

"Ah, here comes our dinners. We are in for a treat."

A young man placed a plate of steaming fried chicken in front of Hannah and then one in front of Ted. The aroma of chicken and spices wafted to her nose, and her stomach growled.

Ted took her hand. "I'll say the blessing."

She leaned toward him to hear his lowered voice thank God for the food. At his "Amen," she raised her head and picked up her fork. Her surprise would have to wait.

They ate in companionable silence except to agree the meal had lived up to its reputation.

The waiter appeared and took their orders for dessert and coffee. As soon as they were delivered, she'd tell him her surprise, confident that her news would lift his spirits.

After the waiter had poured cream into Hannah's coffee and departed, Ted stabbed his spoon into his chocolate sundae and looked her in the eyes, "There's something I need to tell you."

She grinned. "And I have something to tell you too. Can I go first?"

He leaned against his chair back. "By your smile, it must be something good. Go ahead."

"You'll be happy to know I took your advice and applied to Northwestern's law school. I received my acceptance in the mail yesterday."

Lines formed between his eyes. "I wish you hadn't done that."

A sinking feeling washed over her. Had she misread his feelings? But he had tried to convince her to transfer to Northwestern earlier in the summer. Her eyes searched his concerned face. "I thought that's what you wanted."

He plucked his spoon from his ice cream and sighed. "I do want you at Northwestern … I mean, I did. The problem is that come fall, I won't be there." He glanced at his lap then looked up and blinked his watery eyes. "I was waiting until our meal was over to tell you. I'm leaving for England in a couple of days to join their military and fight the Germans."

She gaped at him. She couldn't have heard it right. "Why? You're an American."

"I know, but I'm sick and tired of people thinking my family is rooting for the Germans. Maybe if I do that, the harassment toward my father will lighten up. My brother can't go because he's being trained to take over the company should our father be deported. My dad hates what his former country is doing and that his nephews are in the German army."

"You still have relatives there?"

"Yes. I've only met my cousins once when I was a boy, and we traveled to Germany so Peter and I could meet our grandparents. One good that came out of the trip was after hearing my father speak German the whole time we were there, I wanted to learn the language and asked my dad to speak only in German around me. That's my ticket to getting into the British army. They need translators."

Thoughts whirled in her head. "What about your clerk job at the law office?"

"I told them a month ago I might have to leave earlier."

She gripped her napkin and twisted it into a rope then released it. Nothing like being left out. "Why didn't you tell me this before?"

"We were having so much fun, and I didn't want to put a dampener on it. Nothing was certain until yesterday. The same day you were accepted to Northwestern. My leaving is why we came to the Geneva Hotel tonight. I won't be here to finish off the summer with you. I hope you haven't already withdrawn from the other law school."

Feeling as if he'd delivered a sucker punch to her gut, she blinked at her tears. Didn't she count enough in his life that he'd make such a decision without warning her? "I notified them this morning that I've chosen another school. Northwestern is actually better for me because I can live at my cousin's in Evanston and save money that way."

"But the law school is located in downtown Chicago, not Evanston."

"Cora only lives a block from the streetcar that can take me directly to the Chicago campus." She took his hand. "Aren't you afraid of coming face to face with your cousins in a battle?"

If I'm used as a translator, I won't be on the front line. I'm also boning up on code-breaking. It's not translating German, but that background may help. The code breakers are all stationed in London." A wistful expression took over his face. "If I had my druthers, I'd be applying for flight school in hopes of being assigned to the Royal Flying Corps."

She gaped at him. "That doesn't sound safe."

His eyes twinkled. "I've dreamed of flying ever since the Wright brothers got the first aircraft off the ground when I was a kid. I even traveled down to Florida a couple of years ago and flew on a passenger airplane from St. Petersburg to Tampa." A wide grin filled his features. "It was bumpy and short, but, Hannah, I loved every minute of it. If I can't get into the Royal Flying Corps, I plan to learn how to fly as soon as the war is over. And finish law school, too, of course."

Hannah lifted her glass to her lips then, realizing it was empty, set it down. "I've always thought of myself as rather fearless, unafraid of bucking society, and campaigning for the women's right to vote. But I prefer my feet being on the ground."

He gripped her hand and squeezed it, sending a shiver up her arm. "I don't expect you to understand, or anyone else for that matter. That's why I've never told my parents about my dreams of being a pilot. So, please, no mentions of it to them."

She offered him a slight smile. "I do understand about

dreams. Back in high school, I told my mother about my dream to be a lawyer, and she never said I was crazy, that women don't become lawyers. She told me when she was young, she wanted to be a private detective, and she was going to apply to Pinkertons where they already had lady detectives."

His lips curved upward. "I love it, but what happened? Did she not get the job?"

"She came down with smallpox and met my dad when he was her doctor. She went to nursing school instead. They worked together in his office for many years. I come from a long line of trailblazing women, but that doesn't mean I can't fear for your safety. We only met a couple of months ago, and already I care for you a great deal. I don't want to lose you." She blinked at the growing moisture in her eyes.

His Adam's apple bobbed. "Oh, Hannah, I care a great deal for you too. I need to do this to show my family doesn't support the Germans. I never dreamed you'd move on the idea of switching to Northwestern this fast."

"I wanted to be sure to get in this fall since it was supposed to be your final year there. Is there any chance of you delaying your plans?"

"No. I already gave the British army a letter of intention, and I'm ordered to leave for New York on the train Thursday morning. My ship sails on Saturday."

The first man she'd ever felt this way about, and now he was leaving to go to war. She took a handkerchief from her purse and dabbed her eyes."

He brushed his fingertips along her cheek. "Please forgive me not preparing you better for this. As short a time as we've been seeing each other, I'm falling hard for you, Hannah. I have no right to ask, but please say you'll wait for me."

She turned away. "When I was a child, I begged for a puppy. And finally, we got a puppy. When I wasn't in school, I was with him, and every day I fell more and more in love with him. He even slept on my bed at night. Then my mother learned the hives she had been getting for the past several months were because she was allergic to dogs. They warned me the puppy had to leave, but I refused to believe it. One day, I came home from school, and the puppy had gone to live with someone else. My heart broke in a million pieces. I eventually got over the hurt, but I missed my puppy for a much longer time."

He lifted her hand to his lips and kissed it. "And now I'm that puppy. Let's get out of here." He dropped a couple of bills on top of the check the waiter had left.

They scurried through the restaurant into the lobby and stepped outside. Off to the west, a fading red and orange sky greeted them.

He draped his arm over her shoulders and tugged her to his side. "Looks like we missed the sunset."

She cast about for a response and came up empty. Right then, the sunset was the last thing on her mind.

After they were seated in the car, he stretched his arm around her waist and tugged her closer until they were face to face. She slipped her arm around him as his mouth found hers. Every ounce of her melted at his touch. He pulled away and cradled her face with his hands, looking at her in the dim light. He kissed her again, letting it linger.

He moaned then leaned back until they were eye to eye. "I bet that puppy didn't kiss you like that."

She allowed him a small smile. "Not a chance."

He chuckled. "It was very presumptuous to ask you to wait for me when we've only gone out a couple of months, but when we're together, it feels like we've known each other for years. Is it the same for you?"

Despite the fading light, his gaze still mesmerized her, and now she needed to memorize it. "Yes, it's the same. From the time we swam together at your house, I was drawn to you, and when you showed concern for Suzanne because we'd left her alone, something inside me quickened, and I knew that day would be a turning point in my life. Yes, I'll wait for you, Ted."

He drew her closer. "I was a little worried there. Hopefully, this war business will be over soon. Are you okay with my taking flying lessons if they allow me to?"

"Why wouldn't I be? I would never want to quash a dream you've had since you were a boy."

He gave her a soft kiss. "You just made me love you more than I do already. We only have three days and two nights until I leave. Can you clear your calendar and spend all of them with me?"

Did he realize he said he loved her? "I was already planning on it. Can we stay awake until it's time for you to board the train to Chicago?"

He tipped his head back and laughed. "You don't want to know me when I'm without sleep."

She snuggled under his arm. "Then I'll make sure you get enough. I can't have the man I love be a grouch on the last days we'll have together." She tipped her head back, and he rewarded her with a kiss that sent a shiver clear to her toes.

CHAPTER FIVE

They didn't speak again until he pulled into the circle drive at Safe Refuge. He cut the motor. "I have more to tell you. Are you game?"

A sinking feeling washed over her. "Yes, but let's go to the spring house where it's more private."

A few minutes later, they settled on a glider and faced each other. The light provided by the several gas lamps they'd lit was enough to notice the sparkle put in his eyes earlier by their words of mutual love had faded. Understandable, given all the war talk.

He draped his arm over her shoulders. "What you said back there. Did you really mean it?"

"What did I say?"

He kissed her. "That you love me."

"Of course, I meant it. Did you mean it when you said you loved me?"

"When did I say that?"

When you said my waiting for you made you love me even more."

"Oh, I did at that. I've felt that way for a long while but was waiting until I was sure if you felt the same. I love you with all my heart, Hannah Murphy."

"I love you too, Ted Bauer, with all my heart."

Their mouths sought each other. Lips soft and gentle caressed hers, sending a flood of shivers down her back. He broke the kiss then cradled her face in his hands. "My precious Hannah. Thank you for loving me."

She kissed him. "It's not difficult to do. Now, what else did you want to tell me?"

He sat back and stared straight ahead. "I'm scared for my father. There's talk that if the U.S. joins the Allies, all immigrants who are still German citizens will be required to register, and if they refuse, they'll be placed in internment camps. He's lived here longer than he ever lived in Germany.

"My dad insists he won't register and won't go to a camp. He has a large company to run. He's training my brother, but it's hard for him to give up control. I'm more afraid than ever he's going to be deported.

"A day doesn't go by when my mother isn't in tears. And my decision isn't helping, even though she understands why I'm doing it. Life around my house hasn't been pleasant. It would be worse if they knew my hopes to become a pilot." He looked off toward the lake. "I'm going to miss this place and most of all you." He drew her into a hug and kissed her. "It's a good thing I'm leaving so soon, or I'd be tempted to suggest something crazy like eloping before I leave."

Her breath caught in her throat. His emotions had to be controlling this impulsivity. As much as she was sure she loved him, she was relieved there wasn't enough time. It was one thing to say they were in love, but quite another to marry so fast.

He chuckled. "By your silence, I guess that wouldn't be such a good idea. I know women dream of their wedding from the time they are small."

She shook her head. "I'm not one of those. But I'm not ready yet. Having admitted to each other we're in love is a bit overwhelming."

"I know. We'll have time to do things right when I get back. As I said, I don't expect to be anywhere near the battles and far back from the front line. Unless I make it to flying school."

She held up a hand. "I'm not even going to think about flying school. Just keep telling me you'll be in London, sitting at a desk, decoding enemy telegraphs."

"Agreed. My father is staying in town to accompany me into Chicago on Friday and see me off to New York. We're to have dinner with all my favorite foods Thursday night. I've already told Mother I'm going to invite you. She likes you a lot and insisted I ask you to come. Will you join us?"

She nodded. "Yes. But I hope we'll see each other before then."

He circled his arm around her waist and nudged her closer. "Of course, we will. I thought tomorrow we could take my family's boat and spend the day on the water. Some of the gang you met at my house last June are planning a going-away party tomorrow night, and I already told them I planned on asking you to be my date. Then the next day, maybe you can come to Tranquility Point and stay through the evening meal."

Heaviness filled her chest. In a few hours, her excitement over spending the next school year with the man of her dreams had evaporated with his news of leaving for the war. Now, their declaring their love for each other had her on another emotional high. She needed to be an encouragement to him, not drag him down with her selfish feelings. "I'm proud of you for doing this, Ted."

He kissed her and gripped her hand, pulling her to a standing position. "That warms my heart. "I'll walk you to the cottage."

At the cottage door, he kissed her on both cheeks and then

her lips. Get a good night's sleep. I'll come by around ten tomorrow morning."

"Come earlier and join my family for breakfast. I know my parents would like to say goodbye."

"Eight o'clock okay?"

"Make it seven-thirty. My father has office hours in town, and the girls have school. He drops them off on his way to work."

"Until then, sweet dreams. I love you more than words can describe." He pushed the door open, and after she slipped inside, he shut it.

She leaned her back against the door until his car roared to life, and the crunch of the gravel faded as he drove out onto Snake Road. Tears that had been pressing against the backs of her eyes trailed down her face. He hadn't even left for New York, and she was already a mess. How would she be when he was flying into the war zone? She needed to build a firm resolve to be brave because she had no doubt he would be a crackerjack pilot and not decoding at a desk for long.

Ted returned home and found his mother sitting on the veranda with a knit shawl wrapped around her shoulders. A lantern holding a candle offered the only illumination. She looked up. "Did you have a nice evening?"

If she thought he'd think her composed, her husky voice gave her weeping away. She'd probably spent the better part of the time since arriving home praying for him and pondering his plans. "Yes and no."

"What do you mean by that?"

"The good part of the night is that we both declared our love for each other."

She straightened. "You've only been going out for a couple of months."

"When a man is going off to war, there's no time for societal norms. I knew the minute I saw her at my swimming party last June she was the woman I would one day marry. And don't forget I had a crush on her in eighth grade. That has to count for something."

Mother sighed. "Yes, you were quite lovesick back then. But she was only in sixth grade, so I wasn't too worried. I'm not so old I don't remember how it feels when you first fall in love. I really like Hannah and think you two are good for each other. I hope she doesn't let you down while you're gone. I could shake your father for being so stubborn. If he'd become a U.S. citizen when it became apparent he wasn't ever going back to Germany, we'd be in a much better place."

"I know. I should have told Hannah before now of my intentions. She already went ahead and put in an application to Northwestern's law school, thinking I'd be there in the fall."

"You didn't tell her before tonight?"

"No. I didn't know for sure until a few days ago, and we were having so much fun together, I didn't want to spoil the mood. I kept fooling myself that we weren't really falling in love, and she'd soon move on after I left. I'm elated she loves me, but the timing for her transferring schools is awful."

"Can't she withdraw her application?"

"She doesn't want to. She has cousins living in Evanston and can stay with them rent-free. If this war ends soon, I could be back to school within the year, and that way, we'll be living in the same place. She's coming here my last day for dinner with us."

"Good. The woman who stole your heart should be here."

He turned to go inside. "If it's okay with you and Dad, I'll be taking the *Louise* over to Safe Refuge tomorrow morning to join Hannah and her family for breakfast. We'd like to spend the day on the water before attending my going away party. I hope you don't mind my being with her instead of here." He leaned down and kissed her cheek.

"I don't mind. You two have so little time."

With the saltiness of her tears fresh on his lips, he said, "Don't fret too much. I know God has me in the palm of His hand."

CHAPTER SIX

The next morning, a knock came at the cottage door at seven-fifteen. Thankful she'd decided to be ready in case Ted came early, Hannah opened the door. Her breath hitched as she let her gaze travel from his feet, up to his summer weight trousers to his off-white sweater, and plant itself on his chiseled jaw. She hoped the smile didn't resemble the Cheshire cat in *Alice in Wonderland*. "Good morning. I thought you'd come straight to the big house."

He took her into his arms. "I wanted to say a proper good morning before greeting the family. He leaned down and kissed her. "I have something to show you. Do we have time to sit in the spring house a minute?"

"Sure. Let's go."

They walked hand in hand across the dew-covered lawn to what had become their favorite place to chat and spend time as it gave a sense of privacy, yet they were visible to others. The early morning air felt wonderful on Hannah's face, but what Ted was about to do weighed heavy on her heart.

They settled on the glider, then Ted dug his hand into one of his front pockets. He dropped to one knee and held out a ring.

"This is my promise to come home to you. "I love you, Hannah. Will you marry me?"

She pressed her right palm to her chest. Her heart thumped against her hand as it was going to explode. A lump filled her throat. Had he read her mind? In her tossing and turning during the night, she'd moved from the thought of eloping being too fast to wishing they did have time for a quick ceremony. She held out her left hand. "Oh, Ted. I can't imagine marrying anyone but you."

"I love you my darling, Hannah." He slid the ring onto her finger then stood and pulled her to her feet and kissed her soundly. "It was my grandmother's ring. If it's not to your liking …"

"I love it and love that it has sentimental value."

"Then that's a yes?

"Yes, Ted, I'll marry you."

He kissed the corners of her mouth before claiming her lips." The kiss broke, and he peppered kisses over her face then back to her mouth. He took her left hand and rubbed his thumb over the ring. "I know it's best to keep the engagement to ourselves, given the short time we've been seeing each other and that I'm leaving for the war in two days."

"I agree. I'll not say a word to my parents. Maybe I can wear it on a chain around my neck beneath my clothing. That way, I'll always feel as though you're with me."

He grinned. "I love the idea of you wearing it on a chain." He lowered his mouth to hers, and the kiss quickly deepened, sending swirls of butterflies through her stomach. She wrapped her arms around him and kissed him back with equal fervor. He brought his mouth to her ear and whispered. "When I return home, let's not have a long engagement. I want to be able to have you by my side all night long every night."

"Don't forget we'll both be in law school. Can we afford to marry then?"

"We'll make it work. I only have one more year before I take the bar exam. I'll work as an attorney while you finish up, then after we both have our law degrees, we can start our legal practices together."

She giggled. "I can see the sign on the door now. Bauer and Bauer, Attorneys at Law."

He looked at the ring, still on her hand. "Do you already have a chain?"

"I think so. I'll meet you outside the cottage in a few minutes." She stepped out of the spring house and dashed up the incline, feeling as though she could fly.

In her bedroom, she found the necklace she wanted and removed the pendant. She threaded the chain through the ring then stepped outside the cottage where Ted waited. "Will you please hook this?" He took the chain and she turned her back to him. As he worked to fasten the ends of the necklace together, his fingertips brushed against her neck, waking up the butterflies in her stomach.

"Success." He gripped her shoulders and turned her toward him. "Hannah, I promise to be faithful to you only."

She blinked at the moisture in her eyes and dropped the ring behind her blouse. "And I promise to be faithful to you only."

"There you two are."

They jumped apart and turned toward the voice.

Pop stood at the end of the walkway, a frown marring his face. "We knew Ted was here because his boat is at the dock. Are you coming to breakfast?"

Her face heated.

Ted stuck out his hand to Pop. "Good morning, Doctor Murphy. Blame it on me. I wanted a few minutes alone with Hannah. We were in the spring house."

Her father looked at Ted's outstretched hand, seeming almost reluctant, then completed the handshake. "I understand.

The pancakes are going to cool off if we don't get over there now."

Several hours later, as they drifted along the south shore of the lake, Hannah's stomach growled. She pressed her palm to her tummy. "I can't believe I'm hungry after all the pancakes I ate."

"Me too." Ted stood from his seat. He'd removed his sweater as the day warmed and rolled up the sleeves of his white shirt, exposing muscular forearms that caused her pulse to quicken. He went into the boat's cabin and returned with a basket. "Your lunch is ready, ma'am."

"I thought we were going into town. You've thought of everything."

He carried the basket to the table between their deck chairs and lifted one of its flaps. "I can't promise the fried chicken is as good as the Geneva Hotel's, but our cook makes it quite tasty. And my mother made German potato salad. If you prefer a sandwich, I have a couple of egg salad sandwiches in here too."

"I'll take a chicken leg and a little of the salad. I'll decide later about the sandwich. I imagine there will be a lot of food at the buffet tonight."

He took out a pair of white porcelain plates and placed a chicken leg on each, then added a thigh to one of them and a spoonful of potato salad onto both. He handed Hannah the one with a single piece of chicken, and they settled into their chairs. He took her hand. "I'll say the blessing."

Pleased that he took the initiative to pray over the food, she bowed her head and silently thanked God for placing this special man in her life.

He said, "Amen," and took a bite of chicken. "That's an interesting story your mom told about how she first tasted pancakes made from a mix," he said around a mouthful.

"I know. Pancake mix has been around as long as I remember. I guess a lot of innovations were introduced at the

Columbian Exposition. I hadn't heard about the pancake mix before, but I've heard the rest of the story how she went to the fair with Preston Stevens and caught smallpox when she held a woman's baby who sneezed on her."

"I've always wondered if the scarring on a part of her face was from smallpox. But it's never correct to ask about such things. I'm surprised she'd even want to eat another pancake after that."

"She loves pancakes, but I've never seen her make them from scratch. She's told me at first she was devastated about the scarring but learned through God's help and the help of her caregiver to accept her scars as a badge of honor. I hardly even notice the scars. They've faded some over the years."

He stood and moved to the wheel and adjusted the direction they were heading. "This boat was built by Preston Stevens. He's become a real master at boat building, and now one of his sons is learning the skill."

"That's what I understand. Mama doesn't speak of him much. I get the sense there is a lot more to their history together than she lets on. Did you notice when his name came up how my father stiffened a little?"

He shook his head. "I guess I was too busy looking at your mother and realizing how much you favor her. The women connected to Safe Refuge have all had those captivating Irish green eyes."

Hannah grinned. "The green eyes came from my granny who didn't have any Irish blood. Rory Quinn, my grandfather, was an Irish immigrant, and he was ginger-haired and like a gentle giant. The great fire is what allowed them to cross the barriers of wealthy and poor and marry."

His eyes widened. "I love that story. My heritage is German through and through. Right now, I'm reticent to share that much with strangers. I've heard that some of German descent are changing their surnames to something less German-sounding. The harassment is awful." He set the picnic basket on the deck then moved the table aside and scooted his chair next to hers. "That's much better." He brushed a strand of hair off her cheek. "I want our children to be proud of both sides of their family."

Hannah recovered from the sensation his touch had caused. "I haven't even asked how many children you want to have someday." She hoped he didn't say a dozen or some crazy number like that.

He shrugged. "I've never given it much thought. At least two, but not more than four. How does that sound?"

She took his hand and kissed it. "Perfect."

After the going-away party, Ted drove Hannah home, and they sat in the circle drive for a few minutes, not speaking. Hannah didn't want the clock to pass into the next day, the final full day they'd have together before he'd be away for months or maybe years. Unless… She couldn't bring herself to form the thought.

Ted draped his arm over her shoulders and nudged her closer. "It was a fun evening."

She forced her mind out of her melancholy. "It was."

He tugged on the chain at the back of her neck. "You didn't tell your girlfriends about this, did you?"

She chuckled. "I was very tempted, but I didn't. They sure were curious, asking me what was going on with us. I told them we're seeing each other and are a couple, but that's all. I understand not telling our parents, but why is it so important not to tell our friends?"

"I only want you safe."

"Safe?"

"Yes. As things heat up overseas, your being engaged to the

son of a man, some people consider a traitor could make it difficult for you."

"But you're going to be fighting against the Germans."

He let out a deep sigh. "I'm not there yet."

"I don't think I'll run into problems here. Maybe in the city, but not here."

He pulled her closer. "You didn't notice your father's hesitation to shake my hand this morning?"

"Yes. But surely it wasn't because of that. Pop's very protective of his girls."

"Maybe, but I doubt that was the whole reason." He took her in his arms and brought his mouth to hers, his lips soft and tender. "See you tomorrow morning."

She needed to get inside the cocoon-like safety of the cottage and curl into a ball on her bed. "You don't need to walk me to the door. I'll get out here." She scooted over and climbed out of the car. As she scurried across the drive to the cottage, the door to the big house opened, and Pop stepped out. "Hannah. Come inside for a minute."

Surprised at her father's strong tone of voice, she paused, suddenly feeling like she was five again and about to be scolded.

"Please?"

At least he softened his command. "Okay."

Gravel crunched behind her, and she glanced over her shoulder. Ted's car headed toward the road. Had he heard the exchange with Pop? She approached her father. "Is something wrong?"

"You'll see. Your mother is waiting in the living room." He held the door open, his lips pressed into a flat line.

Chill bumps rose on her arms. Did someone die or become deathly ill? She braced herself for bad news and followed him down the center hall toward the living room.

As Hannah entered the room, Mama rose from the sofa. Something had to be terribly wrong. She never came downstairs wearing a dressing gown after she prepared for bed. "Sit here beside me, Hannah."

She crossed to the sofa. Pop took an upholstered chair a few feet away.

"Since you called this meeting, Nate, the floor is yours," Mama said, her tone even.

Wearing the expressionless face Hannah had seen him use when about to give a patient bad news, her father cleared his throat. "Hannah, it's apparent you and Ted are already becoming serious, and I must order you to stop this relationship immediately."

CHAPTER EIGHT

Hannah stared at her father, then looked at Mama, who kept her gaze fixed on her lap. She brought her eyes back to Pop. The vein in his neck pulsed as though plugged into a socket. She'd never seen him this angry. "I don't understand."

"I didn't expect you to." He paused as though searching for words. "I'm sorry, Hannah, but I … we don't feel we can trust Ted."

Thoughts spun in her head, trying to find a landing place that would make sense. "Trust him, how? He's been a perfect gentleman with me."

He drew in a breath and spoke through clenched teeth. "That's not what I'm talking about. You know, of course, his family is German."

"Of German descent. Ted is an American. Born right here in the U.S." Where was this talk coming from? She'd never heard him speak disparagingly about anyone, no matter their nationality.

He narrowed his eyes. "His father remains a German citizen,

and we don't know if he's in communication with the Germans. He could be a spy."

She straightened and raised her chin. "That's ridiculous. He's as upset with his home country as everyone else is."

"Where has Henry Bauer been these past weeks? His wife is here, Ted's brother comes and goes, but Henry's not been seen in Lake Geneva since the war broke out. He missed the spring Yacht Club meeting two weeks ago, and he never misses that."

So that was it. Was it okay to divulge all Ted had told her about his father over the past couple of days? "He's been at their Chicago home and running his company. He feels less threatened there by people who are talking like you and want to hurt him. In the city, he can disappear into the crowd."

Pop flew to his feet and stood, arms akimbo, hands fisted. "And meet up with operatives undetected."

She bristled. "You don't have to yell. I can hear you fine. He's there running his company."

He narrowed his eyes. "Now you're being ridiculous. Facts are facts, Hannah. For all we know, Ted's brother is also part of the spy ring."

She jumped to her feet and glared at him. "Is that the tale going around now? You were never one to gossip. You're not being yourself, Dad. Ted is leaving in two days for England to join their military and fight the Germans. Why would he do that if what you say is true? Besides, his father is here now to spend time with Ted. He'll be accompanying Ted on the train to Chicago Friday morning."

Pop threw up his hands. "Now you sound like your mother. Maybe Ted is putting up a false front as a shield for his father and brother while they do their misdeeds."

Mama gripped Hannah's skirt and tugged. "Hannah, please sit."

Hannah pivoted, causing her skirt to pop out of Mama's

grip, and glared at her mother. "And sit here listening to this? Has he convinced you of this nonsense?"

Mama released a heavy sigh. "No. He hasn't. But your father is the head of our home and we must—"

"I will not stop seeing Ted." She faced her father. "We love each other, and he needs my support. He's picking me up at the dock early tomorrow morning, and I won't be back until late evening."

Pop's face turned beet red. "You're defying my orders?"

"I don't have to obey you. I'm of age."

The pulsing vein reappeared. "You're still an unmarried woman living under my roof."

"You didn't build this house or the cottage. It's all owned by Mama's family, not you."

"Hannah! This home is your father's as much as it is mine." Mama stood and stared at Pop. "Nate, this has gone too far. You both need to calm down. You know as well as I do Ted is not a German spy or trying to cover up his father's aiding the enemy, which I highly doubt he is doing. You have no proof, and it's not right to be saying these things and giving the man a bad reputation. Hannah is right. She's an adult now, and we are not living in the past where an unmarried daughter needs to obey her father until she has a husband."

Pop waved a hand. "Okay, go with Ted tomorrow, Hannah. He'll leave in a couple of days, and who knows if this summer romance of yours is strong enough to last."

Hannah stepped into her mother's open arms. "Thank you, Mama."

Her mother patted her back. "You're welcome, but don't think you're without fault. Your voice was raised as much as your father's, saying words I never thought I'd hear coming from your mouth."

Hannah leaned back and looked her mother in the eyes. "I'm

sorry. I hate how this war is causing conflicts at home as well as on the battlefield." She faced her father. "Now I'm going to bed, although I doubt I'll sleep much. Perhaps by morning, I'll be ready to apologize for my words."

CHAPTER NINE

The next evening, Hannah followed Ted into his family's dining room. She'd managed to hold back the tears that threatened to appear numerous times while she and Ted walked the shore path around Tranquility Point. And they remained unshed while they sat on the home's veranda holding hands and musing about their future together once the war was over. She continued dry-eyed after that when they snuck out of sight behind a tall pine tree to steal a few kisses. But would she make it until the end of the evening without sobbing when it came time to say goodbye?

He'd asked what her father wanted with her when he'd dropped her off last night. Knowing he'd bring it up, she'd already formed an answer and sloughed it off by saying it was about a personal family matter she wasn't free to talk about. He accepted the explanation and never brought it up again.

As soon as she had entered the Bauer home earlier that day, a sense of deep sadness seemed to envelop her. No wonder with their youngest son leaving for the war. Now, she was beginning to wonder if she should have accepted the invitation to the family's last meal with Ted.

Ted pulled out a chair for Hannah on one side of the large table, then took his seat next to her. Across the table, Ted's brother, Peter, took his seat and ran his fingers through the waves of his thick blond hair. He may have been blessed with good hair, but, in her opinion, Ted had it over him in all other attributes. Besides, she preferred short hair on men. She glanced at Mrs. Bauer, who sat at the end of the table to her right. She'd met her several times in the past and always thought her best feature was her smile. But today, no one was smiling. From the redness around her eyes, the poor woman must have spent the day weeping. She couldn't imagine the pain of watching a son go off to war, perhaps never to return.

"Mr. Bauer looked at Ted from his seat at the head of the table, the lines in his face appearing deeper than when Hannah last saw him at a yacht club event a year ago. He ran his hands over his unusually unkempt snow-white hair, then cleared his throat and looked at Hannah, his brown eyes lifeless. "It's nice for you to join us tonight, Hannah, though I wish it were on a happier occasion."

She managed a soft smile. "Thank you, sir. I'm honored to be here."

His gaze went to Ted. "Son, would you do the honors of saying grace?"

"Sure." Ted bowed his head and began praying in German. After a couple of sentences, he switched to English and asked God to bless the meal and the family's time together that evening. He ended with the German Amen that was slightly different in pronunciation but sounded like the same word.

She raised her head, and he leaned toward her and whispered, "Sorry for the German at first. I said pretty much the same thing I said in English." He looked around the table. "Shall we begin?"

As if on cue, the family maid stepped in from the butler's

pantry with a steaming dish that smelled divine. The young woman set the dish in the middle of the table.

"Schnitzel. My favorite meal at my request." Ted issued a loud sigh.

"But made the Austrian way and not the German." His mother rolled her eyes.

Ted laughed. "Can I help it if I prefer veal over pork chops?" He picked up a serving spoon and scooped a mound of what looked like an oddly twisted noodle, and then added a breaded piece of veal to the serving." He looked at Hannah. "Do you want me to prepare your plate? The dish is too hot and heavy to pass."

She nodded. "But not as big a helping as yours."

He looked at Hannah and whispered, "In case you're wondering, the noodles are called *spaetzle.*"

After serving her a modest portion, he left the spoon in the dish, the handle facing his father as a bowl of green beans was passed.

Hannah's stomach growled. She'd not tasted many German dishes but supposed she'd have to get used to it after the war was over. Already, people were being discouraged from preparing German recipes or at least renaming them an American name.

Peter was the last to fill his plate, and once he finished, everyone began eating. Hannah took a tentative bite and hoped the food tasted as good as it smelled.

A short while later, Ted glanced at her plate. "I guess you enjoyed the schnitzel as much as I do. I hope you left room for dessert. Chocolate cake, German-style." He ran his tongue over his upper lip."

She pressed a palm to her tummy. "You should have warned me, but I'll manage to suffer for your sake."

Peter rested his fork on his plate and looked from Ted to

Hannah. "Something tells me I've missed an announcement from you two."

Ted frowned. "No announcement. We are exclusively seeing each other and have committed to being faithful while I'm away. But Hannah has an announcement." He elbowed her. "Go ahead and tell them."

She frowned, her mind racing. Ted didn't mean the ring that hung out of sight around her neck, did he? She placed her palm to her chest a few inches below her dress's neckline and felt the ring as she gave him a questioning look.

"I'm talking about switching law schools."

At his whisper, she smiled. "I'm planning to attend Northwestern University's law school in the fall. The same school Ted will return to after the war."

Mr. Bauer's eyes widened. "You decided to not go to the University of Wisconsin even though Ted was enlisting?"

"I had no idea what his plans were when I applied to Northwestern. We were both holding off telling each other our plans until they were settled. But, I'll switch anyway. I can stay with my cousin who lives in Evanston near the streetcar that will take me to a stop near the school."

"It's almost like you two are made for each other, isn't it?" Mrs. Bauer asked. "Both lake people and both wanting to be lawyers. Although I have to say, we don't see many lady lawyers. Good for you. If I were younger, I might be tempted to get into a field only populated by men."

Mr. Bauer stared at her. "Louise, I've never heard you say you wanted a career outside of what you do."

"I didn't say I wanted a career other than being a wife and mother. I only mean for young women today, it's exciting to see what they can be. It might have been fun to study pharmacy. I've heard so much talk from you about the different medicines our company is making, and it's always sounded intriguing."

Peter chuckled. "Now that's a job I can't imagine any woman wanting to do."

Mrs. Bauer stared at him. "And why not?"

"Pharmacists have to know a lot about science. Women are never good at science." He pushed his chair away from the table. "I'm too full for dessert. I'll be outside on the veranda where I can enjoy my cigar."

A few hours later, Hannah snuggled next to Ted as they rode in silence toward Safe Refuge in his Buick Roadster. By now, the ache in her heart felt like it was going to explode if she didn't let her tears fall. Only a short time more and she could have a good cry.

Ted pulled into Save Refuge's drive and cut the motor, letting the vehicle silently roll to a stop. He faced her. "I didn't want your family to hear us coming so we could have a few more minutes together. Better yet, can we walk down to the spring house and sit there?"

They walked in silence, and he slipped his hand into hers and wove their fingers together. Hannah shut her eyes, trying to memorize the feel of his palm against hers, including the hardened callouses from his years of rowing. She loved he was taller than her but not so much that when they danced, she could rest her head on his shoulder. And she loved his scent of soap and shaving cream.

They stepped inside the spring house, where he led her to the glider and sat next to her. He drew in a breath and let it out. "I thought about asking you to see my father and me off tomorrow, but my mom and brother will be there, and I won't be able to kiss you goodbye the way I want to. Are you okay with that?"

Relieved that the tears welling in her eyes weren't visible in the dark, Hannah drew in a breath and whispered. "It would only be getting in a few more moments of togetherness. Dragging it out to the last minute doesn't make sense. I've had you to myself the past two days, and they've seen little of you."

He ran a thumb under her left eye. "You're crying. I didn't want to cause you to do that."

"You silly man. When a woman loves a man, and he's leaving for war, she's going to cry."

He kissed the spot where he'd felt the wetness then kissed the same place under her other eye. "I'll have your salty tears of love to remember tonight. I love you, Hanna Murphy. I'll write as soon as I can and let you know my mailing address. It will likely be weeks before you hear, so don't worry." He pulled her into an embrace and held her for several long minutes. Then he leaned back and kissed her on the lips, deeply before trailing soft kisses over her face. She pulled him closer, and his mouth returned to hers.

He leaned back and tugged the ring into the open and slid the ring onto her finger. "This is where the ring should be, not hidden away as if it were contraband. After you get to school, I'd love for you to wear it on your finger." He kissed her. "Best I get you inside."

At the cottage door, he leaned down and feathered his lips over hers. "Goodbye, sweetheart. You'll be in my dreams tonight and every night ahead until we're together again." He reached around her and opened the door. "Now get inside, or I'll stand here all night kissing you to death."

She stepped in, and he closed the door, the same way they'd been saying goodnight all summer. A few moments later, she heard his automobile circle the drive and fade off. She leaned against the wall and slipped her hand into her dress pocket. It landed on what felt like an envelope. She pulled it out and carried it to the living room. She flicked on a lamp and stared at Ted's now-familiar script, *"Do not open unless you get word that I've perished.*

CHAPTER TEN

September 1916

Hannah followed her cousin Cora's husband, Earl, as he carried her suitcase up the stairs to the guestroom while Cora followed behind them. Unless the war ended soon and Ted was able to come home so they could be married, this small room would likely be her home for the next two years. She pushed the thought from her mind. The way things were going over there, an early end to the conflict didn't appear likely.

The only letter she'd had so far from Ted, written a month ago, had him stationed in London, working as a code breaker. The assignment he'd hoped for. She was relieved he wasn't near the lines in France, but that was likely temporary as he'd applied for flight training and felt positive he'd be accepted.

She followed Earl into the bedroom, and he set the suitcase on top of the colorful bed quilt. He looked from Hannah to his wife. "I'll leave you two to yourselves."

When they were alone, Hannah glanced around the cozy

room and faced her cousin. "I don't know how to thank you for allowing me to stay here."

Cora shrugged and absently patted her curly brunette bob. "I'll love having you around. Having lost two of his best employees to the war effort, Earl is very busy doing the work of three men." She plopped into a small upholstered chair. "I wish I'd had a chance to meet Ted. Granny told me he's tall and handsome."

Hannah giggled. "Aunt Callie is right. She might be getting up in years, but she hasn't lost her appreciation of handsome men." She fingered the chain then tugged the ring and a small locket out into the open. "He gave me this ring before he left." She opened the locket. Here's his picture."

Cora came closer and studied the small photo, then ran the back of her thumb over the ring as her eyes widened "This is beautiful. Is there something you haven't told me?"

She couldn't contain her smile. "It was his grandmother's ring. We are engaged, but we've not yet told our parents. We hope to make the engagement official after he comes home."

Cora hugged her. "Congratulations. But why is it a secret?"

"Because of his father being a German citizen. He was never naturalized even though he's lived in the U.S. for many years. Some people are awful toward Germans who immigrated here, and even having a German-sounding name can make trouble for some. Ted wants me to not wear the ring at the lake to avoid people connecting me to the family in that way."

Cora's eyes had grown as large as silver dollars. "I had no idea it was that bad. I live such an isolated life."

She huffed a breath. "You're better off. Believe me. He said once I moved here, I could start wearing the ring on my finger, but I'll be cautious about it." She opened her suitcase and lifted out her underthings and moved them to a dresser drawer. "I don't know how much company I'll be for you. School starts tomorrow, and I'll be needing to find a part-time job."

Cora's mouth turned down. "Oh. I hadn't thought about how you'll have to study and work too."

Hannah stepped over and gathered her in a hug. "We'll make time to be together. Once I know my schedule, it will be easier."

Her cousin's smile returned. "Of course. I wish Earl weren't so set on me staying home. When he lost his workers and couldn't find replacements, I suggested I help out, and he said no wife of his was going to work." She pressed her palm against her stomach. "By now, we should have at least one child. But it doesn't seem God has that in His will for us."

Hannah had forgotten it had been five years since she'd attended Cora and Earl's wedding. She stepped back and looked Cora in the eyes. "I'm so sorry."

Cora's eyes filled. "We haven't shared this with anyone outside of our parents. I've been pregnant twice but lost both babies at around two months." She swiped a palm across her cheek. "Sorry, I can't talk about it without tearing up."

Hannah pulled her closer. "You can cry all you want with me, cousin. I'm so sorry."

They separated, and Cora pulled a handkerchief from her skirt pocket and dabbed her eyes. "Enough of that. I have a pot roast in the oven, and the meal will be ready in about a half an hour. I'll leave you to your unpacking and will let you know when it's time to eat."

"I wondered what smelled so good. But beef is so scarce now. I hate to eat what you have for yourselves."

"Actually, my granny gave it to us to have your first night here. Regardless, you're family, and there should be no restrictions on family … as much as possible, anyway."

Hannah waited until her cousin left the room, before letting her own tears trail down her cheeks. "God, why is there so much sorrow now? Cora longs for a baby, Ted and his family are on pins and needles about his father, and Ted and I are separated so soon after falling in love."

At least she and Pop had come to a truce regarding his suspicions about Ted's loyalty to the U.S. Even so, Ted's welfare was never far from her thoughts and prayers. She was glad to get away to school, hoping the distraction of her law classes would calm her worries.

Later, after helping Cora clean up the kitchen, Hannah curled up in her bedroom chair and began a letter to Ted. She got no further than saying she was now moved into Cora's and ready for her first day of classes when her thoughts went to him, and a familiar daydream took over. She'd managed passage to London and surprised him. He'd run to her, and take her in his arms, smothering kisses all over her face as he did before he left. They'd decide to elope that same day …

"Hannah, wake up."

Her eyes popped open, and she stared up into Nora's face. "You're ready for bed. What time is it?"

"Almost nine."

"My word, I must have slept for almost two hours. Thanks for waking me." She gathered the letter she'd begun from where it fell on the floor. "I didn't get past the first line of my letter to Ted. Oh well, I'll have more to tell him about after my first day tomorrow."

The next morning, Hannah boarded a streetcar that came south down Sheridan Road with a stop at the Northwestern campus before heading into the city and her stop a short distance from the law school. She took a seat and pressed her palm to her chest, feeling the ring and locket. "Oh, Ted," she whispered. "I wish you were here with me now. But I know I'm in your thoughts and prayers and you are in mine."

A half-hour later, she stepped off the streetcar and walked to the law school building. At the entrance, she studied the letter they'd sent with instructions. All she needed was to find the elevator and go to the third floor. She fell in step behind a large group of men and a couple of women. Some split off and went to a hallway on the first floor. Several, all men, except for one woman, pretty with hair almost as black as licorice, entered the elevator with her. Most exited at the second floor, except for the woman who grinned at Hannah. "I'm glad to see I'm not the only female. I'm Clarice Laurent."

Hannah returned her grin. "Let's hope we're not the only two. Hannah Murphy. Do I detect a French accent?"

The woman linked arms with her as the elevator doors slid open. "Only a slight one. I was born in Quebec, but we moved to the U.S. when I was around three. Blame the accent on my French-speaking parents. If we are the only first-year females, we must rise to the occasion and be mighty. I suggest we angle to be in the same study group."

"Agreed."

They found the room for first-year students and stepped in.

"I don't see a female in sight. Do you, Hannah?"

Liking her new friend immensely, she pointed off to their left. "No. But I see two seats next to each other. Let's snag them."

They settled into their seats, and Hannah opened her mouth to ask Clarice if she had lunch plans when a loud male voice interrupted.

"Good morning first years, and welcome to the Northwestern University School of Law orientation day."

By lunchtime, Hannah's brain swam with enough information to make her brain hurt. She'd forgotten how she hated orientation day at any of her schools. Attending classes tomorrow would be easier than today. She looked at her friend as they exited the room. "I think the cafeteria is on the first floor."

Clarice frowned. "I brought my lunch. I'll meet you here in an hour."

"I didn't think to do that. I'm sure you can bring your lunch and sit with me while I eat."

They found the cafeteria and stepped inside the door, almost bumping into a tall man.

Hannah tapped him on the shoulder. "Sir, can you please move aside so we can get to the food line?"

He faced her. "No. I can't, because this is the food line. If they have anything left by the time we get there, it will be a wonder."

Hannah sighed. "Great. Now, what will I do? I don't know the neighborhood well enough to find a restaurant."

Clarice dragged her by the arm into the hall. "I'll share my sandwich with you. I'm not a big eater anyway."

Hannah shook her head. "I can't let you do that."

"Yes, you can. Stop arguing and say thank you."

They found a bench outside that faced Lake Michigan, and after Clarice had handed Hannah half of her peanut butter sandwich, she started to take a bite.

"Do you mind if I pray a blessing first?"

Clarice looked up. "You are different. But it's refreshing. Please go ahead."

Hannah said a short prayer, and they began to eat.

"So, Hannah, do you work somewhere?"

"I plan to look for a part-time job once I figure out where to look. The only work I've done is for my father at his physician's office during the summer doing the billing. Do you work?"

"Yes. As a telephone operator."

"That sounds interesting. Do you like it?"

"Most of the time, unless the traffic is slow, and I have to sit there staring at the board."

Hannah scrunched her nose. "Traffic?"

"Customers calling for assistance." Her face brightened. "Several of the younger operators have left the telephone office and gone back to school. I bet I could put a word in for you, and they'd snap you up."

Hannah shook her head. "I don't know the first thing about a switchboard."

"Neither did I until I got the job a year ago. I have to work at four this afternoon after our orientation. I'll mention you to my boss. I'm sure she'll agree. Come to school tomorrow prepared to go with me for an interview."

CHAPTER ELEVEN

The next afternoon after classes, Hannah joined Clarice on the streetcar that would take them farther south. Clarice had assured that the phone company's building was only a block from the stop, and it would be an easy ride back to Evanston and home.

As the car began moving, Clarice looked at her. "If they hire you, you'll go through training for the first few days, and then you'll begin taking calls for real with an experienced operator. I'll ask if I can be that person for you."

Hannah resisted the urge to hug Clarice. "I don't know what I'd do without you. Yesterday sharing your lunch and today, taking me to a job interview."

"Stop it, Clarice huffed. "I'm not a church person, but I do believe God arranged it all."

She leaned back and looked Clarice in the eyes. "I think you have more faith than you want to admit, saying something like that."

Clarice gave a dismissive wave. "Here's our stop."

A five-minute walk later, they stepped inside a nondescript brick building and took the steps to the second floor. Clarice stopped in front of an open door. "This is where the operators work."

Hannah came closer and peered in. About a dozen women sat side by side in front of a wall of black switchboards. She watched the woman seated nearest to the door as she stuck what Clarice called a cord into a hole in the board, said something, then picked up another cord and poked it into another hole a short distance away. Then, without missing a beat, she pulled another set of cords out of the board, and they snapped back into place at the base. A few seconds later, she repeated the motions with another set of cords. Hannah stepped back and whispered, "I don't know, Clarice. It looks complicated."

"Right now, it can be daunting, but after you're trained, it will be as easy as working a stick shift on an automobile."

She laughed. "I'm not sure I've mastered that yet. I'm glad I'm planning to practice law. Much more to my liking."

"Me too. Let's go. Miss Marshall is waiting for you."

They continued down the hall, and Clarice stopped in front of a door and tapped on it."

"Come in. It's open."

Inside the office, a gray-haired woman rose from behind a desk and smiled at Clarice before directing her focus at Hannah. "You must be Hannah Murphy." She looked at Clarice. "Your shift is about to begin. Go ahead. I'll make sure you two can talk a few minutes after we're done."

Clarice winked at Hannah. "Good luck."

Almost wishing for bad luck after observing the operators maneuvering their cords so fast, she answered with a slight smile.

Miss Marshall gestured to a chair in front of her desk. "Please sit and tell me why you want to be a telephone operator. I know this isn't your lifelong goal."

Feeling more relaxed, Hannah offered the lady a sincere smile. "To be honest because I need a part-time job to help with expenses while I attend law school. It never occurred to me to consider being a telephone operator until I met Clarice yesterday. She insisted I apply. She's tough to say no to."

Miss Marshall laughed. "I'm not surprised at that. She is one of our best operators, and I trust her judgment. If you are in law school, you must have graduated from college."

"Yes. The University of Wisconsin this past June."

The woman's face brightened. "Another Wisconsinite. I'm from Oshkosh. I moved down here when I was promoted to this position. Living in such a big city like Chicago takes getting used to."

"My home town is smaller than yours. I grew up in Lake Geneva. I hope to get back to the lake as much as possible."

A smile split Miss Marshall's face. "Well, I don't see the need for more conversation. I think you'd make an excellent operator once you're trained." She pushed several papers across her desk. "Please fill these out before you leave, and be sure to indicate which days of the week you are available and the times of your last class of each of those days. You'll work no more than twenty hours a week. You can use the table in the break room, which is across the hall from where you saw the switchboards."

Hannah blinked. "When do I report for training? So far as I know, I'll be done by four each afternoon."

"Then there's no time like tomorrow. You'll work from four-thirty until eight-thirty. I'll make sure your hours are the same as Clarice's until you are fully acclimated. I'll get someone to relieve her for a few minutes so you two can talk."

Hannah spent time at the break-room table filling out the forms until Clarice stepped into the room wearing a huge grin. "I knew she'd like you. And she told me I'm to be your sidekick until you are comfortable working on your own. Do you remember how to get back to the streetcar stop?"

"I think so. Thanks, Clarice. You've been a huge blessing to me today. I hope I can do the same for you sometime."

Clarice's face reddened. "You've blessed me by being here. I have a feeling we're going to be lifelong friends. I'd better get back to the board. See you tomorrow."

Hannah finished filling out the papers and left them with Miss Marshall's assistant. Feeling ten feet off the ground, she all but floated to the streetcar stop. As soon as she could, she'd finish that letter to Ted. But first, she already had homework to complete.

Early November 1916

TED ENTERED THE LARGE MANSION, better known as The Admiralty, the current British Naval Headquarters. Time to start another day of decoding. What had sounded exciting and fun at the beginning had now morphed into boredom. He climbed the wide marble steps to the second floor and entered Room 40, which was really a warren of rooms. He walked down the hall to his assigned decoding room, which was no larger than a closet. No windows and with the door shut, very stuffy.

He collected a stack of papers from a tray on the desk. Time to put on his thinking cap. The problem was, the codes he used yesterday were not today's codes. He should be grateful to be working in relative safety, which would please his mother and Hannah, but once he was a trained pilot, he'd be in the thick of things. Never thought he'd say it, but that appealed ever so much more than this.

He drew in a breath and sent up a mental prayer for a clear mind and help to recall previous knowledge that had enabled him to do so well. He skimmed the first message then ran a finger under the first line of numbers and then the second line. He flipped open the current codebook, and suddenly it made sense. He worked fast, deciphering the message. He had an idea what the message inferred, but being he wasn't Navy, he wasn't allowed to offer an opinion. Just translate the code and move on to the next one.

He stood and carried his notes to a basket by the door for pick up, then decided to deliver them to what was the real Room 40 where the analysis took place. One of the naval officers looked up when Ted arrived at the door.

Ted held out his notes. "Special delivery. Looked like it needed immediate analysis."

The man frowned. "Please leave it in the basket for pick up like you've been instructed. Only we can decide if something is urgent."

Ted pressed his lips together. The man's accent indicated he was from Liverpool. Probably had a rough upbringing, and having a high rank and job in the Navy was likely the first time in his life he'd been assigned a responsible task. "Not trying to analyze, but sometimes the notes sit there for a few hours." He turned and started back down the hall."

"Private Bauer, wait."

Ted turned, and the man scurried up to him. "Sorry. My commanding officer overheard our conversation, and he'd like to see the notes now."

Ted handed him the paper, and the man saluted. Ted did the same and walked away. It probably wouldn't do any good, but he'd put in for a transfer to what he originally wanted to do. Use his German as an interpreter.

A few hours later, Ted ran his hand over his short-cropped hair, set his uniform hat on his head, and buttoned his jacket. He saluted to the officer sitting at the main desk in what had been the mansion's reception hall and stepped outside.

At last, he had time to think about something else besides codes. It had been a couple of weeks since he'd had a letter from Hannah. The last one described her mornings working at her father's medical office and how most afternoons her friends came over for swimming off the pier. That was written weeks ago, and he longed to find out how school was going for her. Was she enjoying the classes as much as he did that first year? He'd already written to tell her he was working at the Admiralty Building, which she already knew was the center for the coding department.

After a short trolley ride, he stepped into his rooming house and glanced at his mailbox. The cream-colored envelope he'd been waiting for wasn't an illusion. He grabbed the envelope and grinned at the familiar writing, loving the fancy way she made the T in his name.

Taking the steps two at a time to the third floor, he unlocked his door and stepped into the room. Finally alone, he held the envelope to his nose and sniffed. A faint scent of roses filled his senses, reminding him of the heady fragrance that permeated the air around Safe Refuge during summer. Without bothering to remove his jacket, he plopped onto the bed and tore open the envelope.

My Darling Ted,

By the time you read this, I should be deeply involved in my law classes. This was only the first day, so I don't have much comment since you already know what they are like. I will say I enjoyed it a lot. Can you believe I already have a part-time job? It's definitely from God because I never would have dreamed I'd one day be a telephone operator. The only other woman in my classes works at the telephone office, and she gave me a strong reference. I start training tomorrow afternoon. So, by the time you are reading this, I should be an old hand at connecting calls unless I make some horrible mistake and have already been fired!

It's hard keeping up with news from over there except that I'm happy to know you are in London. I know you're hoping for flight school, but to be honest, I keep hoping this war ends before that happens, and you won't find yourself flying right into danger. I pray for you constantly, asking God to spare your life so that you can come home to me.

I visited your mother a couple of times a week while I was still home. Your father spends all of his time in Chicago now. I think he feels he's not such a sitting duck as he would be in Wisconsin, and maybe he won't have to register if he makes Illinois his permanent address.

I fall asleep every night, holding a pillow and dreaming we're already married, and it's you beside me. Then I wake up and realize it's only a dream. I still wear your ring on the chain, not sure it's safe to wear it on my finger, even here. It never leaves its place around my neck, and somehow that makes me feel as though you aren't so far away after all.

You are my everything, my love, and I live for the day I can put that ring on my finger and announce to the world that we are engaged and about to be married.

All my love and more,
Hannah

He folded the letter and returned it to the envelope. He hated she didn't feel safe enough to wear his ring on her finger. He wanted to return home in one piece as much as Hannah wanted him to. She'd have her answer to her prayer if he didn't get accepted to flying school. Otherwise, he'd have to trust God he'd be kept safe for Hannah no matter where he was assigned.

CHAPTER TWELVE

December 1916

Hannah slipped her arms into her lamb's wool coat and buttoned it up, arranging the fur collar so it would protect her neck from the harsh wind coming off Lake Michigan. She glanced at Clarice, who was working herself into her wool coat. "We had such a nice fall, I can't get used to winter being here already."

Clarice pulled on her gloves. "This is nothing. You should be where I grew up in Vermont. It gets much colder there. I don't know about you, but I'm glad we have a break from our classes for a couple of weeks. Are you sure you don't want to stay here and work with me instead of going to Wisconsin?"

"I'm only going to be in Lake Geneva until the day after Christmas. I wish you'd come home with me."

"I would, but I need the extra money."

Hannah frowned. "No one should spend Christmas alone. I can't imagine."

"Maybe I could take the train up on Christmas Eve and return with you on the twenty-sixth."

Hannah grinned and pulled her wool hat over her head. "That's a wonderful idea. It'll be fun to have you there and show you around my hometown."

"Only if it's warmer than today. Otherwise, I'll prefer sitting near a fireplace."

Hannah laughed. "Agreed."

Clarice linked arms with her as they walked toward the stairs. "Let me stop in the office and make sure they don't schedule me for those days."

Her friend returned a few minutes later. "All arranged. Now let's get to the streetcar and hope there's room for us on the first one. This time of day, it's questionable."

By the time a streetcar arrived that wasn't full, Hannah's feet felt like they'd turned to ice. They found a seat for two and plopped into it. Hannah glanced at Clarice. "I hope there's a letter waiting for me. It's been two weeks since his last one."

"You can wipe that worried look from your face. Ted is safe in London. It's the mail that's slow. I think they sometimes keep the mail bags off the ship if there isn't room. Then the letters must wait for the next ship."

"He's supposed to be in London, but he can't even explain his job to me other than it's decoding. For all I know, the London assignment is a false front for what he's really doing. He could be in France on the front line right now."

"I never thought of that. I hate the way wartime has to be so hush-hush."

"I do too."

After an uneventful streetcar ride, Hannah arrived at Cora's and went directly to the side table in the foyer. She lifted the stack of mail and quickly leafed through the envelopes. Her heart fell. Another day to wonder and fret. She decided to look again, this time taking time to lift one envelope at a time. Halfway through the stack, she paused. Two were stuck together by sealing wax on one of them. Censors always resealed the letter with wax. She separated the envelopes and grinned at the familiar writing. "I'm home," she called out. "I'll be upstairs reading Ted's letter."

Her cousin appeared in the door to the parlor. "I didn't see a letter from him."

"It was stuck to the one on top of it with the censor's sealing wax."

Cora smiled. "I wonder how boring it must be for the censors to read all those letters."

"I can't imagine it myself." Hannah shrugged out of her coat and hung it on a hook by the door, then picked up her tote bag and headed for the stairs.

In her bedroom, she removed her shoes and settled on the bed with her legs curled beneath her. She broke the wax seal and relaxed. Nothing cut out of the letter this time. Ted was learning what he could share and could not.

Dearest Hannah,

I'm hoping this reaches you by Christmas Day. I presume you'll be taking the train to the lake to spend the day with your family, and I'd hate to miss wishing you a Merry Christmas, or Happy Christmas as they say here in London. Oh, how I long to wish you that in person with a long kiss. Hopefully, this conflict will soon be over, and we'll be together again. You'll have to tell me all about your Christmas day and everything you did to celebrate. I hope you'll be able to look in on my mother while you're home.

How are your classes going? I want to recall what was taught in the ones you're taking and wish I were there to discuss them with you and help where I can. I'm glad you've made a friend, and she helped you get a job. Too bad, you can't call me from there so I could hear your voice. Someday overseas calls will happen, but probably in our children's lifetimes rather than ours.

There is so much to say, but I can't except to tell you how much I love and miss you. You are never far from my mind. Remembering your kisses and words of love in my ear is what keeps me going.

Merry Christmas, my darling. May God keep you in the palm of His hand until I return.

Your loving fiancé, Ted

Hannah wiped the tears from her cheeks and pressed her lips to where he'd signed his name. Knowing he'd touched the letter and now, she was touching it with her lips made him seem closer. "Dear God, please keep this man safe and let this wretched war be over soon."

By the time Hannah boarded the train for Lake Geneva the next day, she'd read Ted's letter dozens of times. She'd decided to write back after she was at Safe Refuge and could report on his mother.

She spent the two-hour ride north imagining how Christmas would be if Ted were able to surprise her and walk into the family's living room on Christmas morning. Not exactly realistic, but far better than studying torts as she'd planned.

"Lake Geneva, next stop!"

The conductor's shout broke into her daydream, and she glanced out the window. They were already crossing over Main Street and soon would come the White River and the depot. She buttoned up her coat and tugged on her wool hat. A couple minutes later, the train came to a halt. She stuffed her handbag into her tote next to her textbook, then picked up her suitcase with one hand and the tote with the other.

She followed an elderly woman down the steps to the platform and surveyed the area for a familiar face.

"There's my darling daughter." She turned as Pop approached and gave her a quick hug. "Now that you're here, our family festivities can really begin." He reached for her suitcase.

"I can carry it. I've clothes already at home, so it's light. I'd love for you to take my tote instead."

He grabbed the bag and nearly dropped it. "Whoa, what's in here?"

She chuckled. "Only one of my textbooks and my purse." She hugged him from the side. "Merry Christmas, Pop. I'm happy to be home."

At the car, he stored her belongings in the backseat while Hanna climbed in the passenger seat. He slid behind the wheel and got the vehicle started. "It looks like snow is moving in. I'm glad it waited until you got here. I can't wait to hear all about your classes."

"Oh, you'll get an earful. I love everything. I never thought I'd enjoy school anywhere but at UW, but Northwestern is wonderful."

He turned out onto Broad Street. "I'm glad. You're managing your work at the phone company and homework both?"

"So far. I'm home from work early enough to study for a couple of hours, and I study during breaks between classes."

He turned onto Main Street. "The lake is already frozen over. Not quite safe enough for skating, but if it stays as cold as it's been, it won't be long. Your sisters are anxious to start skating. Have you heard from Ted?"

"I received a letter yesterday. It takes a while for his letters to pass through the censors before they are brought to the U.S. They always arrive a month after he writes them."

Well, at least he's safe in London and not at the front line. I have a sense the U.S. is going to be getting involved before too long. I'm surprised we didn't jump in after the Lusitania was sunk last year. But President Wilson is trying to keep us neutral, as is our dear state senator LaFollette. I think they need to reconsider."

Hannah stared at her father. "I never knew you to be a war supporter."

"I wasn't, but I've come to believe it's sometimes necessary. Has Ted said anything about the war in his letters?"

"He can't, or those lines would be snipped right out of the paper it was written on."

With all the leaves gone from the trees filling the park next to the white frame house that served as the public library, the frozen lake came into view. "I see a couple people out there now," Hannah said. "You better not let the girls know, or you'll never hear the end of it."

Pop glanced over. "If it's safe, it might do us all good to allow them. They are already bored from being on Christmas vacation, and it's only been a couple of days."

Hannah laughed. "I remember those times. Before you know it, they'll be through high school and off to college. Then they'll be so busy on school breaks you'll hardly see them."

"I know, and I'm not liking that idea at all." He turned on Snake Road and soon pulled into Safe Refuge's circular drive.

Mama was out the door before Hannah could extract herself from the car. Her mother wrapped her arms around her. "It's so good to have my first-born home."

"It's good to be here. I love the city, but this is home." She looked around. "Where are the girls?"

"Upstairs, getting ready to convince your father it's time to start the skating season."

Pop laughed. "What did I tell you?"

Mama released her from the embrace. "I thought you'd like to sleep here instead of the cottage since it's only for a few days, but if you prefer the cottage, we'll fire up the furnace."

She shook her head. "Here is fine. Clarice can sleep on the day bed in my room when she arrives."

Upstairs, Hannah went to her room and unbuttoned her blouse to change from her traveling outfit. Her breath hitched. Her necklace! She ran her gaze over the floor. Heart pounding, she rebuttoned the blouse and dashed into the hall, her eyes never leaving the floor as she descended the stairs. If she lost it on the train, she'd be sick to her stomach. She retraced her steps to the coat hooks and opened her coat and felt all around. Nothing.

"Hannah, what in the world are you looking for?"

She faced her mother. "Something precious to me. I have to go outside to the car. She flung the door open and burst through as Pop was stooping to pick something up.

He stared at it and then stood as she raced toward him. "I'm assuming this is yours?" He frowned as he held up the chain, with Ted's ring and the locket dangling from it.

Tears welled in her eyes. "Yes. Thank God, you found it."

"Is there something you've not told us?"

CHAPTER THIRTEEN

Hannah wrapped her fingers around the ring and locket. "May I please have it?"

He kept his grip on the chain. "Not until you tell me what this is about."

She tugged. "You don't want to know."

"It's freezing out here. Let's go inside, and you can tell me there."

She let go. "Okay."

They stepped inside and closed the door. Mama looked from Hannah to Pop. "What's going on?"

Pop cleared his throat. "She dropped this on the gravel outside." He held up the chain and let the ring and locket dangle.

Mama stared at her. "Oh, Hannah. It's a lovely ring, but why didn't you tell us?"

"I didn't want to upset you. Especially Pop."

Mama pulled her into a hug. "I'm very happy for you."

"Would someone please explain what this is about?"

Hannah stepped out of Mama's embrace and looked at Pop. "Ted proposed before he left. We're unofficially engaged, which is why he didn't ask for my hand. I've been wearing it and the locket with his picture on the chain under my clothes ever since. Like it or not, Pop, we're in love and plan to marry when he comes home."

His shoulders relaxed, and he handed her the necklace. "I'm glad you're concealing the ring. It's not good for people to know about your relationship with Ted or for you to see Mrs. Bauer until the war is over."

Tears trailed down her face. "We love each other, Pop, and I won't stop visiting his mother. She's there alone, and my time with her means a lot—to both of us. I know you mean well, but I can't abide by your wishes."

"Hannah. Give your father time to adjust to the fact you aren't a little girl anymore. Let's go to the kitchen. A cup of hot tea will soothe us all."

Hannah and her father sat at the kitchen table, neither saying a word while Mama put a kettle over a flame. She turned and looked at Hannah. "Your father needs to remember how it was when we were your age. Back in the day, I would have done the same thing if I were in your situation." She looked at Pop. "Nate, It's time to stop being caught up in the rumors. We liked Ted when we first met him and said we were glad Hannah had met a fine young man. Now it looks like he's going to be our son-in-law."

Pop's face twisted into a grimace. "This is one time you and I will have to disagree, Mo. I do not want anyone knowing about their relationship. Nor should his name ever be mentioned in the same breath as Hannah's."

Hannah couldn't believe her father's stance hadn't softened. She studied the necklace. "The clasp broke. I'll have to find a different chain."

"I have one you can use." Mama lifted the tea kettle and filled three cups on a tray.

Hannah smiled through her tears. "Thank you." She looked at her father. "I'm not home much anymore. Over Thanksgiving, I told Mrs. Bauer, I'd stop by either Christmas Eve or Christmas Day. I'll be leaving on the twenty-sixth and may not be home again until Easter."

"We can make up a plate of Christmas cookies for you to take to her." Mama set the tray holding their teas on the table. "Since we can't invite her for Christmas dinner, it's the least we can do."

Pop stared at his lap. Several moments passed, and he looked up. "I suppose that's the best way to handle it." He opened his arms to Hannah.

She moved over and sat on his knee. "I may be grown up now and in love with a wonderful man, but you'll always have a special place in my heart as my daddy."

His eyes widened. "You've never called me Daddy before."

"I know, but little children are calling their father's that more than father or papa now. I kind of like it."

He hugged her. "I like it too. Regardless of what your mother said, I do remember what it was like when I fell in love with her. I was so smitten she managed to sell me a dresser I didn't like."

She giggled. "I've never heard that story before. Please tell."

THE TRAIN from Chicago arrived on time, and Hannah slid out from behind the wheel of the family car and approached the platform. Several people stepped off before Clarice appeared at the top of the steps. She spotted Hannah and waved as she descended to the platform with the help of the conductor.

Hannah hurried up to her, and they embraced. "It's so good to see you, Clarice. Let's get to the car. It's freezing out here."

Clarice's brows rose. "Your vehicle has a heater?"

She shook her head. "No, but with the windows shut, it's a lot better than being in this wind."

After a quick drive through Lake Geneva's downtown,

Hannah glanced over at her friend. "I'd like to stop first at Ted's mother's house. I want to drop off a plate of cookies and wish her a Merry Christmas."

"Of course. I can't imagine the poor woman's holiday is going to be very happy with her son overseas and her husband in danger of being interred if we go to war."

"You don't know the half of it. If I tell you more, you've got to agree to not say one word to anyone. Not at my house or in the city at work or at school."

Her friend's face paled. "Good grief, Hannah. Of course, I won't tell."

During the drive to Tranquility Point, Hannah briefed Clarice on the edict Pop had laid down two days earlier and that this would have to be her last visit to Mrs. Bauer for a long while.

As they drove past the pair of stone pillars that flanked the drive into the Bauer estate, Clarice glanced at the estate's name carved in large letters on the columns. "I think they need to change the name. It's anything but tranquil around here these days."

Hannah pulled the automobile to a stop by the home's entrance.

Her friend stared at the stately white structure. "I know you told me Ted's family was well to do, but you didn't say his home was fit for a queen. You go on in. I'll wait here."

Hannah stared at Clarice. Did she not think she was good enough to step into such an elegant home? "You'll do no such thing. You'll freeze out here."

The pair walked to the entry, and Hannah pulled on a chain. Tinkling bells sounded from inside. The Bauer's housekeeper opened the door, and the middle-aged woman's face brightened. "Miss Murphy. The missus will be so happy to see you. Come in, and I'll tell her you're here."

Hannah and Clarice stepped into the foyer and shut the

door. "Gerta," Hannah said. This is my friend, Clarice, from law school."

"Pleased to meet you." The housekeeper offered Clarice a smile before pivoting and entering a door that lead to the kitchen and keeping room.

Moments later, a beaming Louise Bauer stepped into the foyer, her gaze fixed on Hannah. "Hannah, I didn't think I'd be seeing you on Christmas Eve. Thank you so much for coming."

Hannah smiled. "How could I not stop by and say Merry Christmas?" She turned toward Clarice. "This is Clarice Trudeau from law school. My mother sent you these." She held out the plate of cookies.

Mrs. Bauer took the plate. *"Danke Sehr"*

"I presume you said thank you. You are most welcome."

"Sorry. Lately, German seems to come out of my mouth more than English. It was all we spoke at home until I was old enough to go to school. But what with Ted being overseas and Henry and Peter staying in the city, it's not much of a holiday this year."

Hannah's heart ached that she couldn't invite Mrs. Bauer to Christmas dinner. "Then it's good that I came by today. Clarice and I are heading back to the city the day after tomorrow. We have to work the rest of the week."

"Let's sit in the keeping room." Without waiting for a reply, Mrs. Bauer stepped through a door to the left, and they followed her to a small cozy room off the kitchen.

Hannah waited while Mrs. Bauer placed the cookies on a low table and took a seat in a chair to the left of the fireplace. Hannah then took a chair that flanked the hearth on the right. She gestured to Clarice to sit in a chair next to her "The fire feels wonderful. I love this room.".

"Have you heard from Ted? I haven't had a letter in a long while." Mrs. Bauer studied the cookies. "Did you mother make these?"

"Yes, with help from my sisters. I heard a few days ago. But, of course, the letter was written a month earlier. He said nothing has changed, whatever that means. If he tells me more, it gets snipped out by the censors."

"I'm relieved someone has heard. Can you stay for tea? I could have Gerta put on some hot water."

Regretting she hadn't allowed themselves more time, Hannah shook her head. "We'd love to, but my family is waiting, and I need to get the car back for my mother to use for last-minute errands before Christmas Eve celebrating begins."

Mrs. Bauer stood. "Before you go, I have something to give you. I'll be right back."

The woman rustled out of the room, and Hannah looked at Clarice. "I hope she didn't get me a present."

"Maybe she didn't get you one personally," Clarice whispered. "Some women like to have little presents on hand for when they've been given a gift, and they feel they have to return the gesture."

Hannah raised a brow. "For a plate of cookies? I hardly think—."

"Here you go, dear Hannah."

She turned toward Mrs. Bauer, and her mouth fell open. Clarice was right. "You don't need to give me a gift."

Mrs. Bauer held out the gaily wrapped small package. "I didn't get you a gift. Ted gave it to me before he left. He wanted for you to have a present from him even though he couldn't be here to give it to you himself."

A warmth that rivaled the heat from the hearth washed over Hannah as she accepted the gift. What had she done to deserve such a wonderful man? "Oh. I think I'm going to cry."

"You're not the only one," Clarice whispered.

She looked from Clarice to Ted's mother. "Should I open it now?"

"I think you should do it at home alone, not with us watching," Clarice said.

"You're right." Hannah opened her arms to Mrs. Bauer, and they embraced. Hannah breathed in her soft flowery scent. "Thank you for raising your son to be such a thoughtful man, Mrs. Bauer."

The woman stepped out of Hannah's embrace. "I think you should call me Louise. After all, when this war is over, you will be marrying my boy. You're the daughter I never had." She glanced at Hannah's left hand. "Ted told me you're wearing his ring on a chain. Are you still doing that?"

Hannah grinned and tugged the ring out from beneath her thick sweater. "I'm so glad you know. It's right here where it's been since he gave it to me."

Louise's face lit up. "Merry Christmas, Hannah." She kissed Hannah on both cheeks the way Europeans did.

Hanna blinked back her tears. "Hopefully, this messy war will be over soon, and we will all be together again."

Back in the vehicle, Hannah started the motor, and neither woman spoke until they had returned to the state route. Clarice spoke first. "Friend, you better not let go of that man of yours ever."

"I don't intend to. Let's just hope God keeps him safe over there."

"And what a sweet woman his mother is. It must hurt to not be able to invite her for Christmas dinner."

"It does. I pray she never has to hear about my father's edict. I'm not even going to tell Ted."

"Good decision. The mindset everywhere is so anti-German." People aren't considering that a lot of people with German surnames are on our side. I fear what may happen if this war doesn't end soon."

CHAPTER FOURTEEN

Christmas morning, unable to see her clock and not wanting to wake Clarice who slept on a daybed across the room, Hannah gingerly slipped her feet into her bedroom slippers and donned her bathrobe she'd left flung over a chair. She picked up her alarm clock and took it in to the hall along with Ted's present and slipped into the bathroom.

She flicked on the light and stared at the clock. What was she doing waking at five a.m.? She quickly calculated what time it was in London, six hours away. Not yet lunchtime. What was Ted doing? Did he have the day off? On Christmas Day, the first year of the war, the troops on both sides of the front line called a truce and actually sang carols with each other. Nothing like that had happened since. She supposed if it was Ted's day to work, he was working. Especially since he was likely one of the newer decoders.

Too wide awake to get back to sleep, she left her clock in the bathroom and stole downstairs to the kitchen. As she scooped coffee grounds into the percolator basket, she whispered her first prayer of the morning. "Please, Lord, on this day as we celebrate your birth, be with Ted. Help him to remain strong.

Infuse in him the knowledge that my heart is with him on a day when, in normal times, we'd be exchanging presents and being with our families. Please keep all the soldiers safe today and cause this war to end soon." She tucked the basket full of coffee grounds into the pot that she'd already filled with water and lit the flame on the oil stove. She then moved to the kitchen table, where Mama left her Bible every night.

She opened the book and flipped through the crinkling pages, pausing every so often when an underlined verse caught her eye. It seemed almost every psalm had been marked, She stopped to read Psalm Ninety-One

> *I will say of the* LORD, *He is my refuge and my fortress:*
> *my God; in him will I trust.*
> *Surely he shall deliver thee from the snare of the fowler,*
> *and from the noisome pestilence.*

Hannah bowed her head and whispered, "Lord, please deliver Ted from whatever snares he encounters and keep him safe. Be his refuge."

A cough sounded behind her. She jumped and turned.

Clarice stood there in a pink robe. "My goodness, do you always get up so early?"

"I'm sorry. Did I wake you?"

Her friend shook her head. "No. I never sleep well the first night in a different bed. I woke up as you left the room. When you didn't come back, I came looking for you. Blame my worrisome nature. I only wanted to make sure you're okay."

"I'm fine. I woke up, and my first thoughts went to Ted."

Clarice closed the space between them and glanced at the open Bible. "And here I am intruding."

"You're not intruding."

"I am when my best friend's fiancé is off at war, and she's praying."

"I was about to open Ted's gift. Give me about ten minutes. I do want you to see whatever it is."

After Clarice returned to the bedroom with a steaming cup of coffee in hand, Hannah carried her brew and the gift into the living room, She sat in a chair next to the Christmas tree, then lit the lamp sitting on an end table and gave the gift a shake. With a box so small, whatever it was, she likely wouldn't be able to share it with her parents.

Hannah slipped off the ribbon and carefully removed the paper. The red velvet box bore the name of a Chicago jeweler. She was right. She lifted the lid and gasped at the gold heart-shaped locket and chain. She lifted the necklace and ran her thumb over the rose design on its cover. She slowly turned it over and read the tiny words on the back, "Ted & Hannah hearts entwined." She pressed the heart's edge, and the locket opened. During a gathering earlier in the summer, one of Ted's friends had taken their picture together and had given them each a copy. He'd cut his copy of the photo in half to fit their faces into the small frames on either side.

She pressed her lips to his picture and whispered. "Oh, Ted, I miss you so much."

"Is it okay to come in now?" Clarice stood at the door, wearing a stylish red dress with velvet trim. "I actually waited for twenty minutes."

"I hadn't realized it had been that much time. Come and see what Ted gave me. I'm a blubbering mess."

Clarice crossed the room and stared at the locket Hannah held out. "Oh, that's gorgeous."

"Not only that, look at what's on the back."

Clarice read the inscription and grinned. "You are living a fairy tale. Are there pictures inside?"

Hannah opened the locket and turned it so Clarice could see the photos.

She sighed. "I'd like to wear it today. I don't know why my

father has to be so strident in wanting me to keep our relationship quiet. He knows Ted was born in America."

"My goodness, you two are up early." Mama walked into the room, wearing the same green and red dress she'd worn last Christmas, and her gaze went to the locket in Hannah's hand. "What is that?"

"Ted left this Christmas present for me with his mother. Isn't it beautiful?" She held it up, so the heart-shaped locket dangled.

Mama took the locket and let it lie across her palm. "It is exquisite. Your young man has great taste. She turned it over. "Oh, Hannah. It's clear he deeply loves you. May I look inside?"

Blinking at her tears, she nodded.

Mama studied the photos. "Beautiful pictures of both of you. When were they taken?"

"At a gathering last summer at one of Ted's friends. I'm sure Pop won't want me wearing it around here."

"I think you should. And while you're at it, the ring too. I don't like all this sneaking around. That's not how our family does things."

Hannah smiled. "I know, but he's been so touchy."

"If you want, I can prepare him before he sees it."

"Before I see what?" Pop strode into the room wearing gray flannel trousers, a crisp white shirt, and vest, his tie perfectly knotted at his neck.

Hannah gathered the locket into her closed fist and let go of a sigh. "Ted left a Christmas gift for me with his mother. She gave it to me yesterday, and I just opened it." She uncurled her fingers and held up the locket.

He stepped closer and studied the jewelry. "That's quite lovely. Why would you not want me to see it?"

She shrugged. "I didn't want to upset you knowing how you feel about keeping our relationship quiet."

His face slackened. "I'm sorry you feel that way. To be honest, I've regretted some of the things I've said. I've been meaning to apologize but didn't know how. He took the locket from her, turned it over, and read the inscription. "Let's get this around your neck where it belongs."

She smiled through her tears. "Best we wait until I wash. I still have to dress. Does this mean you're okay for me to wear the ring on my finger?"

He pursed his lips for a couple seconds. "I'm wary only because of the growing sentiment toward all of German descent. I'm sure it's fine to wear it on your ring finger once you're back in Illinois. Now go get dressed. We still need to eat breakfast and get to church by nine."

Before dressing, Hannah slipped the ring onto her left hand and admired it for a moment. One day, God willing, she'd be able to wear it in full view all the time with Pop's blessing. She quickly dressed, then Clarice helped her fasten the locket around her neck. She paused in front of her mirror, loving how the pendant looked against her dark green velvet dress. She gathered up the presents she'd found in the city for the girls. "Let's go before my sisters stage a revolt."

"It's about time you two got here." Pop stepped out from the kitchen, wearing a bib apron and holding a spatula.

"Sorry, we got to talking." Hannah and Clarice went to the living room, and she nestled her gifts among the other presents under the tree. "Something smells good."

"Blueberry pancakes." Annie piped up from where she sat on the floor, ogling the gifts. "Pop is making us wait to open gifts after we eat breakfast."

"Well then, we'd best get to the breakfast table and eat fast." Hanna turned and linked arms with Clarice. "You are about to eat the best blueberry pancakes in the world."

CHAPTER FIFTEEN

April 6, 1917

Clarice ran up to Hannah at the streetcar stop near the law school, her face flushed. "I'm glad I found you. With our short attendance day, I wasn't sure I would. We're in!"

Hannah stared at her. "In what?"

"The U.S. just declared war on Germany and joined the allies. Things are going to start changing around the telephone office and everywhere else."

Hannah sagged against a streetlamp and gasped for air.

"Hannah, are you okay?"

She gave herself a mental shake. "Yes. I think so. For a minute I couldn't breathe. I'm concerned about Ted and what this might mean for him."

"Isn't he still in flying school?"

"I think he was to complete it last week. I've been pushing that out of my mind because that means he'll be soon flying over Brussels and engaging in battles and dropping bombs."

"Yow, I'd be nervous too. I didn't think about that. He'll switch over to the U.S. military now, won't he?"

"What he can say is so vague. The U.S. is in the process of developing an air division. He anticipated staying with the Royal Flying Corps initially. The RFC flies out of their own airfields since they are only across the channel from the action."

"I'm surprised he could tell you that much."

"I learned how to fill in gaps by going to the library and reading the British newspapers." A shiver raced down Hannah's back as reality slammed her in the gut. No longer could she be assured Ted was in relative safety.

"Well, that shows how interested in the details of warfare I am. Were you headed home?"

"I was planning to meet Cora and Earl at church for Good Friday services. But right now, all I want is to call my family, hear their voices."

"I bet the switchboards at work are lighting up like a dozen Christmas trees because of a lot of people wanting to do the same thing."

"You don't want to call your mother?"

Clarice looked off. "We're not really as close as I let on."

"I suspected that from things you've said. You're welcome to come with me to my cousin's if you don't want to be alone."

"I think I'll head over to work and see if they need help."

Hannah grimaced. "You would say that. Now I'll feel guilty about going home."

Clarice waved her off. "Don't. If I were you, I'd do what you're doing. Maybe I'll be your operator when you make the call."

Hannah's transportation came shortly after Clarice's. She squeezed into the crowded car, and, not finding a seat, she gripped a pole. The usually quiet streetcar hummed with dozens of conversations. She closed her eyes as the tension-filled air seemed to wrap around her.

"It's about time the U.S. came out from hiding. We'll show those Krauts they can't bully other countries around."

She glanced down at an older balding man who sat on a nearby seat.

The man next to him nodded. "I agree. We'll show the Bosch they can't push people around like they've been doing. I wish I were younger and able to join up."

On the other side of the aisle, a woman sniffed into her handkerchief. "I'm scared my Ernest is going to be called up. He's my baby." Her seatmate comforted her with an arm over the woman's shoulders.

Hannah said a silent prayer thanking God she only had sisters and that Pop was too old to be drafted. It was enough to worry about Ted, especially if he'd become a pilot.

By the time she arrived at her stop, she was grateful for the peaceful quiet street her cousin lived on. As people began coming home, she doubted it would be silent for long. She stepped into the house, and loud sobs filtered into the foyer. She scurried down the long hall and entered the kitchen. Cora sat at the kitchen table, weeping into her folded arms. Hannah placed a hand on Cora's shaking shoulder. "Cora, I'm home. What's wrong?"

Cora raised her head and stared at Hannah through her red eyes. "Oh, Hannah, I'm glad you came home. When we heard the news, Earl decided to stay at work, and I've been here weeping ever since. I'm afraid Earl is going to be called to war. I was feeling safe because the president has said we were going to stay neutral."

"Isn't Earl too old? He's almost thirty."

She dabbed her eyes with a handkerchief. "The cut off is thirty-one. They have to register by June."

"I didn't realize it went into the thirties. I would think they'd first draft the younger men. And I heard several men on the streetcar say they planned to sign up. Maybe enough will enlist, and Earl won't be drafted."

She sniffed. "I hope you're right. I'm glad you came home early. I thought you were going to church from school."

"After I heard the news, all I wanted to do was call home and didn't want to wait."

Cora nodded. "I understand. I called my mother already."

Hannah stepped into the hall and dropped into the chair beside the small table that held the candlestick phone. She put the earpiece to her ear and tapped the switch hook several times. An operator came on the line. "Hello. How may I help you?"

She didn't recognize the voice. "I'd like to call Lake Geneva, Wisconsin. The number is five-four-seven."

She waited through the silence, visualizing the steps being taken to make the connection.

Pop's voice came through the line. "This is Doctor Murphy."

"Pop, it's Hannah. I'm glad you're home. After I heard the news, I wanted to call you."

"Hannah. I've been thinking about contacting you, but I thought you'd be at church."

"I should be, but we didn't go."

"We stayed home too. By the way, it appears I'm not alone in my suspicions about Henry Bauer."

She let out a sigh. "As I've said before he's been living in Chicago because—"

"I know, but the afternoon papers are posting a warning to all Germans who have never become U.S. citizens. They're now called enemy aliens, and restrictions such as curfews and limits on how far they can venture from home are going into effect. I'm glad you're not at home and being tempted to visit Mrs. Bauer."

Her chest tightened. "Louise Bauer has been an American citizen since she was a baby. There should be no danger in visiting her."

She heard him take a deep breath. "It's difficult to know who to trust. Have you heard from Ted?"

She swiped at a tear trailing down her cheek. "Not for about two weeks. I'm scared. There's something I didn't tell you about what he's been doing."

"Don't tell me he's a spy for the Brits."

She rolled her eyes. "He's been taking flying lessons from the Royal Flying Corps and will soon be serving as a pilot for them. Now that the U.S. is in the war, I'm not sure how that will work, once we have our own air service in place. But no matter who he's affiliated with, he's going to be in danger."

Silence filled the connection. "The man is either more courageous than I gave him credit for or a fool. Do his parents know this?"

"I don't think so. He talked about waiting until he was a certified pilot. Maybe by now he's written to them and the letter is on the way."

"Let's hope so."

"A part of me wants to come home, but, at least for now, I intend to stay in school and continue working for the phone company. I expect the switchboards will be busier than usual. I'll give Louise a call and ask her to let me know if she hears anything from Ted."

"Good idea to stay put. If I don't hand your mother the earpiece, she's going to have a conniption fit. Here she is."

Her mother's voice came through the connection. "Don't bother repeating what you told your father. I only want to say I love you, my dear daughter. I think we're in for a long struggle, and we will be praying for Ted and all of the other young men who will be going to war."

"Thank you, Mama. I love you."

Hannah hung up the telephone and returned to the kitchen, where Cora was pouring hot water into a pair of cups. "Hot tea sounds good. I'm glad I called home. Things are worse than I thought for Ted's family. His father in particular." She took a seat at the table.

Cora set a steaming cup in front of Hannah and sat across from her. They sipped in silence for a few moments. Cora cleared her throat. "Are you planning to return to Lake Geneva until the war is over?"

"The law school is filled with young men, many of whom will likely be drafted. I'd think they would have to suspend classes once the draft starts. I'm sure the telephone company will need me to take on more shifts." She wrapped her hand around the heart locket. "I'm scared Cora. What if I never see Ted again?"

"Hannah, listen to you. Didn't you just tell me I shouldn't worry about Earl being drafted before it happens? The same goes for you and your fretting about Ted."

At her cousin's words, the tears Hannah had managed to keep corralled trailed down her cheeks. Cora came around the table to embrace her. "God has both our men in His hands, and we need to trust Him. While you were on the phone, I remembered something Granny used to say to me. Don't borrow trouble before it happens."

Hannah leaned back and managed a smile. "My granny used to say the same thing. Do you suppose our great-grandmother said it to them?"

Cora shrugged. "Probably. Not a bad thing to pass on through the generations."

"I'm going to repeat those words to myself whenever I feel worries coming on."

Cora retook her seat and picked up a Bible that was sitting on the table. "The better thing to remember is what God's word says." The pages crackled as she flipped them. "Here's what I'm looking for." She slid the Bible across the table and pointed at the page from Philippians and the words she'd underlined.

> *Be careful for nothing; but in everything by prayer and*
> *supplication with thanksgiving let your requests be*
> *made known unto God.*
> *And the peace of God, which passeth all understanding,*
> *shall keep your hearts and minds through Christ*
> *Jesus.*

Hannah looked up. "Thank you. That's perfect. Do you always mark up your Bible?"

"I do with the scriptures I want to remember."

"That makes sense. I usually jot verses in a notebook. But that one got past me. I think the next time I write Ted, I'll share this verse with him."

HANNAH STEPPED into the telephone office's lunchroom, somehow finding comfort in the room's sterile appearance. She sat at the table and picked up a copy of the *Chicago Daily Tribune*. The large headline seemed to scream at her: U.S. AT WAR.

"You came after all." Clarice stepped in, carrying an apple and dropped into a chair across from Hannah.

"I couldn't stay at home without feeling guilty. I tried calling Miss Marshall to let her know I was available, but I couldn't get through. I thought maybe the ride down here would help me clear my thoughts, but the streetcar was noisy with everyone jabbering about the news. It was impossible to think or pray. Miss Marshall says the boards are fully staffed through tomorrow morning, but she added me to the next five afternoons instead of the usual three. It's going to cut into study time, but it's the least I can do to support the war effort."

Clarice took a bite of her apple and chewed a few moments. "I'm on the same schedule too. We can study together during our dinner breaks."

"We're needed here, but I can't help but feel there must be something more we—or I should say I—can do. A part of me wants to drop out of school until it's over. Then I want to stay. Ted isn't done with his law classes yet, and if I finish before him, I can support us both while he catches up. But will there even be classes to attend with so many of our classmates being drafted?"

"I've been thinking about temporarily dropping out too. Communication is going to be very important in the war effort. We are needed right here on the boards even if it's only to connect neighbors and family members." Clarice finished off her apple and tossed the core into the trash.

Hannah sighed. "My father told me the government is already warning noncitizens—namely the Germans—that they're being watched and if they break any laws, they will be severely prosecuted. Pop thought the limit for German residents on how far they can travel from home is only a mile. Fortunately, Mr. Bauer's Chicago home is in Lincoln Park, and his office is on the northside. It might be more than a mile, but not by much. How can those people survive if they can't go to work?"

Clarice's eyes widened. "That's probably the plan. It sounds like they're almost forcing them to return to Germany."

"It's even worse. All residents who are still German citizens will have to register as enemy aliens and carry an ID card."

"What about Ted's mother?"

"She was born here to naturalized citizens. Their Lake Geneva property is in her name, and Bauer Pharmaceuticals is in Ted's brother's name."

Clarice's eyes widened. "Has the government said they will seize their property?"

"Not yet, but it's been mentioned. I hope to head up to Lake Geneva on the weekend and visit Ted's mother. My father isn't going to be happy, but I must do it, even if it means being ostracized by my own father."

CHAPTER SEVENTEEN

Two Weeks Later

Hannah boarded the train for Lake Geneva, thankful the phone company didn't need her for the weekend. She selected a window seat and slid her small suitcase onto the rack above. Hannah invited Cora to join her at the lake for the weekend, but her cousin wanted to be home for the few hours she and Earl had with each other. She hated leaving her because Earl continued to work long hours, and too much time alone was wearing on Cora.

Already, a dark cloud had settled over the law school as people seemed to be frozen in time, waiting for the first draft notices to appear. Talk of the school temporarily shutting down seemed to be on everyone's lips. That would suit her fine. She couldn't concentrate on classwork with Ted and other men she knew being in harm's way. The conductor's shout of, "All aboard," along with a loud hiss outside the window interrupted her thoughts.

The young man next to her cleared his throat, and she glanced over. He looked vaguely familiar. Had she seen him at church or school? Before she could ask, he faced her. "I've seen you in one of my law classes. I don't believe we've met. My name is Will O'Brien"

She offered a soft smile. "Hannah Murphy. I was trying to place where I'd seen you before."

"There aren't too many women enrolled in law school. I knew immediately where I've seen you. Where are you headed?"

"Lake Geneva. What about you?"

"Williams Bay. The end of the line. My father is a caretaker on one of the estates. I withdrew from school today and plan to enlist on Monday."

Not wanting him to see the grimace on her face, she turned away. It was all happening too fast. She gathered her emotions and faced him. "That's very brave of you."

His expression turned grim. "I'm scared to death, but a man has a duty to his country."

"As do women. I'm thinking about withdrawing from school myself. I can't go to the front line, but I'd feel guilty staying in school while men like yourself are in danger. Were many others withdrawing when you were there?"

He nodded. "Quite a few. We were told that the university is trying to figure out how to keep the classes going, but with so many of draft age, suspending classes until the war is over will likely happen. They told all of us that when we return, we can pick up where we left off. I have to tell my parents today I'm not waiting for the draft to enlist. I'm the first O'Brien to get a college degree, and I know they'll be disappointed. Do you live in Lake Geneva?"

"Yes, but on the lakeshore. The Safe Refuge estate."

His face lit up. "Rory Quinn's property?"

"He was my grandfather. You've heard of him?"

"Yes. My da talks about Rory a lot. Says he helped him get his job as a caretaker working for the McCraes on the Blackloft estate."

She grinned. "We're almost neighbors. That's only a short walk down the shore path from Safe Refuge."

"We are at that." He frowned. "I don't remember any Murphy's living in that house, only the Quinns."

"My mother is a Quinn. My father is Nate Murphy. Until a few years ago, we lived in town in the same house as his medical practice.

"Of course. Now I make the connection. Doctor Murphy has been our doctor for as long as I can remember."

She chuckled. "Small world, isn't it?"

"It is at that. I guess we never met because I attended Woods School, and you probably attended a private school."

She shook her head. "My parents sent me to public school in town. My Aunt Katie and grandmother both taught at Woods before they had children. Where did you go to high school?

"Williams Bay." He yawned. "I'm going to try to nap if you don't mind. I haven't gotten much sleep this whole week."

"Nor have I. Nice to meet you, Will O'Brien." She pressed her head against the back of the seat and closed her eyes, wishing the knot in her stomach would subside. Will lived close to Safe Refuge, and yet they'd never met. Despite her parents' efforts to keep the family from being considered upper class like most of the lakeshore families, it still happened. War was a great equalizer.

Subdued chatter floated through the car. As the voices rose and fell, snatches of the conversations became background noise. Would older men eventually be drafted? Would the Germans be able to make it to our shores? Would the government really detain Germans who never became U.S. citizens, or, worse yet, deport them? She managed to tune most of it out, letting the click-clacking of the train's wheels become a sort of lullaby.

"Yeah, I heard Henry Bauer is under surveillance along with his son."

"I thought his son was over in England serving with their army. Doesn't sound traitorous to me."

Her eyes popped open. The voices seemed to come from the seats behind her.

"Not that son. The one who works at Bauer Pharmaceuticals in Chicago."

"They better watch out. I hear the government might start seizing the property belonging to German citizens."

"If that happens, Tranquility Point will be no more."

"I heard it's been put in his wife's name."

"Isn't she German?"

"Don't think so."

The conversation moved on to something else, but the words whirled in her thoughts. If only she could contact Ted and tell him what people were saying. At least Ted's reputation seemed to be intact. No matter what Pop thought, she must visit Louise Bauer as soon as possible. Surely the government wouldn't seize Tranquility Point, would they?

The train arrived in Lake Geneva, and Hannah glanced at Will. "Here's my stop. My father is meeting me at the city dock with the boat. I'm sure he wouldn't mind dropping you at Blackloft."

Will thought a moment then shook his head. "Sounds inviting, but my da is meeting the train in Williams Bay. He'll be on his way from Delavan, and there's no way to contact him. Thanks for offering, though."

Hearing him call his father the Irish "Da" caused a sweet memory of hearing her mother call her father "Da." Hannah wished Will safety and blessing along with her goodbye and stepped off the train. Her yearning to spend time on the water as soon as possible had prompted her to suggest Pop pick her up at the Lake Geneva pier. Nothing calmed her more than being on Geneva Lake.

She shifted her small suitcase from her right hand to her left and began walking down Broad Street. A northwesterly breeze buffeted her back. Grateful she'd chosen to wear the wide-brimmed hat that tied under her chin, she stopped to fasten the top button on her wool coat. It may be spring on the calendar, but that didn't mean warm breezes in Wisconsin. Those didn't usually come until May.

Automobiles, along with an occasional horse and wagon, traveled up and down Broad Street. As she approached Main Street, the sidewalk filled with shoppers, mostly women with woven baskets over their arms, likely picking up groceries for tonight's supper. Since it was a school day, only children below the age of six were around. To look at the town, one wouldn't guess the U.S. was now at war.

She crossed Main Street and glanced over at the Geneva Hotel. Memories of the dinner date she had with Ted before he shipped out flooded into her thoughts. Despite his announcement about enlisting in the British army, having admitted to each other they'd fallen in love, they walked on air that night. "Lord, please keep Ted safe wherever he is and whatever he is doing. Please protect Will, the man I met on the train, as he heads to war."

She arrived at the dock and spotted Pop waving from the *Doreen*, the family's steam yacht Grandfather Rory had acquired for his family. She loved how the boat still served her generation.

She approached the boat and handed her suitcase over to her father, where he stood on the vessel. He set it on the polished wood deck and held out his hand. "Welcome aboard." Instead of letting go of her after she stood next to him, he pulled her into his embrace. "Hannah, my girl. I'm so glad you're here."

She leaned back and looked him in the eyes. "It feels good to be home."

"How long can you stay?"

"I have to be back by Tuesday afternoon for a shift at the telephone company."

His brows arched. "No classes?"

"I don't know yet. Only a few women are enrolled, and most of the men are of draft age. The school may have to temporarily shut down."

He stepped out of her embrace. "That makes sense. The same thing is probably happening in medical schools." He began untying the ropes from the pilings. "We can talk more about it at the house. Your mother is anxiously awaiting your arrival and preparing your favorite beef roast dinner."

Her stomach rumbled. The first pang of hunger she'd felt since Monday when news of war became real. "Beef roast sounds wonderful. Probably the last we'll be able to enjoy in the coming months."

He put the boat in reverse and backed away from the dock then got it moving forward out into the open water toward Safe Refuge. "You're right about the roast. I got the last one at the butcher yesterday, and he doesn't expect any more in. Most beef is being allocated to the training bases. Chicken is in far greater supply."

"I'm sure I'll enjoy every bite. Since there's an hour's worth of light left, would you mind heading up shore past home? Nothing calms me like a boat ride."

He grinned. "Your wish is my command." He got the boat running parallel to the shoreline. Over on shore, her sisters stood on the Safe Refuge dock waving. She waved back. "The girls are wondering why we're not coming their way."

He laughed. "They're very anxious to see their big sister. But it won't hurt them to wait a little longer."

Blackloft, the estate where Will lived, came into view. "I sat next to a man on the train who is planning to enlist on Monday. His father is Blackloft's caretaker. You might know him. He said you were his doctor."

Pop's eyes widened. "Will O'Brien?"

"Yes."

"I had no idea he was old enough to enlist. I haven't seen him in a while."

"He's attending law school with me. I didn't know him as he attended Woods School and went to high school in the Bay." She looked out at the water and waited for it to soothe her troubled soul. "Pop, I feel so small. Here Will grew up only a few properties down from Safe Refuge, and I never met him. I hate how our paths never crossed."

"I get how you feel, but if he'd attended the same public school in town as you, you would have met him. Remember, you didn't live at Safe Refuge until a few years ago and had lots of friends in town."

"I know, but I was at Safe Refuge more than home during the summers, and none of my summer friends were from town. I hope that when Ted and I are married, we can live in town in a regular house like I grew up in at first and let our siblings have the lakeshore homes."

His lips turned down. "I'm sorry you feel that way. Have you thought about how you can use the blessing of a home like Safe Refuge to help others? Don't shun it so quickly. Since we'll be at Tranquility Point in a few minutes, do you want to stop and look in on Louise Bauer?"

She gaped at him. He really had changed. Was she ready to face her future mother-in-law and have what may be a difficult conversation? "I don't like dropping in on people unannounced. Besides, it's getting chilly, and Mama is probably wondering where we are. I'll get settled and drive over tomorrow."

CHAPTER EIGHTEEN

As Hannah and her father made their way up the incline from the lake, Mama stepped out on the veranda steps wearing an apron over her long-sleeved blouse and skirt. Her hairstyle was much shorter than the last time Hannah had seen her. "It's about time you got here. The girls said you zoomed right past them half an hour ago."

Hannah embraced her mother. "I love your bobbed hair. I'm sorry to confuse you. I wanted some additional time on the water to clear my head of all the war talk. Not that I expect the chatter to disappear now that I'm here."

Her mother pulled an envelope from her skirt pocket and handed it to Hannah. "It won't. This arrived in today's mail. Ted must have thought you would be here rather than in Evanston by the time it made it this far."

She stared at Ted's familiar scrawl and smiled. "He said he might start sending my letters here, but I didn't expect one so soon. I'd like to read it alone. I'll share later what he said."

Pop picked up her suitcase. "I'll help you get this over to the cottage."

"I think I'd like to sleep in my old room, at least for tonight. I don't want to be alone just now."

Pop looked at her mother. "Is the room—"

"Ready for her?" Mama grinned. "I was hoping she'd want to be with us. Yes. Fresh sheets are on the bed."

As they stepped into the house, Margie and Annie scampered up, both wrapping their arms around Hannah from either side. She laughed. "My goodness, what a wonderful welcome. I've missed you girls."

Annie leaned back and looked up at her. "We missed you too, and Ted. When is he coming back?"

She hunched down until she was eye level with her little sister. "I wish I knew, Annie. He's in Europe right now fighting the bad guys."

"That's what Pop told us. He showed us on the globe where he is. But when is he coming home?"

Hannah drew in a breath. "Probably not until everyone agrees to stop fighting." She stood and gave her father a look that said, 'help me out.'

Pop shrugged. "You're on your own. Nothing I said satisfied her." He continued to the stairs.

"You're silly, Annie." Margie lifted her chin. "Maybe you're too young to understand."

"I am not too young." Annie turned on her heel and ran down the hall after Pop.

The aroma of roast beef caused Hannah's stomach to growl. "That roast smells divine," she called out to her mother. "I promise I won't be long." She headed to the stairs, hoping Annie wasn't waiting for her to continue peppering her with questions for which she had no answers.

At her room's door, neither Pop or her sister were in sight. Assuming they must have returned to the lower floor by way of the back stairs, she dropped into the upholstered chair in front of the large window, then opened the locket Ted had given her at Christmas and stared at his picture. Oh, how she yearned to feel his arms around her, his lips against hers. At least with his image before her, while she read his letters, it seemed he wasn't so far away. She slid her finger under the envelope's flap and lifted out the folded paper and began to read.

My dearest Hannah,

I miss you so much, my love, and wish this horrible war was behind us so we could be together. I don't know if the following information will get through the censors, but I'm going to try. I'm soon to make my first run over the enemy, and by the time you get this, I'll have made several more sorties. I know you pray for me daily, and I covet those prayers. It's exciting and scary at the same time. I'm no longer stationed near London. I can't disclose my location, but I can say I won't be at the front line, so please don't worry. Being in the air is safer than being a sitting target in the trenches. Regardless of this being wartime, I have to say, outside of meeting you, this has been the best time in my life. I can't explain what it feels like to be flying through the air with the beautiful English countryside below me.

I wrote to my parents about my pilot training, and by the time you receive this, they should have received their letter. I expect nothing has changed regarding my father. If you can, please continue to check on my mother. My brother has enough on his hands, keeping the company running. He's hoping to receive a deferment since I'm enlisted, and our mother is alone in Wisconsin.

I fall asleep every night with you on my mind and dream of your sweet kisses. I can't wait to come home to you and hold you in my arms forever.

All my love,
Ted

She picked up the envelope to see the postmark. Three weeks earlier. Faster than most of his letters. She read his last words for at least the dozenth time, and a tear dropped from her cheek onto the paper, smearing the word 'love' near his signature. She reached for a pillow and hugged it to her chest, trying to pretend it was Ted. She tossed it aside. Pretending was no use. "Lord, please keep him safe. I love him so much, but You love him more."

A knock came at the door. "Hannah, are you okay?"

"Yes. Mama, come in."

Her mother stepped into the room, a concerned expression on her face. "I heard you crying clear into the hall. Did Ted have bad news?"

She sat up. "I don't know if it's good or bad. He can't tell me much but, I read between the lines. It appears he's now certified to fly and is flying what he calls sorties over the enemy. He insists flying a plane is safer than being on the ground. I'm not sure I agree." She sniffed and blew her nose into her handkerchief. "Guns can shoot down a plane."

Her mother sat next to her and pulled her into a hug. "I was reading Psalm Ninety-One this morning, and I think it's a good psalm to read every morning while this war is going on." She reached over to the nightstand and picked up the Bible, keeping her other arm around Hannah.

Hannah pressed her face into her mother's shoulder as the sound of the Bible's thin pages being turned filled the air.

"Here it is. Listen." Mama's soft voice rose and fell as she read the soothing words aloud.

> *"He that dwelleth in the secret place of the most High*
> *shall abide under the shadow of the Almighty.*
> *I will say of the LORD, He is my refuge and my fortress:*
> *my God; in Him will I trust."*

Hannah leaned back and looked into her mother's green eyes. "How do I know I'm dwelling in God's secret place?"

"Do you live by the commitment you made to Him when you were in grammar school?"

"Yes. Most of the time."

A soft smile lifted the corners of her mother's lips. "None of us are perfect. That's why we need Him every day of our lives. I fully believe He has Ted in the palm of His hand, as he likes to say, and you as well. If it's His will for Ted to return home and you two to have a life together, it will happen."

Hannah blinked her tears away. "Why do you always have the right words to say?"

"I had a wonderful teacher during one of the biggest trials of my life."

"I know. Mrs. Ambrose."

"I wish you could have known her. The Lord took her way too early. At least you were able to know her for a little while."

"I remember her sparkling blue eyes and hair as white as snow. I always thought she was a beautiful angel."

Mama hugged her. "And what is remarkable is that even as a child, you saw through her scarred face to the beauty beneath."

"The same as you, Mama. I don't see your scars, either."

Mama's hand went to her left cheek, the scars not now as prominent as they had been. "It's hard to think that right after I had smallpox and the scars appeared, I thought my life was over."

"But Pop loved you despite your scars." Hannah covered Mama's hand with her own and squeezed it. "Each generation has its trials to bear. Our family certainly has." She stood and crossed the room to the mirror over her dresser. "My face may be scar-free, but it's full of red blotches. I'd better splash some water on it. I need to put up a brave front for my little sisters."

After changing from her traveling dress into a blouse and skirt, Hannah returned to the first floor and found her parents in the kitchen, Pop slicing the roast and Mama dishing green beans into a serving bowl.

"Any news from Ted other than that he misses you?" Pop asked.

She glanced at Mama. "You didn't tell him?"

"No. As long as you're here, Ted's news is for you to share, not mine."

"I don't mind if you share with Pop. He's now a pilot and has begun flying for the Royal Flying Corps. All he can say is that it's safer in the air than in the trenches on the ground."

Mama let out a sigh. "I hope he's right, but I don't know which is worse. His poor mother. I know it's selfish, but I'm glad we only have girls, and my husband is too old to be drafted."

The following morning, after a restless night, Hannah joined the family at the breakfast table in the kitchen. "Good morning, everyone."

Her sisters, wearing similarly styled school dresses, were already seated one on either side of Pop, who wore his usual work clothes of suspendered trousers and a long-sleeved white shirt and tie. Once at the doctor's office, he'd don a white lab coat.

"Good morning, Hannah. Do you want coffee this morning?" Mama approached from the stove, carrying a coffee pot.

"Yes, please. That's all I want. I'm still full from last night."

Pop cleared his throat. "You need to eat more than that. Breakfast is the most important meal of the day."

She rolled her eyes. "Thanks for the advice, Doctor Murphy. I think I'll survive if I wait until lunch to eat."

Mama poured coffee into a cup that sat in front of Hannah. "I happen to agree with your father, but it's your choice. Are you planning to visit Louise Bauer this morning?"

She nodded. "Yes. I was wondering if I could use your car."

"That's fine."

"I'll call first to confirm she'll be home and wanting a visit."

"I wouldn't do that." Pop forked a mound of scrambled eggs."

She stared at him. "Why? It's not polite to drop in unannounced."

"What if they're listening in on her phone calls?" He lifted the eggs to his mouth and paused the motion. "They're already monitoring Henry Bauer in the city. Even though Louise is an American citizen, she's still his wife. And he owns the largest pharmaceutical company in the U.S. which used to be owned by a large German corporation."

"He transferred ownership of his company to Ted's brother, and Tranquility Point is in Louise's name only."

"I hardly think that matters to some. If you have an ounce of German blood in you or are related to a German, you're suspect. Look how fast I became suspicious of Ted."

She pushed her coffee away. "I don't think I can even stomach this." She scraped her chair back and moved to stand.

"Please stay. We need to pray."

She looked at her father. "Okay." She bowed her head as he prayed for the United States military and the allies. When he shifted the focus to Ted and his family, she perked up, silently agreeing as he asked for protection on the Bauers and for the government to act responsibly toward all people of German descent.

Pop said, "Amen," and looked up. "Annie, why the tears."

The child's lower lip trembled. "I'm scared. What if the Germans come to America and take away my friends, Rolf and Emma. Their grandparents live in Germany. Rolf told me his parents bought him a U.S. Army suit, and they're making him wear it around their neighborhood so people know they aren't for Germany."

Mama took Annie's hand. "Honey, there's a wide ocean between America and Europe. It takes days to travel here on a ship. Germany isn't going to invade our shores and, if they would, they'd be stopped at the east coast. We're miles from there."

"But what about the people who are against Rolf and Emma's family? They live here."

Mama looked at Pop with pleading eyes, but he just stared as if he had no answer.

Hannah drew in a breath and let it out. "Annie, right now, people are trying to figure out who they can trust. Some people who only came from Germany a short while ago are afraid for their families who still live there. They know what it's like to live under a cruel government. Not everyone is against Germany, nor are they for Germany. The Bible tells us to be kind to all people and live at peace with them as best we can." She stood and walked to the door. "I'll be upstairs." She stared at Pop. "After I call Louise."

Pop's face reddened, and he opened his mouth. Mama placed a hand over his closed fist, and he pressed his lips together.

Hannah scurried to the stairs, not wanting to hear what was sure to be a heated conversation.

An hour later, Hannah slipped her arms into her coat and set her hat on her head. At the door, Mama handed her the car key. "Be careful. I know how you like to drive fast."

Hannah sighed. "I'll be taking it a little slow. I usually love my visits with Louise, but now that we know Ted is in harm's way, it's going to be hard. She didn't say anything about receiving his letter. Thanks for calming Pop for me. I hate this war and how it's tearing families apart. I want to do something more to help than working at a switchboard."

Mama drew her into a hug. "You're welcome. He loves you so much and doesn't want to see his girl suffer. This is a pain for which he has no medicine, and it frustrates him. I love you too. Not only because I gave birth to you, but because you remind me so much of me when I was your age, and that scares me. I know what it's like to feel passionate about someone or something. Please be careful."

Hannah blinked away her tears. "Oh, Mama, I'm not as brave

as you. You were ready to travel the world. The world beyond is a scary place. What I'm most driven by is the need for women to stick together. A lot of our men are taken from us because of this war, and many won't be returning. Men haven't always made wise decisions for our country. There must be something more we women can do rather than sit at home rolling bandages. That's the only thing I've heard that's available for women to do."

"You are definitely my daughter. I'm sure bandages will be needed, and someone has to roll them. If you want to do more, figure out what it is, and fight for it and never give up. Go and bring comfort to Louise. I'm sure she needs it."

As Hannah drove west, she reflected on how it was almost a year ago when she and her friends had taken the same route to Tranquility Point, where she and Ted first became reacquainted. They frolicked in the water without a single care in the world except to get to know each other. At what point was it that she'd fallen in love with him? Was it during their playful banter while they raced each other through the water, or when he showed concern over how they'd ignored Suzanne? All she knew for sure was by the time she returned home, she was confident that one day she'd marry Ted Bauer.

She turned between Tranquility Point's stone pillars and drove down the long winding lane and came to a stop at the home's entrance. The house appeared deserted, but Louise had assured her she'd welcome her visit.

She walked up to the entrance and pulled at the ringer. A few minutes later, the door swung open, and Louise Bauer stared at her with vacant eyes. She held up an envelope. "This just came from Ted. Louise opened the door wider. "Are you sure you want to be seen visiting me?"

Stunned at the woman's pale complexion, Hannah's heart ached. "I'm not afraid of bullies."

The creases on Louise's forehead deepened. "Come in. I'll fix us some tea."

She stepped inside, and Louise turned a knob on the door, and a loud *click* sounded. "I never thought I'd see the day when I have to be locked inside my own home. Especially at the lake."

"I don't remember that bolt lock being there. Have you been bothered by people?"

"Only by some boys who looked to be in their teens. They came up from the shore path and threw eggs at the windows and shouted nasty names. Peter called a locksmith in town and ordered bolt locks installed on all the doors. I've been afraid to go outside to wash the mess off the glass."

Hannah's stomach burned hot. "Did you recognize them?"

She shook her head. "I presume they were from Williams Bay since we're closer to the Bay than Lake Geneva. They're scared boys. Another year or two and they'll be old enough to be drafted. Please don't make a fuss. I don't want any trouble.

"We've got enough to worry about with Henry being so stubborn. I begged him when we became engaged to become a citizen, and he said he would when he had time. It never happened. Now I live in fear he'll be deported." Louise started walking toward the kitchen, and Hannah followed. "I let the help go a few weeks ago. I was down to Gerta and the outside man. I hated doing that, but I was afraid for their safety. With me living here alone, I don't dirty the place much. I hired the landscaper who took over your grandfather's business to mow the lawn and clear snow come winter."

They entered the kitchen, and Hannah found the cabinet that held the dishware. "Wouldn't your help be safer here?" She took down a pair of cups and saucers.

"I think they went back to the city. They're both U.S. citizens and won't have a curfew. They've probably found work in service already."

After Louise prepared their tea, they settled at the kitchen table. Hannah wrapped her hands around the hot teacup letting its warmth seep into her hands. "It's kind of chilly in here. I never thought about it. Do you have a coal furnace? So many of these older homes don't."

"Thankfully, when Henry bought the property, he had a furnace installed, thinking we'd like to spend our Christmases here, which we did while the boys were small. I was about to head to the cellar to shovel coal. That's not important right now. How long have you known about Ted's pilot training?"

She startled at the question. "Before he left, he said he hoped to be trained to fly airplanes, but asked me to not say anything to you or Mr. Bauer. He didn't want you to worry."

Louise huffed a breath. "As if I could worry any more than I already have been. The English Channel isn't very wide."

"I know. He mentioned two letters ago that his instructors have given him high praise. I'm sure he'll be fine." If only she could believe her words.

Louise took Hannah's left hand and rubbed her thumb over the ring finger. She directed her gaze to Hannah's neckline. "Do you still wear the ring?"

Hannah tugged the chain out from beneath her sweater and let the ring dangle. "Yes. On my finger while at school, but here I wear it this way."

A smile filled Louise's face, and for the first time since Hannah had been there; a twinkle appeared in the woman's eyes. "Such a beautiful ring. Does your father still object to your seeing Ted?"

"No. They've always liked him. Both he and my mother pray daily for him and know we're planning to marry as soon as he is home. He thought it best to not publicly wear the ring while I'm here. He's only looking out for my safety and yours."

"I don't see how it would matter. Ted is an American citizen and is serving overseas with the allies."

"You've already have had trouble with those boys."

She waved a dismissive hand. "Only because they hear their parents talking. Everyone is scared of someone these days. Emotions are high. It's up to you, though."

Louise was right. Her man was fighting the Germans, and she should wear the ring he gave her with pride. Hannah eased the chain clasp around to the front and undid it. She removed the ring from the chain, slid it onto her finger, then held it up to the overhead light. "I love how it sparkles. It's really so beautiful."

Louise grinned. "More so on your hand than around your neck."

"You're right. I'm going to wear it like it's supposed to be worn."

Louise took her hand and squeezed it.

They chatted for a few more minutes, then Hannah pulled the ring off her finger.

Louise's eyes rounded. "What are you doing?"

"I'm going to wash the egg off your windows, and when that's done, I'll shovel some coal into the furnace. I don't want to be wearing my ring while I'm doing that." She slipped the ring into a pocket of her shoulder bag. "Show me a pail and whatever you use to wash windows."

"Have you ever cleaned windows before?"

Hannah laughed. "My mother made sure I learned how to cook, clean house, and wash a window or two. And now she's doing the same with my little sisters. Annie may be only going on eight, but she already knows how to dust the furniture and wash dishes without breaking any. I intend to raise my own children the same way should God bless Ted and me with a family."

Louise's eyes sparkled. "I'll get an old shirt of Ted's to put on over your pretty sweater."

Hannah was finishing up washing the last of the half dozen windows the hooligans had defaced when Louise came outside with a steaming mug in her hand. "I brought you hot cocoa. I've been keeping some German chocolate in the back of the pantry. I think you deserve to taste its richness. And it will warm you up."

Hannah accepted the cocoa and sipped. "Oh, Louise, it's wonderful. Much better than what my family used to buy. Thank you. This is the last window, and to be honest, I'm glad it is." She sipped the drink and, happy to see it had cooled enough, she drained the cup. She handed Louise the empty mug. "Show me where to dump this dirty water and rag, and after I take care of the coal, I'll be out of your hair."

"I did the coal while you were working on the windows." Louise chuckled. "You'd better be sure to get that mustache off your upper lip. Set the things inside the door over there, and I'll take care of them."

Back inside, Hannah grabbed up her purse and returned her

ring to her finger. "I need to get the car home. Mama has to be somewhere within the hour."

The women hugged goodbye, and Hannah scurried out to her vehicle. It wasn't until she was halfway home that she realized she never took off Ted's shirt.

CHAPTER TWENTY

The following Monday

Hannah slipped into her chair at the dinner table, determined to keep an upbeat attitude if only for the sake of her sisters. After Annie's tears the other night because of her friends at school, she'd worked hard to shield her own concerns.

Pop said grace, then looked around the table at each of his daughters as a soft smile emerged. "My precious girls, how was your day?" He picked up a serving bowl and dished a large scoop of macaroni and cheese onto his plate. He passed the bowl to Margie and glanced around the table. "Where's the meat?"

"It's meatless Monday, starting this week." Mama accepted the macaroni from Margie and scooped some up. "They haven't banned sugar, though. There's cake for dessert."

A frown marred Pop's forehead. "I'm not sure if meatless applies if the meat was prepared on Sunday, and it's leftovers."

"I'm not sure either, but I thought it best to start right away. We'll have the leftover pork tomorrow. Be prepared for

Wednesday, though, when we go without eating wheat products."

He picked up his fork and stabbed at a clump of macaroni. "A little less wheat in our diets won't hurt us." He ran his gaze over his daughters. "As I asked before, how was your day?"

Margie shrugged. "Everyone at school is sad. Mrs. Viner's son left for the army today, and she could barely get through the reading lesson without sniffling. I don't like war."

Hannah patted her sister's hand. "None of us do. Have they said anything about what the students can do to support the troops?"

"Not yet."

"I'm sure they will in days to come. But one thing we can do as a family and individually is pray for the safety of all those going to the war front," Mama said.

"Like Ted." Annie's small voice popped up.

"Yes, like Ted," Mama glanced at Hannah's hand. "When did you start wearing your ring?"

Hannah held up her hand, still not used to seeing the ring there. "While I was visiting Louise. She suggested I wear it. I think seeing it gives her pleasure since it was her mother's ring. I've not worn it around the house but decided this morning I would."

Pop sipped his water. "I heard the U.S. Air Corps is ramping up and will soon be sending men to Britain and other countries for training since the U.S. won't be ready to train them for a while. I wonder if Ted will be involved with that. I'm not sure I'd want to go to war in a flying machine, but being up high has got to be safer than being dug into a trench. Raise your head up above ground to look around, and you can have it blown off."

Annie let go of a sob. "I don't want Ted's head blown off."

Mama directed a hard stare at Pop. "Nate, please be careful what you say."

"You're right." He looked at his youngest daughter and patted her hand. "I'm sorry to scare you, Annie. Ted isn't in a trench. He's high up in an airplane. I'm sure he'll be fine."

A vision of Ted's airplane being shot out of the sky filled Hannah's mind, and she swallowed back a sob. "You don't know that." She pushed away from the table. "I'm not hungry. I'm going for a walk."

Ignoring her mother's pleas to return, Hannah stepped out onto the veranda and immediately regretted not grabbing a wrap. The warm spring day had turned dark and wintry. More reflective of her mood. She took the steps to the lawn then folded her arms against the sharp breeze coming off the lake. After reaching the shore, she began walking the path toward town. "God, I don't want to complain. Many people are in worse situations than us, but please keep Ted safe and bring him home in one piece."

She passed Snug Harbor and recalled idyllic summers when, as a child, she often spent time playing there with the Sturges children. By the time she reached the next property, bits of icy precipitation slapped her face. Anyone with good sense would turn around. How must it be for Ted, flying those airplanes with only a small windshield and a pair of goggles to protect him from the elements? This was nothing by comparison. She couldn't join the army or fly a plane, but there had to be some-thing a woman could do to help besides avoiding meat one day a week. She pivoted and headed home.

By the time she arrived back at Safe Refuge, she'd made up her mind. She was going to drop out of school and devote her time to the war effort.

"CORPORAL BAUER, you're to report to Hanger four immediately."

Ted looked up from the notes he'd been making on the best

way to train the new Americans who were to arrive any day." He frowned at the private. "Do you know why?"

"Sorry, I don't."

He tossed his pencil on the desk and stood. "Thank you, Private Jones."

The private returned Ted's salute, then turned on his boot heel and left.

Ted grabbed his regulation belt and strapped it around his waist. He tugged at the bottom of his jacket to be sure it hung correctly. As he passed a small wall mirror, he paused to make sure his tie was on straight.

He made his way to the hanger and stepped into the office.

A young private looked up from his work. "They're waiting for you out there." He pointed to a door that led to the hanger.

Inside the hanger, he spotted a group of men wearing what looked like brown U.S. Army uniforms standing next to his RFC commanding officer. Sergeant Thomas turned as Ted approached. "Here's Corporal Bauer now."

The men saluted, and Sergeant Thomas spoke first. "The first American trainees have arrived, and they've been assigned to you. Help them get settled in Barracks Three and show them around the base. Tomorrow you'll begin by reviewing what they already know about operating an airplane, and you can determine yourself who is ready to actually fly and who isn't."

Ted nodded and looked over at the half dozen men, all standing at attention, arms down at their sides. Some appeared eager, and one or two looked scared to death. He smiled. "At ease, men. Let's head over to the barracks, and we can talk there."

"Here are copies of their paperwork." Sergeant Thomas handed him a large brown envelope."

Ted tucked the envelope under his arm. "Gentlemen, follow me."

CHAPTER TWENTY-ONE

Early December 1917

Hannah sat in the break room, sipping a cup of coffee that tasted more like water. She pushed it aside and tugged over the newspaper that lay across the table and chuckled.

"First, bad coffee and now, yesterday's paper."

"Who are you talking to?"

She looked up at Clarice, who stood in the door, a wide grin across her face. "Myself, I guess. What's with the dazzling smile?"

"Oh, Hannah, our hopes to be more involved are being realized. We're going overseas." She laid what looked like a government bulletin on top of the newspaper. "I'll have to return it to the bulletin board, but I wanted you to see it first."

Hannah's heart raced. "You better not be fooling me." She picked up the document that bore the emblem of the U.S. Department of Defense and read the first paragraph. "Why would General Pershing be ordering telephone operators to the war zone?"

"Read the next paragraph. The troops are using telephone cables to communicate at the front, and they need switchboards to connect the calls. One of the other operators told me the soldiers can't move the cords around as fast as women." Her grin returned. "They need us, girl."

Hannah read the next paragraph, and her hopes shattered. She handed the paper back to Clarice. "They only want French-English speaking women. That leaves me out."

The smile on Clarice's face dissolved. "I hadn't thought of that." She pursed her lips as if in thought. "You've got time. They won't be testing the applicants for a month or so. I can teach you. You're a quick study. Look how you've aced your tests in law school. I've already been teaching you some French phrases."

Hannah huffed a sardonic laugh. "That's because the tests at school are in English. I doubt being able to say please pass the salt in French is a qualifier. You're a shoo-in. You've been bilingual since birth." She palmed away the lone tear trailing down her face.

Why hadn't she taken French back in high school? With law school classes suspended, she had time to do more. And joining the effort on the same side of the globe as Ted could possibly allow for them to be together on occasion. A vision of Clarice and Ted meeting up in a quaint French town, away from the front, entered her thoughts, and she fought down the ugly claws of jealousy attempting to wrap themselves around her heart. She pushed the idea out of her head. Clarice would never try to be anything but a friend to Ted.

"I'll come over tonight, and we'll get started on the lessons." Clarice picked up the document and scurried toward the door. "I'll see you at the boards. Chin up."

THAT EVENING as Hannah dried off the last plate from their dinner, the doorbell rang. She handed the towel and plate to Cora. "That's probably Clarice. She said she was coming over this evening."

She opened the front door and stared at the book in Clarice's hand. "I know that can't be a law book since the school is now on hiatus."

Clarice pushed past her and into the home's foyer. "You're going to have your first French lesson tonight."

Hannah raised her hands. "Don't waste your time. There's no way I will learn French well enough to speak to the French operators and get calls transferred. They're looking for fluent French speakers like you."

"You won't know unless you try. Now, where is a place we won't be interrupted?"

Hannah pointed at the staircase. "Upstairs in my room. Let me tell Cora where we'll be. I'm expecting a call from my parents, and we'll have to be disturbed if it comes while you're here."

Clarice cocked a brow. "Everything okay at home?"

"As well as it can be with food shortages. Though a doctor never goes out of business, my dad is doing a lot of doctoring without charge. But they're comfortable so far.

"I'm more concerned about Ted's mother. To save on heating costs, she's closed off her home's upstairs and has made a bedroom for herself in the library on the first floor. Ted's brother comes about once a month, and my father has been going over there periodically to check on her. My parents say if worse comes to worst, she can stay at our place in the cottage."

"Your dad really made a turnabout."

"Yes. For which I'm grateful. He's lost a few patients because people think he's aiding the enemy. But most people are smart enough to know better."

Cora stepped into the front hall from the back. She looked at their guest. "How are you, Clarice?" Her gaze went to the French book. "I hardly think you'd need a textbook on French."

Hannah's friend shook her head. "I don't but Hannah does. Did she tell you about the opportunity that's being given to telephone operators who speak French?"

Cora raised her left brow and cast a look at Hannah. "She did not."

Hannah sighed. "That's because it's not an opportunity for me. I don't speak fluent French like Clarice. But she thinks I'm smart enough to speak like a Parisian within a month. She'll soon see I'm hopeless." She turned toward the stairway. "We'll be in my room if a call comes through for me."

The pair climbed the steps and sat on Hannah's bed, facing each other. Clarice opened the textbook and turned to the first lesson. As soon as she began explaining irregular verb usage, Hannah held up a hand palm out. "Stop, stop, stop. I don't know an irregular verb from a regular one in any language. Did I tell you I dropped my Spanish class in high school and had to take it during my first year in college because I lacked the foreign language requirement? It was the only college class I got a D in."

Clarice stared at her. "Not you."

"Yes, me. I love you for wanting to teach me, Clarice. I know in my gut you are going to pass the test and fly through the interviews like a champ. I'll find a different way to serve right here at home."

Clarice wrapped her arms around Hannah. "I don't want to go without you. If you can't speak French, then I won't even apply."

Hannah worked her way out of her friend's embrace. "You'll do no such thing. You are exactly the kind of person they are looking for. I've been following the news on the Woman's National Farm and Garden Association. Hilda Loines, one of the founding members, is strong on the idea of starting a Women's Land Army here in the U.S. It's similar to what women in Great Britain have been doing since the war began. The women fill in for the farmers who have gone off to war, by planting and harvesting crops, taking care of the animals, and anything else that needs doing."

Clarice burst out laughing. "You? I can't picture you plowing a field and getting all dirty."

"I've got horticulture in my blood. My grandfather was a landscaper and florist, and my Aunt Katie and her husband own a farm not far from my home. Their son and son-in-law work on the farm because my uncle is disabled from a farm accident. If the younger men are called up, they'll need assistance. I'd like to help Wisconsin get its own WLA chapter. The Woman's Farm and Garden Association is having its annual conference next week in New York City, and I've decided to attend."

Clarice blinked. "Why didn't you mention this before?"

"Because I kept pushing it away from my mind. That announcement at the telephone office today convinced me this is the way I can serve at home. It's what God wants me to do."

"I didn't know your grandfather was a laborer. I thought you were born with a silver spoon in your mouth."

She huffed a breath. "Oh please. I'm nothing like that. My father is not from wealth, it's my great grandfather who bought that land and built Safe Refuge. My mother's father was an Irish immigrant and worked as a janitor at a mission school in Chicago before the fire. He and my granny met there. The great fire changed everything. As I understand it, my granny was not one to flaunt her wealth. After they married, my grandfather learned about landscaping, and that led to his becoming a well-known florist and landscaper around the area.

A knock came at the door and Cora stuck her head in. "Hannah, your mother is on the telephone."

Clarice picked up the book. "We're done. I'll let myself out. Tell your mother I said hello."

Hannah smiled. "Thanks for understanding. See you tomorrow at work."

In the downstairs hallway, she went to the telephone and lifted the earpiece to her ear. "Hello, Mama."

"Hannah, did I call at a bad time?"

"Not at all. I was upstairs. How are things there?"

"They could be better. Louise Bauer was taken to the hospital this afternoon. Your father arrived home a few minutes ago and said he took out her appendix, and she's doing fine."

A sinking feeling washed over her. "Why didn't you let me know sooner? I would have caught the last train out. I'll let them know tomorrow I'm needed at home."

"There's nothing for you to do here. She'll be in the hospital for at least a couple of weeks, and we're arranging for her to convalesce in the cottage when she's released. I didn't want to call you until we knew for sure what was wrong. When the caretaker's boy went over this afternoon to take some eggs to her. She didn't answer, and he let himself in with his keys and discovered Louise in bed and in a lot of pain.

"He immediately called your father's office. Nate asked me to drive her directly to the hospital in Elkhorn. He met us there and after examining her, took her into surgery. The infection was caught before the appendix burst, or it could have been far worse. Ted's brother is coming on the train tomorrow, but he probably won't stay for more than a day. I hope Henry has been told about it. We telegraphed the internment camp office down in Georgia, but we've not heard back."

"Are they letting Ted know?"

"I don't know. I suppose it would fall to his brother to send a wire, but if she's going to be okay, maybe it's better to not tell until she is up and around. I hope she doesn't reject our offer of staying in the cottage."

"She may insist she'll be fine at Tranquility Point, but stress you don't mean forever. Only until she's herself again. I'm planning to request I be removed from the rotation all next week as I'm attending a conference in New York City on Thursday and Friday. I can stay with you until early Tuesday morning."

"A conference in New York this close to the holidays? Don't forget Louise won't be released for at least a week or more."

"I'll be back before Christmas. I'll explain when I get there."

CHAPTER TWENTY-TWO

Saturday morning, Hannah stepped off the train, surprised to see Mama waiting for her on the platform. She stepped into her mother's embrace, and realizing at once how much she needed Mama's hug she didn't release her hold for a long while. She leaned back and took in Mama's hollow-cheeked face. "Where's Pop?"

"He had an emergency at the hospital."

"I hope not involving Louise."

"No. She is settled and comfortable, awaiting your arrival in the cottage. We brought her home yesterday. Since your father is her doctor and I'm a nurse, it was decided she's in as good of hands as the hospital, and she was released early. Your Aunt Katie is with her now."

"Probably better since she's your only patient and won't be exposed any germs. I only hope you're not taking on too much. I can see the fatigue in your face."

"I slept at the cottage last night since it was her first time there. Louise slept like a baby. Me not so much. I thought maybe you could sleep there while you're here."

"Of course, I can stay with her. After all, she is going to be my mother-in-law."

Hannah began working her glove over her left hand, and Mama glanced at the ring. "Have you been given any trouble about being engaged to someone of German descent?"

"No. I say my fiancé is flying for the RFC and expecting to be transferred to the U.S. Air Corps soon. That's the end of the discussion. After they've given me sympathetic looks, that is."

They reached Mama's car, and Hannah walked to the passenger side and placed her suitcase onto the backseat. She shut the backseat door and prepared to slide onto the front passenger seat.

"You take the wheel," Mama said. "I know you love to drive."

Hannah grinned. "You sure?"

"Yes, but don't drive it like a race car."

Hannah sat behind the wheel and reacquainted herself with the dashboard while Mama settled in the passenger seat and wrapped a blanket over her legs.

Hannah laughed. "Now, I know why you let me drive. So you can snuggle under the blanket."

Within minutes they were rolling down Broad Street toward the intersection at Main Street. Hannah glanced around. "Looks like you got some snow. It must have stopped at the state line. We've yet to have any."

"We did. Be sure to watch for ice patches," Mama warned. "I used to love snow, but the older I get, the less I like it. It's unsafe to drive on snowy streets."

She glanced at her mother. "That doesn't sound like you. You've always loved everything about life and whatever it threw at you."

"I think that stopped when Annie was born. Your father delivered both you and Margie at home, and everything went well. Not so with Annie. I went into labor after you and Margie had gone to bed since it was a school night. She came quickly, but I didn't stop bleeding, and your dad had to rush Annie and me to the hospital. They halted the bleeding and insisted I stay there for the next week. He refused to leave us there, and very early the next morning brought us home."

"You never told me that." Hannah made a right turn onto Main street. "When I got up the next morning, you and Annie were both in your bed. You must have come home shortly before I got up."

"We called Katie to come to stay at the house before we left for the hospital, and as soon as we arrived back home, she returned to the farm. We were settled before you or your sister got up. That birth took a lot out of me."

"I remember being surprised to see her with you since her due date wasn't for another month. But I was too wrapped up in school and my friends to pay much attention to how tired you must have felt. I'm sorry for being so ignorant of your condition."

"You weren't ignorant. I made sure you didn't know and took lots of naps while you were in school. Your granny was there almost round the clock to help."

Hannah turned the car into Safe Refuge's property and parked in front of the home's entrance. As they climbed out of the car, Pop pulled in and parked his Model T coupe behind them. He jumped out, not bothering to close the coupe's door and, using long strides, approached Hannah, his arms open. "I arrived in time to welcome you home." He wrapped his arms around her and held her tight for several beats. "Good to have you home, Hannie-girl."

Warmed at hearing his childhood nickname for her, she stepped out of his embrace. "I only came from Chicago, not the war."

"I know, but with all that's going on, it feels like we need to all be here together. You should have brought Clarice with you."

"She has to work. There's a good chance she'll be leaving for France soon, and she wants to get as many hours in as she can."

His brows rose. "France during wartime?"

She explained why they needed telephone French-English speaking operators in France then said, "She has to be tested, but I have no doubt she'll pass." She picked up her suitcase. "I'll get settled in the cottage and say hello to Aunt Katie and Louise. Is she strong enough to join us for dinner?"

Pop shook his head. "Give her another few days. We'll prepare a tray, and you can take it over after we eat. Go ahead and invite Katie to eat with us, but she'll likely decline. With the guys sure to be called up soon, they prefer to have the family together for supper as many evenings as possible."

Hannah made her way to the cottage and let herself in. Careful to not make a lot of noise, she headed for the stairs on tip-toe. In front of Louise's room, the floorboard creaked, and she winced.

"Is that you, Katie?"

Louise's voice sounded strong but not as robust as usual. "It's Hannah, Louise. I'm sorry if I woke you. I'll take my suitcase up to the bedroom and be gone in a jiffy."

Footfalls sounded on the stairs, and she turned to see Aunt Katie, her graying blond hair pulled back into a bun at the nape of her neck, descending. A broad smile split her face. "I'm glad you're back. I need to get home and get supper started. If I don't, Jake will try, and that always spells disaster."

Hannah laughed and pulled her aunt into a hug. "Pop said to invite you to stay for supper, but that you'd probably decline."

Aunt Katie chuckled. "He knows me well. Hannah, I don't know what we'll do if Dylan and James are both drafted. If one stays, then maybe Jake can do some of the light work. But it's going to be tough."

Hannah's heart squeezed. "I may have a solution for you, but it won't come as quick as a week or two. I'm attending a conference next week in New York, and hopefully, I'll come away with answers."

Her aunt narrowed her eyes. "I don't understand."

"I'll share more when I know more."

"Hannah Murphy, don't you dare leave without coming in here."

At Louise's command coming through the door, Hannah winked at Aunt Katie and whispered. "Go on home. I'm here now." She set down her suitcase and opened the door. Louise sat up in bed, her long silver hair spread out on the pillows like a fan. She grinned and held her arms open. "Hannah, my daughter, if you aren't a sight for my sore eyes. What were you and Katie talking about?"

Hannah scooted across the room and bent into Louise's hug. "Nothing but war talk. Her son and son-in-law are of draft age."

The older woman frowned. "I thought farmers were exempt."

"They are, but they have one son only, and their son-in-law also works for Jake. It's complicated." She looked Louise in the eyes. "It's so good to see you. Your hair is beautiful. I had no idea it was so long."

Her lips lifted into a smile. "I call it my silver crown. Sometimes I wish I could wear it bobbed like yours. Henry loves my hair, and he'd be very disappointed to see it cut off if I did it before he returns home."

Hannah ran her gaze over Louise's silver locks. "If my hair were as beautiful as yours, I'd never cut it."

"Whatever do you mean? You were such a carrot-top when you were a child, but now your hair has become a rich mix of red and brown. And those beautiful waves."

Hannah picked up a hairbrush from the nightstand. "Thank you. We all want what we don't have, don't we? Would you like me to brush your hair?"

Louise sat up. "I'd love it. It's hard for me to brush it after my surgery." She leaned forward. "If you bring it all over my shoulders to the front, you should reach most of it."

Hannah drew a wooden straight-back chair next to the bed, then started to draw the brush through Louise's hair. "I hear you've had a rough few days." She stroked the hair as she talked.

"The only thing better would be if you and Ted were both here. But that won't happen for a while. I've not heard a thing since he wrote to say he was flying those airplanes. I pray every day for his safety. Between Ted in the war and Henry in the internment camp, I'm constantly worrying. At least with Peter running the company, he's exempted. Do people die from worry? If so, I should have been dead months ago."

Hannah swallowed against the mass growing in her throat. "I don't think worry being cause of death is valid, but the stress from worry can certainly weaken the heart. My father said you came through the surgery well and are strong. Have you heard from Mr. Bauer?"

Louise shook her head. "I think he's afraid to write to me because it might cause me to be seen as a collaborator. Lord have mercy, I've never set foot in Germany except once when we took the boys there to meet their grandparents. Yet I might be suspicioned as a German sympathizer if I'm not careful. I worry about your family keeping me here. You know how paranoid everyone is these days."

Hannah nodded. "I do."

Louise took Hannah's left hand and ran her thumb over the ring. "I'm sorry I encouraged you to wear the ring on your finger. Maybe you should put it on your chain like you used to."

She shook her head. "No. If Ted is in the war, fighting for the U.S., I want to wear his ring. He's the one in danger. Not me."

CHAPTER TWENTY-THREE

Hannah stepped into the big house and sniffed the air. She made her way to the kitchen as Mama was lifting a golden roast chicken from the oven. "It seems whenever I come home, you are always cooking something that makes me ravenous."

Mama smiled as she set the bird on top of a pair of trivets already arranged on a counter. "Katie brought it over when she came. They're culling their flock. Did she tell you her concerns about running the farm?"

"Yes. And I'm glad. It's given me more of a reason than ever to attend the conference in New York City next week."

Her mother scowled. "What is the organization?"

"The Woman's National Farm and Garden Association. Their annual conference is at the Astor Hotel, December eighteenth to the twentieth. I signed up not so much to become a member, but to hear Hilda Loines speak. She's very high on organizing a women's land army in the Chicago area, and I'd like to get in on the ground floor. I've saved enough from my pay at the telephone company for the train and hotel. I'll only be gone four nights. Home in plenty of time to get here for Christmas."

"I've heard the term 'women's land army,' but have no idea what it is."

"Basically, women train to do farm tasks and fill in on farms where the men have been drafted. They are called farmettes. I'm hoping to convince Mrs. Loines to let me start one in Wisconsin."

"It sounds interesting." Mama lifted a pot of potatoes from the stove and strained the hot water into the sink. "Can you grab the masher from the drawer and start mashing these?"

Hanna gathered what she needed for the task and set about mashing the potatoes. "Britain has a very functional WLA, as it's called. It's the model for what they are doing here in the States."

Her mother turned off the flame under a saucepan of green beans, carried the pan to the sink, and drained off the water. "Too bad your grandfather isn't alive. He'd have loved to know more about this women's land army."

"He wouldn't have objected to women doing men's work?"

"Not at all. My father had all of us children learning all we could about plants and the soil. My brother was mowing lawns on the estates by the time he was twelve. He made some pocket money that way, but I don't think he enjoyed it taking him away from his summer fun." She laughed. "Maybe that's why he chose not to follow in Da's footsteps."

"It's sad that the business had to be sold to someone outside the family."

"It is, but at least the man who bought the business was someone we can trust to come and go on the property to use the greenhouse." As soon as you're finished with the potatoes, I'll get your father in here to carve the chicken."

A short time later, the family settled around the table in the dining room. Margie stared at the platter of sliced chicken. "Is it right for us to be having such a meal when others are not as fortunate?"

Pop scowled. "What brought that on? We were given the chicken by your Aunt Katie from their farm, and we are grateful for it. I assure you we will be eating from it until it's picked clean, and then your mother will make chicken soup from the bones. Nothing is going to go to waste."

Margie straightened. "We heard at school, fresh produce isn't in our markets like it used to be because so much is being sent to those in England who are worse off than us."

Pop heaved a sigh. "We are already observing meatless Mondays and wheatless Wednesdays. This is Friday, so I think we're okay to eat chicken today. Shall we say a blessing on the food?"

Everyone bowed their heads, and Pop thanked the Lord for the gift of the chicken and asked that people all over their county and beyond would have enough to eat. He also prayed for safety for the U.S. soldiers and particularly for Ted, that he would come safely home to Hannah and Louise, and the conflict soon would be over.

Before raising her head, Hannah dabbed her eyes with her napkin. She looked up to see both Pop and Mama staring at her.

"Are you okay, Hannah?"

She looked at her mother. "Yes. When Ted's name was said in the prayer my tears erupted."

Mama rested her palm on top of Hannah's hand. "You're in love with him, and his welfare is never far from your mind even when you are thinking about other things."

"Thanks. I entrust Ted's safety to God every morning when I wake up and again at night before I go to sleep, and at least a dozen times more throughout the day, but I can't seem to stop the tears."

She glanced around the table. "Why are you all staring at me? Let's eat. Margie, can you pass the potatoes?"

After dinner, Hannah prepared a plate, then placed the meal in the still-warm oven to keep while she helped with the dishes. She had just filled the sink with sudsy water when Mama shooed her from the kitchen, saying the younger girls can take care of the rest.

"I won't argue with that. Louise must be wondering where her supper is."

She took the plate from the oven and made her way to the cottage. Balancing the plate in one hand, she pulled the door open with the other and stepped halfway into the darkened hall. Her foot hit something solid, and she fell forward. The plate flew out of her hands and shattered on the floor. Landing on her stomach, she tried to draw in a breath and couldn't. A moan sounded, but it wasn't coming from her. She raised her head as her eyes adjusted to the low light and gasped.

"Louise, what happened?" She forced herself up and crawled to the older woman, then pressed two fingers to her neck as her dad had taught her. Feeling a faint heartbeat, she scrambled to her feet and stepped onto the broken plate and nearly took another tumble. "Louise, don't move. I'll get my father." She raced across the flagstone path to the house, flung the door open, and yelled. "Pop, come quick! Louise has fallen!"

CHAPTER TWENTY-FOUR

December 1917

Ted shrugged into his heavy flight jacket. As scared as he always was before taking off, a rush of excitement soon pushed out his fear. Today would be different. Two of the guys he'd trained in the second group of Americans were flying with him in their own aircraft. John Dyer, the trainee who was to occupy the plane's seat in front of him, woke up with an unsettled stomach but insisted he was fine. Ted hoped John didn't lose his cookies while in the air. The first time into combat usually meant jumpy nerves and the inability to think fast.

He'd have given the guy a pass, but it wasn't his decision to make. He almost looked forward to his upcoming transfer to the RFC's base in France. Once over there, he'd not be training anymore and would serve in the RFC until the Americans arrived.

He trotted across the dirt toward his plane and came alongside John. "How's the stomach?"

John shrugged. "Better."

They checked the fuselage. The four bombs were in place, and ammo was loaded into the guns attached to either side of the plane's nose. Thankfully, they were positioned so they couldn't shoot the plane's own propeller.

He climbed up into the pilot seat and fastened himself in, while John did the same in the front seat. After tugging his leather helmet down and fastening it under his chin, he reached beneath his shirt and pulled out a chain that held a metal cross, his dog tag, and a small locket. He popped the cover on the pendant and smiled at the image before pressing his lips against Hannah's photo. He hadn't heard from her in a long while. He hoped the last letter she wrote would find its way to him here in England before he transferred. Snapping the cover closed, he dropped the chain beneath his shirt and moved his goggles in place. "Lord, please grant me protection and bring me safely home to Hannah and my family."

Forcing his emotions and thoughts of Hannah and his family from his mind, he started the engine. As he taxied across the bumpy ground toward the runway, he mentally rehearsed the flight plan and all the dips and turns necessary when flying into German territory with its labyrinth of trenches and tunnels. During his first run, he'd been puzzled by the stretches of roads lined on either side with square holes. When he realized the holes were cellars, all that remained of row after row of family homes, he became nauseated. He hated war now more than ever, and it broke his heart that his father's people had caused so much of this.

He stopped at the end of the runway, and one of the newer trainees walked up and got his propeller rotating. Without another thought, Ted taxied down the bumpy runway, increasing his speed. As his biplane lifted off the ground, he glanced over his shoulder, assured that the other plane was also aloft. They flew parallel to each other and gave a thumbs up as they reached the English Channel. Ted tensed. Reports said the Bosch was still a good dozen miles inland, but he had to be prepared. He approached the Western front, identifiable by its zigzagging arrangement of trenches, and began making turns and changing altitudes every half-minute, all designed to keep the Bosch's shots unable to touch them. Ten minutes from now, he'd arrive at his target and drop the bombs. The Krauts wouldn't have time to react if everything went as planned.

A shot rang out from below, and he turned and climbed to get a better view. The other plane was still with them. Their target was just up ahead. He scanned the ground, looking for the flower beds he was told were in front of the Bosch's camou-flaged barracks, all the while keeping the roller coaster flight plan.

"There are the flowers!" John shouted back to him.

Spotting the red and yellow blooms, Ted's pulse accelerated. He brought the plane up and then down in a swoop and released his two bombs while John did the same with the two bombs under his control. A moment later, the explosions sounded, followed by several other explosions. Both planes had made their marks as planned. He made a wide turn to check for damage as a sizeable cumulous cloud floated overhead, causing the aircraft to stand out as if in a spotlight. *Nothing like shouting out here we are!*

A shot came from below and its bullet pinged against the fuselage.

A dial on his dash spun. He was losing either oil or fuel.

Another shot rang out and John slumped in his seat.

A knot filled Ted's throat. *Blasted Bosch. Blasted cloud.* He uttered an oath under his breath. *Keep your head, Bauer.* He had to get out of enemy territory before they crashed.

The plane was descending too fast. Praying John was only

wounded and not dead, he pulled back on the yoke, willing the aircraft to climb. One more minute in the air, and they'd be past the front.

The plane's nose went down.

He closed his eyes and braced himself.

CHAPTER TWENTY-FIVE

December 18, 1917

Hannah stood from her folding chair and applauded along with the rest of the women in the large ballroom. Hilda Loines was all she expected the woman to be and more. She'd done the right thing by coming to this conference. Never had she felt so right about a decision since the day she accepted Ted's marriage proposal.

She had to speak with Mrs. Loines, and that would have to happen today because she was due back at work day after tomorrow. With the brother of one of the operators having been killed at the front and another out because of illness, her time off had been cut short, and she had tickets for tonight's train to Chicago.

By the time she wormed her way through the crowd from her back-row seat, a large group of women had huddled around Mrs. Loines. Hannah planted her feet firmly behind what appeared to be the end of the line. The queue was inching forward at the pace of a turtle, but she wasn't leaving. She shifted her weight from one foot to the other, wishing she'd worn flat shoes instead of the high heels.

Her stomach rumbled, and she checked her wristwatch, a practical purchase made before the trip. It was well past the scheduled lunch break, and she prayed someone from the conference didn't whisk Mrs. Loines away before she reached the head of the line. It didn't appear the speaker was of a mind to hurry anyone along. With only four others ahead of Hannah, a woman scurried up to the speaker and held out her arm to stop the next woman in line. She pulled Mrs. Loines aside and whispered something. Mrs. Loines shook her head and said loud enough for everyone to hear, "These women have waited well over an hour to speak with me, and I'll not deny them. Just bring me a sandwich."

The organizer's eyes widened. "Are you sure?"

"Yes. I'm quite sure. These ladies are giving up their lunch hour. I can do the same."

Hannah relaxed. What a wonderful example.

A half an hour later, Hannah approached Mrs. Loines and waited while the woman took a bite of the sandwich that was brought to her. Her own stomach growled for the umpteenth time, but she didn't care. If Ted could endure all he'd been experiencing, she could handle a missed meal."

Mrs. Loines swallowed and dabbed her mouth with her napkin. She looked passed Hannah's right shoulder. "You in the tweed jacket, would you mind finding someone to bring me more water? I promise you'll regain your place in line."

Not looking at all put out, the dark-haired woman scurried off in the direction of the registration desk, and Mrs. Loines smiled at Hannah. "Now, what is your name, and what can I do for you?"

She stepped forward and shook hands with the woman. "Mrs. Loines, I'm Hannah Murphy. I'm from a small Wisconsin town located a short distance over the state line from Illinois. I was excited to hear about your plans for an Illinois Women's Land Army, but Wisconsin desperately needs a WLA. The state has many dairy farms and crop farms. I'd like to help get one started. We can use my aunt and uncle's farm near my family home for training. My uncle has limited abilities, and his son and son-in-law are planning to enlist if they can get help. There are crops to be tended and animals to be cared for. How can I get a WLA started in Wisconsin?"

She drew in a breath as unbidden tears clouded her eyes. "I'm sorry, Mrs. Loines, for talking so fast, but I had to get it all in, and I know your time is limited."

"Please call me Hilda." The woman pulled a handkerchief from her purse and handed it to her. "It's fresh, please use it. I have a feeling there is more than the war effort that is bringing those tears to the surface."

Hannah nodded. "Yes. My fiancé has been flying with the RFC and will soon transfer to the U.S. Air Corps when it's up and running. His father immigrated from Germany years ago but has never become a U.S. citizen. He's now interred in Georgia. I've not heard anything from my fiancé in weeks…."

Hilda retook her hand and squeezed it. "My word, you have had a lot on your shoulders. Are you willing to learn? Being a farmette is hard work."

"Yes. My grandparents escaped the Great Fire in Chicago, and my grandfather was a landscaper and florist until he died a few years ago. I learned a few things from him. I can do this. I know I can."

The woman smiled. "I'm teaching a class this afternoon on the WLA. Come to that, and after it's over, I'm finished for the day. We can sit together and do the paperwork. We're just getting the Libertyville, Illinois training farm put together to have it up and running for training by March. I have two women ready to move in there right after the holidays to get things organized. You could join them there. Each state has its own WLA, and so far, Wisconsin hasn't come on board. Perhaps by your using your family's farm as an associate of the Illinois WLA under your leadership, the state will come around and want to help. Can you be in Libertyville after the first of the year?"

She wanted to hug the woman but held back and grinned. "Oh, yes. Thank you so much."

"I should be the one saying thank you. Now go and get some food. I'll see you at two o'clock when the class begins."

TWO DAYS LATER, Hannah brought her lunch bag into the breakroom to keep until lunchtime. Clarice turned from pouring a cup of coffee and startled. "Hannah, what are you doing here? I thought you weren't coming back to town until tomorrow."

Hannah yawned as she placed her lunch on the counter next to several other lunch bags. "They didn't tell you? I had my time off cut short because of Dorothy's brother's death and Edna being sick. I caught the late train out of New York night before last and arrived in Chicago at ten last evening. I'm working the seven a.m. to four p.m. shift today. Trying to sleep on a train is impossible, and I was too wound up to drop off quickly when I got to bed at Cora's last night. I hope the boards are quiet today."

Clarice shrugged. "They're so-so. How was the conference? Was it worth the trip?"

She grinned. "Oh yes, very much worth it. In fact, I have to tell Miss Marshall that December thirty-first is my last day here. I'll be working at a new job starting in January."

Clarice's brows rose. "Doing what?"

"Farming." Hannah laughed. "Shut your mouth. Actually, I'm going to be training in Libertyville at a farm the Women's Land Army has set up to teach how to be a farmette. After a month or two of training, I plan to take my new knowledge north to Lake Geneva and start a similar training farm on my aunt and uncle's farm."

Clarice jumped from her seat and scurried to the other side of the table. Hannah stood, and they embraced, both saying at the same time. "I'm going to miss you."

Hannah looked her friend in the eyes. "When are you supposed to leave for your training in New York?"

"Not until after the first of the year."

"Then, you have a standing invitation to join us for Christmas like you did last year."

"That would be wonderful, but I'm hoping to get home to Vermont for the holiday. Only God knows when I'll next be able to see my mother. If that doesn't work out, though, I accept your invitation."

"Oh, Clarice, I'm glad. You should see your mother before taking on such a huge responsibility in a very dangerous part of the world."

Clarice looked off then back at Hannah. "My thoughts exactly. How are you going to learn about farming when it's winter, and planting won't start until spring?"

There was that imaginary wall again. At least she was going home for Christmas. "I wondered about that myself. But the training farm has milk cows, and they need to be tended year-round. My aunt and uncle also have a few, but not a huge herd. Come spring, there will be plenty to do at my family's farm. I'll prepare for planting season and recruit women to join the WLA."

"So, once you head up to Wisconsin, you'll be there and not come back to school?"

"Ted and I both intend to get our law degrees from North-western when the war is over. I'll be back, probably as Hannah Bauer." She felt her grin dissolve. "I'm worried, Clarice. This is the longest I've gone without a letter from Ted."

Her friend waved away her concern. "It's the war and Christmas time. I'm sure both have slowed down the mail."

What Clarice said made sense, but she still had a bad feeling that had been in her gut for several days, and it wouldn't go away.

ON SATURDAY, Pop met Hannah at the train in Lake Geneva with a borrowed a truck, having been warned she was bringing a large trunk.

The moment she stepped into the house, she went to the hall side table and sorted through the morning mail. Her heart fell.

"Were you looking for mail from Ted?"

She faced her mother. "Yes, I was hoping he'd continued to send mail here. I've heard nothing in a long while. Has Louise heard anything recently?"

Mama shook her head. "If something was wrong, wouldn't Louise have heard from the government?"

"That's what keeps me hopeful. I'm going upstairs to change."

A few minutes later, she returned downstairs wearing a wool skirt and thick sweater. She donned her winter coat and wrapped a long wool scarf around her neck. "I'll be in the spring house."

A worried expression filled Mama's face. "But it's so cold out."

"I'm warmly dressed, and the spring moderates the temperature somewhat. I won't be long. I need to be alone, and the spring house is the last place Ted and I sat together before he left." She stepped into the parlor and tugged a knitted afghan off the back of a chair. "I'll take this for fortification."

Relishing the bite of the frigid wind on her face, Hannah entered the spring house, and her heart fell. She'd forgotten Pop always stored away the furniture during winter. There was nowhere to sit but on the cover that protected the spring. After wrapping the afghan around her shoulders, she sat on the edge of the cover and bowed her head. "Lord, I know something is wrong. Even if I get a letter today, it would have been written at least three weeks ago. A lot can go wrong in three weeks. Please watch over Ted."

"Hannah?"

At Mama's voice, she opened her eyes and turned. Her mother held out a yellow paper. "This came a few minutes ago for Louise. She wanted to bring it to you herself, but she's not yet strong enough from that fall to walk down here in the cold."

Hannah held out her shaking hand. "I knew something was wrong. He's dead, isn't he?"

CHAPTER TWENTY-SIX

*H*annah took the paper from Louise and read.

Mr. and Mrs. Bauer,

The United States Army and Royal Flying Corps regret to inform you that your son, Theodore Bauer's plane was shot down over Belgium by the German Army two weeks ago, and he has been declared missing in action. Efforts to locate him and the plane wreckage have been hampered by weather and that his last known location was in occupied territory. The allies will make every effort to locate the wreckage and update you. You and your family have our deepest condolences.

A sob pushed through Hannah's throat, followed by a loud wail. She fell into Mama's arms. "I knew something was wrong. How did I know?"

Mama patted her back like she'd done many times when she was small. "Because you and Ted have that special connection. The same way your father and I do, and the way my parents did. It goes beyond being in love. Let's pray, then Louise needs comforting too."

By the end of their prayer, both were sobbing, and Mama handed Hannah a handkerchief. "Take comfort that God knew about this before it happened, and if Ted didn't survive, he's with Him now, and if he is alive, God is watching over him." She looked out at the lake. "See the moon rising in the east? I think that's a sign from God that He sees you and knows your pain. One way or the other, you will be with Ted again."

Hannah blew her nose and stuffed the handkerchief into her coat pocket. "I'll probably find that more comforting after it sinks in."

Mama took her by the hand. "Come. Louise needs us."

As if in a trance, she let Mama lead her to the house. They found Louise sitting at the kitchen table, eyes closed and rocking Annie back and forth on her lap.

Louise opened her eyes then ran a hand over Annie's head. "Child, I need my lap back. Thank you so much for comforting me."

"If you need me again, Miss Louise, let me know." Annie slid off Louise's lap and wrapped her arms around Mama. "Is Ted dead?"

Mama patted the girl's head. "We don't know, honey. He might be lost is all. Why don't you find Margie and tell her dinner will be a bit late. If you two want a snack to hold you over, that's fine."

Hannah sat next to Louise, and they fell into each other's arms for several moments. Louise leaned back and spoke in a shaky voice. "Sweet Hannah, promise me you'll always be in my life. You are already like a daughter to me."

An ache rose in Hannah's chest, wanting to make it all right again for the woman. "Of course, I will."

Louise's lower lip trembled. "I'm worried about Peter and my husband. I need to notify them. I doubt the government will do that."

"I'll help you. There's a verse from Philippians that says

we're not to worry about anything and turn all our concerns over to the Lord. You'll have to look it up as I'm not good at memorizing scripture or remembering the exact verse numbers."

"When do you have to be back in Illinois?"

"I'm not working at the telephone company anymore. Women are signing up to substitute for the farmers who are being drafted. It's called the Women's Land Army. I'm to help start one in Wisconsin, but first, I must be trained at a small farm in Libertyville, Illinois."

Louise's brows rose. "I can't imagine you working on a farm."

"Nor could have I a few months ago." At least she got their thoughts off Ted for a few moments.

"Will you still want to do that now that … Ted is missing?"

"Yes. Now more than ever. The Krauts took down our Ted's plane. They must be stopped. I'm sure he'd want me to continue as I planned."

A sizzling sound came from the stove, and Hannah turned toward her mother. "Bacon at dinner time?"

"Why not?" Mama laid another strip of bacon in the cast-iron skillet. "Maybe having breakfast for dinner will start a new trend. Katie brought us some eggs. We may as well use them while they're fresh. Louise, do you want to join us?"

Louise pressed her hand to her stomach. "I can't eat anything."

Mama looked at Hannah. "I suppose that's true for you too?"

Hannah shrugged. "I'm not very hungry, but I need my strength for what's ahead. Yes. I'll eat."

Louise grunted. "Well, maybe I should have an egg and toast."

Hannah smiled at her. "I was hoping you'd say that."

After Hannah got Louise settled in her room at the cottage for the night, she went to the cottage's new telephone in the parlor and put in a call to Clarice, hoping she wasn't working late.

Her friend answered right away.

"Hey, it's Hannah."

"Didn't I only say goodbye to you yesterday?"

"Yes. But I need to talk." A sob pushed through her throat. "Ted's missing in action."

"I can be on the morning train."

"Oh, Clarice, thank you. But aren't you planning a trip to your mother's for Christmas?"

"I can do both. I'm to be there until after New Year's Day. If I'm a couple days late, it's no problem."

"I'm not going to pretend that I won't love having you here. I'll reimburse you for the fare."

"No need. It's what friends do for each other. See you tomorrow morning."

She replaced the receiver on the cradle and stared out the window. She'd always had girlfriends growing up and through college, but never one like Clarice. She somehow knew they'd be friends for life.

A few minutes later, Hannah let herself into the big house, relieved that everyone had gone to bed. She should, too, even though she was sure she wouldn't sleep a wink and probably wouldn't for several days. Stepping into her room, she stared at her trunk that Pop had brought up while she was in the springhouse. Was that only a couple of hours ago? It seemed like at least a week. She raised the trunk lid and dug down beneath the clothing until her hand settled on what she was looking for. She lifted out a stack of letters—all Ted had written since he shipped out—and stared at the top envelope. The one that he gave her with instructions to not open unless she received word that he had been killed.

The telegram said he was missing in action, but don't most people die in a plane crash? She slid her finger under the flap then stopped and placed the envelope at the bottom of the stack. Moving in slow motion, she removed her blouse and skirt and tossed them aside. Not bothering to find her nightgown in the trunk, she climbed into bed. Maybe tonight was all a dream, and she'd wake up with Ted still in England safe and healthy, and there wouldn't be any need to open that envelope.

CHAPTER TWENTY-SEVEN

January 4, 1918

utterflies danced in Hannah's stomach as Pop turned his car into the training farm's lane. Finally, she had something else to do besides moping around her parents' house and scanning the daily papers for news of the war. Being involved with the WLA was somehow causing her to feel closer to Ted wherever he was. Although his status hadn't changed, she believed he would be found alive.

They pulled up outside a large farmhouse, and a woman wearing bib-style dungarees and knee-high boots came down the steps.

"Looks like your welcoming party is here." Pop opened his door and climbed out while Hannah did the same, feeling very overdressed in her wool skirt, shirtwaist blouse, and jacket. Pop came up beside her

"You must be Hannah." The woman lifted a hand, glanced at it and laughed as she stuck it out to Hannah. "I had to check first to make sure it was clean. I've been building chicken coops. Blanche Corwin."

Hannah returned the woman's smile as she shook her hand. "I'm Hannah Murphy, and this is my father, Doctor Nate Murphy."

Pop glanced around. "I'm very impressed with what I see so far."

Blanche shrugged. "This is nothing. Wait until March when the trainees start arriving. And now, with Hannah willing to start a similar operation in Wisconsin, it's very exciting. Hannah, let's get you settled first. Then we can talk." She looked at Pop. "Doctor, if you need to get back to Lake Geneva, we can take it from here, but you're more than welcome to see where Hannah will be living for the next couple of months."

Her father grinned. "If I don't see her quarters for myself, her mother won't let me forget it. I have orders to pay close attention and bring home a thorough report."

Blanche laughed. "Sounds like something my mother would say. Come along. Let's get out of this cold."

Inside the house, they passed by a cozy sitting room with a fire blazing in the fireplace, then climbed the stairs to the second floor. They walked down a narrow hall until Blanche stopped in front of a closed door. "Your home away from home." She pushed the door open and allowed Hannah to step past her.

The twin-sized bed covered by a faded flowered bedspread, a highboy dresser, and an upholstered chair were about all the small room could hold. Not as nice as her room at home or the one she had at Cora's, but comfortable and functional. She stopped next to the bed and stared at a poster on the wall of a young woman in bib overalls like those Blanche wore, holding a hoe. Tears erupted, and she fished her handkerchief from her pocket. "I'm sorry. I've never been this emotional until—"

"I know that picture gets to me too," Blanche said. "I think all of us can relate to that woman."

"It's not her," Hannah said. "It's the ghostly line drawing of the soldier behind her and those words, 'Get behind the girl he left behind him.'"

"Her fiancé went missing in action in early December," Pop gently explained.

Hannah looked at her father and hoped her expression of gratitude conveyed her appreciation.

"I'm so sorry. I had no idea. I'll take it down immediately." Blanche bent over the bed and worked one of the tacks out of the wall.

"Wait, don't do that."

Blanche faced her. "But it's making you cry."

She shook her head. "I'm over it now. I hadn't seen that poster before. The soldier's profile is so like Ted's. It took me by surprise. I kind of like that I am the girl Ted left behind, and I need to be behind him and the other men over there."

A soft smile broke out on Blanche's face. "I fully understand. I have a brother serving over there, and that's how I feel about the poster." She pointed to her right. "We all share the bathroom just down the hall. It even has a tub. Not all farms have indoor plumbing. Doctor Murphy, do you want to see it?"

He shook his head. "No need. I've seen enough, and I need to get back home for afternoon office hours." He took Hannah in his arms. "We'll miss you, Hannie. Feel free to call collect anytime you want to hear a voice from home." He kissed her on the cheek. "No need to walk me out." He nodded a goodbye to Blanche and stepped out.

Hannah picked up her suitcase and opened it on the bed. I expect I'd better get out of these city clothes."

Blanche crossed to the dresser and pulled one of the drawers open. There are three pairs of bib overalls in three different sizes in here and several long-sleeved pullover shirts. Once we know which fits you best, we can exchange two of the bibs for the correct size. We're issued three pairs each. I'll be downstairs in the room with the fire going. Join me there once you're settled."

After changing into the overalls that fit best, Hannah carried the other two pair downstairs.

Blanche sat on the edge of a sofa cushion, hunched over papers strewn across the coffee table. She looked up and grinned. "Those fit like they were made for you. Put the discards on that chair over there and sit next to me."

"I'm glad they look better than they feel. It feels strange wearing clothing intended for men." Hannah placed the discards on the chair and sat next to Blanche. "This is such a cozy room."

"It's the only room we're using right now. We make sure the furnace is stoked each night when we need some heat in the upper rooms."

"You say 'we,' but so far, you seem to be the only person here."

"There are two of us. Alice Bensen has a part-time job at a bank in town. She works there three days a week." She handed Hannah several pamphlets and a few papers with typing on them. "I want you to spend today reading. The papers describe the operation of a training farm located in New England—our model for this farm. The pamphlet describes the various farm activities WLA farmettes might be asked to do. Things like plowing, planting, cultivating, and harvesting, Also, milking and taking care of chickens, pigs, goats, or what-have-you. We hope to train the women in as many of these tasks as possible during the few weeks they are here. I'm about to make some tea. Would you like some?"

Hannah nodded. "That sounds wonderful, but please don't feel you have to wait on me."

"Today, I wait on you. Tomorrow you're on your own. Do you take milk and sugar? I can only offer one teaspoon of sugar, but we have plenty of milk since our cows need to be milked daily. Nothing like milk fresh from the cow."

"I'm fine without sugar, but I agree about the milk. I've tasted it a few times at my aunt and uncle's farm."

By the time Alice, a tall woman with honey-blonde hair twisted into an up-do, returned from her bank job, Hannah had read all the material Blanche had given her. She hadn't felt as excited or nervous since her first day at law school. While they waited for Alice to change into her overalls. Blanche took Hannah to the kitchen located at the rear of the home.

"We're fortunate to have a complete kitchen with a cook-stove, refrigerator, and indoor plumbing. The last place I served, we had to go outside to a pump to get water. Do you know how to cook?"

"Yes. My mother taught me early on how to cook and do for myself. I often help her in the kitchen when I'm home." Hannah walked over to the stove and grabbed a potholder. "Do you mind if I see what smells so good?"

Blanche laughed. "Go ahead. It's beef stew. Nothing special."

Hannah lifted the lid, and the aroma of beef, spices, carrots, and gravy wafted into her nose. Her stomach rumbled for the first time since she heard the news about Ted. "It smells pretty special to me. We only have beef about once a week now."

"The beef was a donation from one of our supporters. That's good, you know how to cook. Most of the women I've trained barely knew how to boil an egg."

"One bank teller is now changed and ready for the cows." Alice stepped into the kitchen, her lengthy hair now plaited into a long braid that hung down her back.

Blanche snickered. "I think you look better as a farmette than a teller."

Alice laughed. "I agree. Ladies, I think the cows are calling us. Are we ready to bundle up?" She grabbed a wool cap from a hook on the wall and pulled it over her head.

At the backdoor, Blanche handed Hannah a wool hat similar

to Alice's. "You'll need this in addition to your coat and scarf. The wind is wicked out here."

The threesome stepped outside, and the wind slapped Hannah in the face. She bent and pushed on, following the other two. Despite her thick jacket, the wind forced itself through the coat's weave, and by the time they reached the large red barn at the far side of the yard, she was chilled clear to her toes. It was clear the thin lace-up boots she wore today were not enough. She should have worn the work boots and thick socks she'd borrowed from Aunt Katie.

Inside the barn, four black and white cows lay curled up in the hay, each in their own stall.

Alice announced each one's name and said they were usually outside, but because of the day's cold wind, they didn't have the heart to turn them out after that morning's milking. Already, Hannah was overwhelmed from all her reading, and, now, it appeared she was going to learn how to milk. She'd take writing a legal brief over farming any day.

Blanche grabbed a couple of tools from hooks on the wall and handed one to Hannah. "Now for one of the less appealing jobs. This is a shaving fork. Jab it into the straw, lift it out, shaking as you go until the cows' droppings are all that's left. Then toss them in the wheelbarrow." She walked to an empty stall and demonstrated the task, then handed Hannah the tool."

Hannah scrunched her nose and laughed. "I think I prefer the milking."

Alice gave her a hard stare. "We take turns, but when working on a farm, you'll often have to do both jobs. Tomorrow you'll milk, and I'll clean the stalls. Don't mind the cows, just work around them. When you're done, come back to the house and wash up. We'll have the beef stew ready."

What happened to the affable woman she met a short while ago? She saluted Alice. "Aye, aye, Ma'am."

Alice and Blanche laughed as they stepped outside. Was this

a test of sorts to see if she had what it took to be a farmette? Like it or not, she'd show them she had what it took and more. She shoveled the fork into the straw and lifted it.

The door to the outside flew open, and Blanche and Alice stepped inside. "Surprise! We were only fooling. You don't have to clean the stall tonight." Blanche said. "We'll get all the stalls cleaned out tomorrow morning after the cows are gone."

Alice snickered. "It was all I could do not to return your salute. Let's go have dinner."

Later that night, after a hot bath, Hannah donned a long flannel nightgown, then slipped between the clean sheets on her tiny bed and stared at the ceiling. "God, you have blessed me so much in many ways, but You know the one thing I want is to know for sure Ted is alive and healthy. You can see him wherever he is. Watch over him and bring him safely home in Your due time." She rolled over on her side, hugged the pillow she'd brought from home to her chest, and fell asleep dreaming it was Ted.

CHAPTER TWENTY-EIGHT

Three Months Later

Hannah stood next to the family car in the warm April sun and drew Blanche and Alice beneath each of her arms. "I could not do what I'm about to do without you two. Thank you for all you've taught me." She released them and looked over at Mama. "I can't believe how warm it is today." She shrugged out of her cardigan sweater and tossed it into the car.

Mama stared at her tan arms and gasped. "I had no idea you worked outside, exposing your arms."

She laughed. "Of course, I did. The days have been warm and sunny, and long sleeves are too hot when doing heavy work like plowing. I like the look of a tan." She looked from Blanche to Alice. "I can't believe it's time for me to go already."

"You know we're right here, and Bea Morrison will be there in Wisconsin to help in a few more weeks," Blanche said. "Now, get on home and get that training farm going." She looked at Alice. "Come on, we've got the new trainees to orientate."

Mama handed Hannah the car key. "You take the wheel. I'm

not used to driving this far, and I'm more comfortable being a passenger."

Once they were on the main road heading north, Hannah glanced at her mother. "How is Louise doing? Whenever I've asked over the phone, all I've heard is 'fine' before the subject is changed."

Mama sighed. "She's fine physically, but I'm not sure emotionally. Not knowing if Ted is dead or alive is wearing on her."

"He's alive, Mama. I feel it in my bones."

Mama let out a sigh. "I hope you're not setting yourself up for a huge letdown. It's been months since he went missing."

"I refuse to think any other way."

A couple of hours later, they pulled into the Safe Refuge drive. "Leave your suitcase in the car," Mama said. "Your father can bring it in the house when he gets home."

Hannah laughed. "I don't need to wait for Pop." She jumped out of the car, opened the backseat door, and grabbed the suitcase by its handle, hoisting it off the seat. "You can close your mouth, Mama. Let's get inside." She started across the gravel toward the cottage door, then stopped and set the suitcase on the ground. "Why is Ted's Buick here? He's not … is he?"

Mama scooted over. "Oh, Hannah, I should have warned you. With your new duties and your having to go back and forth between here and the farm, Louise thought you should have his car."

Hannah forced a laugh. "I knew it was too good to be true. I'm relieved because I was wondering what I'd do for transportation. What a good idea."

They continued to the cottage, and Mama opened the door for her. Hannah stepped inside and set the suitcase on the floor outside Louise's bedroom door. "It's Hannah, Louise!"

"You get yourself in here now!"

Hearing Louise's much stronger voice coming from the

living room, Hannah chuckled and stepped into the next room. Louise smiled as she set her book on a side table and stood from the sofa, her arms open.

Hannah scurried into the embrace. "It's so good to see you up and dressed."

Louise glanced at Hannah's arms. "And it's good to see you looking tan and …" She ran a hand over Hannah's muscled arm. "Strong. How are you dealing with no news for so long?"

"Being busy and learning new things has helped me to not fixate on the situation, but nights are difficult. When I crawl in bed as dead tired as I am because of all the physical work, I still don't fall asleep for a long while. By the way, thank you for loaning me Ted's car."

"It's not a loan. I'm giving it to you. I'm sure he'd want you to have it. How long are you here for?"

"Until the war is over. I'll be up very early every morning and will head straight to the farm. There may be times I'll stay overnight there, but most of the time I'll be here in the evenings. At least that's the idea."

"I'm glad you plan to be here to sleep. At night, my thoughts go crazy, I think maybe the Germans took Ted as a POW. But, he's not on any POW list the Germans have provided. Can they be trusted to tell the truth?"

"I doubt it. My friend Clarice is in France working the switchboards back of the front. She promised to ask around once she arrived if anyone knew anything about the crash, but that's not panned out. She's working almost every day. At least if I keep busy with the WLA, knowing what we farmettes are doing is so needed, I'll manage. Europe needs the food our farms produce to keep the allied soldiers strong."

"I envy you being able to do what you do. There's nothing for an old lady like me."

"You're not that old. If I may ask, how old are you?

Louise dropped her gaze to her lap. "Forty-Nine."

"That's not old. You're only a few years older than my mother, and she plans to help at the farm a couple days a week. Why don't you come with her?"

Louise's eyes widened. "I've never worn pants in my life."

"You can wear a skirt if you prefer, but I've become so used to wearing overalls I hated putting on a skirt this morning. If you don't like it, you don't have to come back."

"But I don't have any pants."

"We have overalls in all sizes at the farm. We'll find you a pair. I'll let you and Mama know when we're set up for you two to help."

CHAPTER TWENTY-NINE

Ted woke and squirmed on the narrow cot that had been his bed for what seemed at least a year. Overhead, heavy footfalls sounded on the floor above. The Germans were still there. He turned and coughed into his pillow to muffle the sound. The irritating cough seemed to be worsening and likely wouldn't improve until he was out of this dank cellar. If the Germans ever found out that Walt and Herta Janssen were harboring an Allied soldier in their cellar, they'd be shot on sight, and so would he. He had no idea what caused them to care enough to help him, and it gutted him to even think how they might suffer for their kindness.

He pulled a soiled handkerchief from his pocket and looked at the crude map his commanding officer had scribbled on it. His so-called escape route given him the same day they crashed. It might have worked if he'd not been knocked out. But praise God for Walt Janssen. He had no idea how the old farmer had somehow managed to free him from the wreckage, get him to the farm, and then down the narrow cellar stairs and onto the cot. He remembered insisting they not leave John, that he needed rescuing too. Walt's answer was short and to the point,

"He's gone, and you're not." He'd wavered between consciousness and brain fog the entire time and once laid out on the tiny bed, he'd slept for several days.

He stuffed the cloth back in his pocket. He should ask Walt to burn it, but it helped him to remember that the Lord gives us a way out of our troubles much better than a map. He had no doubt Walt was sent by God to find him.

Between the old couple's broken English and his fractured French, they'd managed to communicate enough that he understood when he heard heavy footfalls overhead, he had to be very quiet as it meant the pair of German officers who bunked at their house on their days off were upstairs. It was only because of the Janssen's willingness to host German officers that they were able to continue to live in their home.

He stretched out his good leg. The one that was mangled in the plane crash hadn't had any feeling from the knee down for weeks. Herta still worked to keep it from getting infected by daily cleansing the wounds with alcohol, but he was certain if he ever got out alive, he'd have to have it amputated. Something that would have already been done if he'd been taken prisoner.

He'd somehow lost his dog tag along with Hannah's picture and the cross. Walt said they weren't on him when he came upon the wreckage. The tag had to still be in the wreck.

Assuming he was reported as MIA, how was Hannah dealing with the news? Would she want a one-legged man for a husband? She didn't seem that shallow, but if it repulsed her, he'd have to quietly slip out of her life, and she could move on to a whole-bodied man.

Voices sounded overhead. He was directly under the Janssen's spare bedroom, and he often entertained himself by eavesdropping on the Germans. They mostly talked about their families and how much they missed them. He supposed they were ordinary people like him, wanting the war to be over so everyone could go home. What if one of them was his cousin?

Not out of the realm of possibility. War was evil. Hopefully, this would be the war to end all wars.

His stomach growled. He was nearly out of the bread and dried nuts he had to keep himself going when the Germans were there. The Janssens kept the cellar door covered by a rug, and the Krauts had no idea it was there. To try to bring him food while the Germans were around was too significant a risk to take. They'd already stayed two nights instead of the usual one, and he'd not heard any sounds of them packing up to leave.

His thoughts turned to last summer when he and Hannah used to sun themselves on Safe Refuge's pier after a swim. They always kept a respectable distance between them except for their clasped hands. If he thought hard enough, he could almost feel her hand in his.

Upstairs, the outside door slammed, and he startled. He blinked and glanced around, before returning to that summer day. Hannah had joked that if her mother saw her now, she'd scold her for ruining her skin by getting a tan. He'd said he didn't care if she had tan skin. She would be as beautiful with a tan or without one. He smiled at the memory of her stealing a kiss and thanking him for being so progressive. He had no idea what loving her had to do with progressiveness, but if it pleased—

Furniture scraped across the floor overhead. Someone was going to open the cellar door. He forced himself to roll off his bed onto the dirt floor and tucked himself under the cot. The trapdoor to the upstairs creaked open, and he held his breath.

Please, Lord, don't let it be the Germans.

The footfalls on the stairs were too heavy to be Herta's.

He was doomed. They were doomed.

"Ted, my *freund*. You must be hungry. No?"

He poked his head out from under the bed. Walt Janssen stood over him, holding a tray. "The Bosch stay two nights. We were worried. Here. Let me help you back to bed. Then you will eat."

Ted inched out and tried to sit up, but he'd weakened in the two days he'd laid there without sustenance. Walt set the food tray on the side table and assisted him onto the bed "You need new linen. Herta will bring soon." He arranged Ted's pillow behind his back and set the tray on his lap.

A delicious fragrance wafted into his nostrils, reminding him of one of Mother's Sunday dinners. One that wasn't German. He looked up at the old man. "Lamb?"

Walt nodded. "Ja, Germans bring. I didn't want to know where they got it. They aren't all bad. Just some of them." He reached beneath the bed and dragged out the chamber pot, then turned and climbed to the main floor, and the trapdoor closed. Sounds of the thin carpet being plopped down and furniture relocated indicated it would be a while before Herta came with fresh bedding.

He picked up the spoon and jabbed it deep into the stew. He had to remember to eat slowly, or his stomach would revolt despite how starved he was.

He lifted the spoon to his lips and closed his mouth around it.

Outside of remembering Hannah's kisses, this was about as close to heaven without being there he could be. He'd definitely take his time, letting it last as long as possible.

CHAPTER THIRTY

At the sound of a car horn, Hannah stepped out of the farmhouse's backdoor and waved as her mother brought her vehicle to a stop. The passenger door opened, and Louise emerged with a nervous smile on her face. "I'm here, Hannah. Now find me some pants to wear."

She laughed. "It's about time. It only took me a month of coaxing to get you here. Come in, both of you."

They all stepped into the kitchen, and Aunt Katie turned from the sink and hugged Mama. "Good to see you, Maureen." She looked at Ted's mother. "Louise, I'm glad you came."

Louise nodded. "I'm happy to be here. Have you heard from your men at all?"

"Letters from our boys come piecemeal. So far as I know, both are okay."

While the women chatted, Hannah went into a spare room that had become the training farm's office. She returned to the kitchen and handed two pair of bib overalls to Louise. "If you prefer to wear the skirt you have on, you'll be fine. You and Mama will be preparing the soil for the vegetable garden. No matter what you'll wear, you'll need these rubber boots. It's very muddy over there. She handed each woman a pair of galoshes. I'll be working with the trainees, plowing one of the fields."

Louise looked at Mama. "Since Maureen is wearing overalls, I'll do the same." She took the two pairs from Hannah. Show me where to change."

As they walked toward the bathroom, Louise said. "I had no idea when you said you were farming, you meant doing such heavy work as plowing."

Hannah smiled. "Someone has to do it, and with the men gone, it's up to us women. At least Uncle Jake is here to teach as much as he can. In fact, he'll be working with you and Mama at the garden."

With Louise settled in the changing room, Hannah returned to the kitchen and looked over at the breakfast table where her four trainees were finishing breakfast. "Ladies, it's time to hit the field."

A short time later, she stood in the pasture, facing her trainees. "Some farms will have motorized tractors. The owners of this farm do not. To plow with horses, you begin with gathering the animals and hitching them up to the plow. Have any of you worked with horses before?"

A tall brunette named Roxanne raised her hand. "I grew up on a farm. We had workhorses, but I never did anything but ride them when I was little."

Hannah smiled. "Well, you have more experience than most of us. Unlike our parents and grandparents who needed horses for travel, we've already become accustomed to automobiles. To call these two mares, you whistle like this." She held up a hand and pressed her fingertips to her tongue. She blew hard, and a loud whistle filled the air.

Both horses stopped grazing and trotted over to the group.

Eyes wide, one of the women said, "I doubt I could make a whistle like that."

Hannah laughed. "Two weeks ago, I didn't think I could either. My uncle showed me how."

The trainees followed behind Hannah as she led the horses over to the barnyard. She stopped beside a plow and faced the women. "We're lucky that my uncle's plow has a seat, and we don't have to walk behind it. I'll explain how to hitch the horses to the plow as I'm doing it. Later each of you will have a chance to try. This is where you need to take notes."

The trainees pulled out small notebooks and pencils, and Hannah explained how to harness the animals and then how to attach the plow to the horses, making sure the long pole, called the tongue, was comfortably between the two horses.

She climbed onto the seat, picked up the reins, and clicked her tongue. The horses began moving slowly to a corner of the field, as Hannah explained what was happening as her students walked alongside her. At the edge of the field, she halted the horses with a loud "whoa," and lowered the plowshare to the dirt, praying she'd be able to keep the horses going straight, and got them moving. She glanced behind her and smiled at the sight of the blade dragging through the dirt and turning it over. She stopped the horses and waved the women over. "Who wants to try first?"

Roxanne's hand went up.

The sun stood high in the sky as Hannah, and the trainees stepped into the kitchen and inhaled the aroma of simmering chicken and dumplings. Her stomach growled. "Aunt Katie, that smells wonderful. When do we eat?"

Her aunt turned and ran her gaze over Hannah and the others. "As soon as you wash up."

Hannah let the trainees use the washroom first, and by the time she returned to the kitchen, Mama and Louise had joined them. She stifled a chuckle at the sight of Louise with a dirt smudge across her rosy cheeks. "Looks like you two have been working as hard as us."

Uncle Jake limped into the kitchen. "You finish plowing the field already?"

Hannah chuckled. "We got half the field plowed despite the many times we stopped so each woman could take a turn. We'll be back to work as soon as we eat."

A couple of the trainees, who'd returned from washing up, groaned and pulled faces.

Hannah rested her fists on her hips. "Sorry to be such a hard taskmaster, but the work has to be done."

Roxanne stepped over and gave Hannah a side hug. "We're just teasing you. I actually love working outside and the accomplished feeling when you look over what you've done in a few hours."

"I agree." Mama began placing napkins at each place at the table. "I'm so proud of what you are accomplishing here, Hannah. I wish your grandfather could see you working in the dirt."

Hannah couldn't stop grinning. "I wish I could have known my grandfather longer. Sometimes I feel as though he's not really gone when I walk through his greenhouses. I know I'm not called to be a farmette for the rest of my life, but for now, it gives me pleasure to help this way."

LATER, after Mama and Louise left for home, Hannah stayed to have the evening meal of vegetable soup with the trainees before returning to Safe Refuge. She parked in the drive but didn't move to get out. Instead, she ran her hands over the steering wheel as a memory of a ride she and Ted had taken in the car filled her mind. He'd reached over and tugged her as close to him as he could. She'd asked if it was safe to drive one-handed, and he'd laughed, saying maybe not, but he'd take his chances. They were so in love and carefree. "Oh, Lord, I miss him so much. I cannot shake the feeling he's still alive. Please show me if that's crazy thinking or if it's true."

She climbed out of the auto and headed into the house where she found Pop alone in the living room with the evening paper.

She greeted him with a quick hug and sat on the ottoman in front of him. "Where's Mama?"

"She took a hot bath, and I've not seen her since. She's pretty achy tonight. I expect she's already gone to bed."

She chuckled. "I'll probably find Louise in the same condition. Maybe worse since she's older. I'll let them know they don't need to return tomorrow."

"They both intend to. Using sore muscles is the best cure for them anyway. How are you doing? You look like you could use a bath yourself. You've got mud halfway up your arms."

"And likely stink too. I'd better get to the cottage. I'm almost asleep on my feet. I take it there was no mail for me."

He frowned. "No and nothing for Louise either." He stood and took her hand, pulling her to her feet and into a hug. He leaned back, his eyes misty. "I know you want more than anything to hear that Ted survived the plane crash. I do too, but I'm afraid the odds are against that. Hannie. But know that I'm here for you."

CHAPTER THIRTY-ONE

Summer 1918

Hannah stood at the farmhouse's bathroom mirror and towel-dried her hair. The chin-length bob looked good without a lot of fuss, for which she was thankful. She hung the towel on its rack and examined her tanned and freckled image. What would Ted think of it when he saw her? She corrected herself … if he ever saw her. As much as she tried to think of him as being in heaven, as logic seemed to dictate, she couldn't.

She wrapped herself in her bathrobe and stepped across the hall into the office to dress in her traveling clothes. As much as she loved teaching women about farming, it felt good to wear regular clothes for a change. Hilda Loines was in town for only two days, and Hannah was grateful to meet with her tomorrow morning about expanding the Wisconsin WLA beyond this farm and two others farther north. She'd heard recently a dairy farmer near Madison needed help. If the man could manage for another month, she could assign him one of the recruits coming next week for training.

She gathered up her purse and overnight bag and headed for the kitchen, where she found Aunt Katie washing up the last of the dinner dishes. Hannah set down her things and picked up a dishtowel. "Are you still okay with taking me to the depot?" She dried a glass. "I think we should leave in about fifteen minutes."

"It's going to be tight. But we'll make it work." Aunt Katie gestured with her head toward the table at the far side of the room. "Hannah, this is Carl Johnson. He owns a farm over toward Delavan and has been waiting to speak with you about getting some help this week."

She gave her aunt a questioning look.

Aunt Katie shrugged and mouthed, "He wouldn't take no for an answer."

Hannah bottled a sigh. Why now? She only had Bea Morrison as a co-trainer since they were between trainees. She turned and crossed the room to stare into the deepest blue eyes she'd ever seen.

The man stood, rising to a height that had to be at least six feet. He came around the table and held out his hand. "Pleased to meet you, Miss Murphy. It sounds like I came at a bad time."

She placed her hand in his, appreciating the roughness of his work-hardened skin. A shiver trailed up her arm, and her breath hitched. Hoping she didn't appear as red as she felt, she withdrew her hand and stuck it in her skirt pocket. "I can only give you ten minutes. I have a train to catch."

His easy-like smile revealed a pair of dimples. "No problem. This won't take long."

She glanced at her purse, resting beside her overnight bag, where she left them on the floor. To put Ted's ring on now would only draw attention to the message she needed to convey —she was taken. Or was she? Handsome as he was, how could she be attracted to him so quickly when she loved Ted and clung to the possibility he was still alive?

She offered him her best business smile. Whatever the

farmer wanted, she'd take care of it, and he'd go away. As she lowered herself into the chair opposite him, she asked, "What can I do for you, Mr. Johnson?"

He sat and looked her in the eyes. "Our farmhands were called up a couple of months ago, and I had my cousin helping me. Now he's broken his leg. I have a field of sweet corn that's ready for harvest. Can one of the farmettes help me for a few days? I need to get it to the markets around the county by the end of the week. With the canneries buying up most of my other corn, fresh is rarely available in the stores."

"I'm so sorry, Mr. Johnson. All the ladies we've recently trained have already reported to their assignments. I can add you to our waitlist, and when the next group of trainees is ready, I'd be happy to assign one to your farm. But that won't be for another month."

He grimaced. "The corn is ready now."

Her heart squeezed. Wasn't this what the WLA was formed to do? Her family was able to start their own victory garden on Safe Refuge's land, but if they hadn't been blessed that way, meals would be even skimpier than they'd become. Maybe she could send Bea to his farm for a few half days until the crop was picked. "If you had help mornings only, which I know is the best time to pick sweet corn, would that help?"

The telephone rang in the hall and Hannah moved to stand.

"Continue your conversation, Hannah, I'm expecting a call." Aunt Katie scooted out of the room."

Mr. Johnson grinned, and the dimples reappeared. "I'll take whatever help you can provide. I'd be happy to drive over here to get her."

She returned his smile. "That won't be necessary. We trainers have our own cars."

Aunt Katie rushed into the room. "The Wade's heifer just went into labor and looks to be breech. Mrs. Wade needs someone to watch her boys while she assists her husband. I need to take you to the train immediately."

Hannah jumped up. "I'm ready now." She looked at her visitor. "Mr. Johnson, I'll be back in town tomorrow and will let you know then what arrangements I could make for you."

He scraped his chair back and stood. "I can take you to the train. If you don't mind riding in my truck."

"Why would I mind?"

He lifted his broad shoulders and let them fall. "It's kind of dirty."

"Dirt never bothers me. You should have seen me an hour ago." She looked at Aunt Katie. "Thanks to Mr. Johnson's kindness, I have a ride. You get over to the Wades."

Hannah waited while Mr. Johnson placed her overnight bag in the truck-bed then spread a blanket over the passenger seat.

He stood back, seemingly satisfied with his handiwork. "Time to take your seat, madam."

She had no choice but to accept his proffered hand and was relieved at the absence of a shiver. She slid onto the lumpy seat and clasped her hands in her lap. Whatever that sensation was before, it had passed.

He started the motor and put the truck in gear. "You said the depot in Lake Geneva. Right?"

"Yes." This was only a ride to the train, so why did she feel as if her heart was going to pound itself right out of her chest?

Pangs of guilt assaulted her. She needed that ring on her finger now. She unclasped her purse and slid her right hand into the inside pocket, where she always kept the ring when she was at the farm. Finding it, she worked the ring out of the purse and started to slide it onto her finger. The truck hit a bump, and the ring slipped off her finger and bounced against the gearshift, making a loud *ping* before it dropped to the floor beneath his feet.

He frowned and glanced down. "What was that?" The truck veered toward the side of the road and he yanked it back.

She bit her lower lip. She couldn't pretend she didn't notice.

"I dropped my ring. When we get to the depot, we'll have to look for it."

He frowned and glanced at her. "Okay. He returned his focus to the road. "Have you always lived around here?"

Relieved to have the topic changed, she relaxed. "Yes. I grew up in Lake Geneva, but now my family lives on the lakeshore in a house my great-grandfather built. Did you grow up on your farm?"

"Yep. It looks like we lived close by but never met. I'm grateful you WLA ladies are helping out us farmers."

"We're happy to serve to help get food to our troops and to those people in England."

By now, they were heading down the hill into town, and the ride would soon be over. She still didn't know how to explain the ring. What was wrong with her? She was an engaged woman and was always proud to show off the ring and talk about her Ted.

He parked the truck at the depot, and she waited for him to get out first so she could look for the ring. Instead, he reached down between his legs and lifted his hand with the ring wrapped around the tip of his little finger. He studied the gem a moment. "It's beautiful."

"Thank you. I never wear it while working at the farm."

She took the ring and slid it onto her finger.

"Looks like you have a special person in your life."

Not missing a shadow of disappointment on his face before it dissolved, she nodded. "My fiancé's plane was shot down over Belgium six months ago. He's missing in action."

He winced. "I'm so sorry. It must be awful not knowing what happened."

"He went down in occupied territory, which makes it difficult for the Army to do reconnaissance. Some think after six months with no further word, I should accept the fact he'll never be located, and his status will change to killed in action. I need more confirmation before I can accept that."

Mr. Johnson rolled his window down. "I hear the train whistle. Best we get you over to the platform." He opened his door and jumped to the ground.

He circled around the front of the truck and opened her door. She stared at his outstretched hand and then at the ground below. Too far to exit without his assistance.

"Miss Murphy, is something wrong? The train is almost here."

She gave herself a mental shake and let him take her hand as she slowly lowered her foot to the ground without one chill running up her arm.

The train whistle sounded, and he reached into the back of the truck and lifted out her bag. She held out her hand. "I can take it from here."

"Nonsense. I'll carry it over to the platform."

They arrived next to the track as the large black locomotive lumbered into the station, belching steam as it screeched to a stop.

"Have a good trip." He turned and headed in the direction of the truck.

She picked up her bag, climbed the steps, and glanced over her shoulder. He was almost to his truck. She waited a moment to see if he'd turn around. But he didn't.

THAT EVENING AT CORA'S, Hannah hung up the phone and slumped in the chair.

Her cousin approached her. "Hannah, what's wrong?"

"Can we talk in private?"

"Of course."

They made their way to what had been Hannah's room less than a year ago and sat side by side on the edge of the bed.

Hannah ran her gaze over her cousin's concerned face. "I feel like I'm cheating on Ted."

Cora's mouth fell open, and she glanced at the ring on Hannah's left hand. "It's been a long time since he was declared missing, who can blame—"

She held up her hand, palm out. "As far as I'm concerned, he's still alive."

"Are you seeing another man?"

Hannah shook her head. "Today, a farmer came to the training farm for help. He's a handsome young blond with piercing eyes as blue as Geneva Lake on a cloudless day. When we shook hands, a shiver raced up my arm. The same thing happened when I first met Ted. I tried to ignore it, but it's hard to disregard a heart-stopping smile and dimples like his."

Cora gave a gentle laugh. "You're smiling at the memory. Was that all that happened?"

"I was sure I'd be able to get away from him since I was leaving for the train, but Aunt Katie received an emergency phone call, and the farmer offered to take me to the train. I had no option but to accept. While we were on the road, I tried to fish my ring out of my purse, and it fell right under his feet. I was so embarrassed. When we got to the depot, he found it."

Cora's brows rose. "And that was all, right?"

She shook her head. "When I said I was engaged to Ted, I saw disappointment on his face. He must have been attracted to me too. I told him Ted had been declared MIA. I wish I'd not have told him that. Now, he might think there's a chance. I prayed the whole train ride for God to forgive me and give me strength."

Cora took her hand. "I don't know that there's anything that needs forgiving from the Lord. The war plays with our emotions in ways that aren't normal. You're a young, attractive woman, Hannah, and plenty of heads would turn at the sight of you."

She let out a sigh. "It was the first time in months that I forgot about the constant ache in my heart. Ted was—is—so perfect for me. How could I even be attracted to someone else?"

She fell into Cora's arms. "I love Ted with all my heart, and I miss him so much."

Cora patted her back. "Of course, you do, and hopefully, this war will be over soon, and you two will be back together. You probably won't need to see this man again, right?"

She leaned back. "He needs immediate help with his sweet corn, and I have no one fully trained and able to help but me and Bea, my co-trainer. I called her and she was about to call me. Her mother has taken ill, and she needs time off for a while. There's no one else." She stood and went to her overnight bag and pulled out her nightgown. "I'm probably making a mountain out of a molehill. I'm to meet with Hilda first thing in the morning. I'll catch the afternoon train back to Wisconsin. Pray that Bea's mother has a full recovery overnight." She let out a sigh. "I'm going to bed."

CHAPTER THIRTY-TWO

Two days later, shortly after dawn, Hannah arrived at the Johnson farm. Bea was only able to work mornings, but preferred to work with the trainees. Before leaving the car, she stuffed her feet into her rubber galoshes then found Mr. Johnson in the barn. As she approached, he tossed aside the broom and dustpan he held and grinned. "I'm surprised to see you here."

"We had it scheduled for Wednesday, right?"

"Yes. I was under the impression …." He shook his head. "Never mind. I'm glad you're here."

"I did plan to send my co-trainer, but she's working with our new trainees this morning, so you're stuck with me."

"I would never consider your company as being something I'm stuck with. I appreciate your coming." He ran his gaze over her bib overalls. "I was wondering what you ladies wear."

She laughed. "Farm work doesn't lend well to skirts and heels. We farmettes are like one of the guys when we're on the job."

He grinned, causing his dimples to appear. "Let's get this corn harvested."

Relieved to have felt no shivers or elevated heart rate, she followed him out the back of the barn and over a rise to a large cornfield.

He glanced at her. "Did you bring a hat? The sun gets brutal as it rises higher."

She gave him a thumbs up the way Ted described the corps men doing in one of his letters. "Right here." She reached in her back pocket and pulled out the floppy hat that had been part of her uniform all summer and secured it on her head.

Mr. Johnson pushed his cap back and laughed.

"Does it look that funny?"

He shook his head. "Not at all. I don't know why I laughed. Here you are giving of your valuable time to help me, and I'm making fun of your hat."

She supposed she should have felt self-conscious, but his easy-going manner wasn't troubling. She allowed him a smile. "No worries. I'm not offended."

"Good. Have you picked corn before?"

"Only what we grow on our property at Safe Refuge. We started a little garden this year."

"Then, you at least have an idea of the process."

They arrived at the cornfield, and he showed her how to take hold of the top ear of corn on each stalk then give it a sharp twist. After it popped off, she was to toss it into a nearby wheelbarrow, then take the next stalk, and do the same thing, moving the wheelbarrow down the row with her. When the wheelbarrow was full, he'd help her load the corn into a burlap bag for transport to the markets he served.

"One more thing," he said. "You don't want to take the lower stalk if it's small. We call those nubbins. We'll collect them later for the needy. The corn is still okay to eat and can be prepared in different ways."

She offered him a smile. "Your concern for the needy warms my heart. I'm sure some must feel forgotten with all the attention being given to the men in the war or those in need in Great Britain."

He answered with a shrug, and she returned to her task. It appeared the man found compliments uncomfortable. An appealing trait.

They worked in companionable silence, for which Hannah was grateful. It was bad enough having him so close while he worked on the next row.

Please, Lord, may Bea's mother have no downturn tomorrow, and Bea will be available to take over here.

"My side is done. How are you doing?"

His question burst into Hannah's mental prayer, and she jumped.

"I didn't mean to startle you. You must have been in some deep thought."

"Only wondering how things were going at the training farm. I guess I'll find out soon enough." She worked the ears off the last stalk in her row and tossed the corn into the wheelbar-row. It was okay to fib sometimes, wasn't it?

"Why don't we take a break? There's a water pump over yonder. The best spring water in Walworth county."

She took her handkerchief from her back pocket, and blotted her forehead. "Show me the way."

They walked toward a small rise at the edge of the field and approached a red-handled pump. He grabbed a tin cup that hung on the side of the pump and handed it to her. "Ladies first."

She held the cup under the spout and water gushed into the cup, causing the metal to chill her hands. He stopped pumping and grinned. "Go ahead. Taste it."

She took a drink. The icy cold water ran over her tongue and down her parched throat. She wiped her mouth with the back of her hand and grinned. "It's as good as the spring water we have on our property. Maybe even better. Forget selling your corn. You should bottle this stuff."

He chuckled. "I've thought about it, but who would buy water?"

"Can I have seconds?" She stuck the vessel under the faucet, and he pumped, stopping when the water reached the rim. She drank it down and handed the cup to him. "Your turn. I'll pump."

After he gulped down his water, he handed her the empty cup. "Want more before we go back to work?"

"I'd better not, or I'll float back to the field." She glanced down the incline, past the barn to the two-story house beyond. "You said the other day you inherited the farm. Was that what you intended to do all along—take over the farm from your dad?"

He refilled the cup and drank its contents. "I planned to attend the university and study agriculture. I thought maybe I'd go into ag research. But Dad died, and I had no choice but to stay on here."

"I graduated from the University of Wisconsin last year. If you'd been able to attend there, we might have met on campus."

A grin split his face. "Possibly. But, our paths wouldn't likely have crossed. I'd have been spending all my time in the university barns while you were attending sorority parties."

She frowned. "I was in a sorority, but it wasn't all parties. I wasn't drawn to medicine the way my parents were, but I wanted education beyond the university. That's why I started law school last fall."

He bent and pulled at a weed until it broke free of the soil. "No one's gone to college in my family. This man you're engaged to. He attend college too?"

A lump filled her throat. She didn't want to hold her education over him in a way that would feel superior. Yet she couldn't lie. "Yes. But not at the same schools. We met at a swimming party at his parents' home. He was in law school until last fall when he joined the British army, then switched to the Royal Flying Corps."

His face fell. "I hate that I missed out on college."

"Education is necessary for a man if he wants to be a doctor or a lawyer, but you had as great an education right here working with the soil and crops. You have to understand the weather and the best time to plant and harvest. You're running your own business, earning a living, and making food that doctors and lawyers need to do their jobs, serving others."

A heart-stopping smile filled his face. "I've never thought about it that way. Best we get back to the corn."

By noon they'd finished a second row and congratulated themselves on accomplishing as much as they did in one morning. He grinned at her. "We worked well together. If you come back tomorrow morning, we might be able to finish most of the field."

"I thought you said through Friday. Tomorrow's only Thursday."

"I did say Friday, but I don't want to hold you up, you being shorthanded and all."

She shook her head. "Your corn is important too. I set time aside for you tomorrow and Friday."

"Thank you." He grabbed up half a dozen ears of corn and handed them to her. "For you to take home."

She held the corn to her chest as she walked down the row toward her car. Mr. Johnson was a very nice man. She'd send Bea here tomorrow. The two of them might hit it off.

CHAPTER THIRTY-THREE

Hannah stared at Bea. "I'm surprised you're so reluctant to help Mr. Johnson. It's only until noon. It's a lot more pleasant picking corn than doing the indoor teaching that's next on the curriculum."

Bea pulled a face and shrugged. "What if my mother takes a downturn, and I'm needed at home?"

"The caregiver will call here, and I'll call the Johnson's, and his mother will get the message to you to leave at once. Please do this for me. I'll be happy to pinch hit for you someday."

A few minutes later, she waved Bea off as she left. Hannah didn't believe crossing one's fingers really brought one luck or a hoped-for blessing, but she crossed her fingers on both hands anyway and looked up at the cloudless sky. "Please, God, let the two of them hit it off."

When the trainees arrived from where they spent the night at a nearby farm, Hannah had set out the printed lessons and worksheets in front of three place settings at the kitchen table.

"Good morning, ladies. I hope you slept well."

The short brunette named Edith yawned. "I did until I heard

the rooster crow. I thought they didn't do that while it's still dark."

"Really?" the red-haired woman named Helen, responded. "I didn't hear a thing until this one on my left yelled at me to get moving."

Lil, her almost-black hair knotted in a bun at the back of her head, shrugged and lifted her hands. "What else could I do? When I spoke gently, you snored on."

Edith crossed her arms. "Oh, hush, Lil. I don't snore."

"Yes, you do," the other two said at once.

Hannah burst out laughing. "Well, I can see we're off to a good start. It's time to quiet our hearts. Prayer always helps me to do that. Please bow your heads while I invite God to join us." Ignoring Edith's eye roll, she bowed her head and thanked God for the beautiful day and to please bring peace into their midst. She ended with praying for the troops who were in harm's way at the front and in the air. She looked up happy to see the women's heads all remained bowed. After a few moments of silence, she gave up on the hope someone else would want to pray and said, "Amen."

She looked around the table. "Now, before we begin, if anyone wants coffee or tea, hot water is in the tea kettle on the stove, and coffee is in the pot to the left of the teakettle. Grab a cup and prepare whichever you want. We'll get started in five minutes."

Two hours later, she glanced at the kitchen clock on the wall, surprised it was already ten o'clock. The ladies had responded well to the lessons and, although the discussion was lively, it wasn't mean-spirited. "Time for a break. Use the bathroom if you need to. I'm ready for a drink of water after all the talking I've done." She went to the sink, set a glass under the pump, and worked the handle a few times. As the water gushed out, memories of yesterday when she and Carl were at the spring flowed into her thoughts. His water was far more refreshing than the well water here, and so was Carl's company.

Her breath hitched. When did she start thinking of him as Carl and not Mr. Johnson? She didn't call him by his first name to his face, did she? She retraced yesterday morning as best she could. Surely if she had, he would have said something, wouldn't he? She lifted the glass to her lips and drank.

"Hannah? Are you okay?"

She pivoted and looked into Edith's caring face. "Yes, I'm fine."

"Good. I was worried when you didn't answer me. I bet you were thinking about that man of yours."

She blinked. How did she read her mind? Of course, she didn't mean Mr. Johnson. She pushed out a smile. "My Ted is never far from my thoughts."

Edith nodded. "I understand. It must be hard not knowing his status."

"It is. Did you want a drink of water?"

"Yes, in fact, we were wondering if you have a pitcher to fill with water that we can keep on the table."

Hannah clapped her hands. "That's a wonderful idea. I should have thought of that." She opened a cabinet and found the pitcher she'd seen Aunt Katie use and set it in the sink under the spout. "You pump, and I'll make sure it doesn't overflow."

Over the next two hours, Hannah covered the care of chickens, pigs, and other smaller animals the women might encounter on their assignments. She'd leave the discussion of cows and milking for the afternoon. All the while she was speaking, Aunt Katie was busy at the counter fixing beef stew and biscuits, and the smells were causing Hannah's stomach to growl.

She closed the notebook that held her teaching material. "In case you haven't guessed by the wonderful aromas my aunt is bringing to the room, it's dinner time. Please clear the table of your materials and be back here in ten minutes."

Edith raised her hand. "Why is lunch called dinner?"

"Good question. Because farm people work hard all morning and need extra energy to continue working through the afternoon. The noon meal is the larger meal of the day. The evening meal is called supper."

"That makes sense." Edith pushed her chair back and stood. "First dibs on the bathroom."

The women had just left the kitchen when Bea burst through the door. "Am I glad that's over. That man is impossible to work with. I think he said five words the whole morning."

Hannah's heart sunk. Evidently, crossed fingers still didn't work. "Really? He was the opposite yesterday. We must have talked about a dozen different things."

"Apparently, I don't have what it takes to loosen his tongue. No wonder he's still a bachelor. One week living with him would drive me nuts. I'd feel as if I were having conversations with myself."

Aunt Katie stepped over. "Did you try asking questions?"

"Yes, and made sure they didn't require a single-word answer. What a bore." She looked at Hannah. "Tomorrow is all yours. How did your morning go?"

"Very well, and we stayed right here, going over the lessons. No phone calls. The women are ready for outdoor work."

The trainees returned to the kitchen, and Hannah managed to steal away to the washroom. She shut the door and said in a whisper. "Lord, why couldn't they have gotten along? I'm shocked he was so quiet with her. Now I have to go over there tomorrow. If at all possible, let us hear something today about Ted. Hopefully, good news that he's found and is okay."

CHAPTER THIRTY-FOUR

Friday morning, Hannah prayed the whole way to Mr. Johnson's farm that she'd not slip up and call him by his first name. He'd never called her anything but Miss Murphy. This was a business association, and nothing more.

She pulled into the barnyard and parked next to a shiny black Oakland touring sedan. The expensive automobile looked out of place in the humble surroundings. Who would come to a farm this early in the morning driving a car like that?

A door slammed, and she turned toward the sound.

Wearing bib overalls, Mr. Johnson ambled down the steps and across the yard. "Good morning. I expected Miss Morrison again."

Hadn't Bea explained to him she couldn't return? "Um, something came up, and she couldn't make it. Looks like you're stuck with me again."

He laughed. "Like I said before, I'd hardly call it being stuck. You're a good worker and get the job done fast."

She scowled. "And Miss Morrison wasn't?"

He studied his feet then brought his gaze back to her. "Yes, and no. She worked fast but wasn't much of a conversationalist."

She stifled the laugh, fighting to break free. "That's odd. She never shuts up when we work together. But isn't that what's expected of a good worker? Less chatter means more accomplished."

"You're right, of course. I work alone so much, I enjoy some conversation when doing a mundane task like picking corn."

She offered a gentle smile. "Mundane for you, but not for someone who's never picked corn before. She was probably focused on doing it correctly. How much is left to harvest?"

"Only a couple of rows. We should be done by noon if we get started right away. I finished feeding the pigs and chickens a few minutes ago, and didn't get out to the field as early as I'd have liked."

She glanced at the fancy car. "Don't you have a visitor?"

"No. Why?"

"Not many farmers I know drive an Oakland."

A crooked smile lifted the corners of his lips. "Well, now you know at least one."

She gaped at him. "That's your car?"

"Yes, ma'am. When my dad died, he left me a sum he said I should spend on an automobile of my own choosing because I deserved something nice to use when I wasn't working."

"It's a beautiful car."

"That it is. Let's get busy and get the corn harvested."

At the field, Hannah surveyed the rows of stalks. "You did say there were only a couple of rows left to do. Does that include the nubbins?"

"When you and I picked, the nubs weren't ready, but now they are. I've got a couple of bushel baskets to fill with them after we finish the last two rows. I let the word out that anyone who needed nubbins to come by the farm tomorrow morning, first come, first served."

"Aren't you concerned the first to come will hog them?"

"They haven't yet. I think those that have less are kinder than those who have a lot. Those that have a lot are always scheming to get more, but those who don't are grateful for what they do have."

Moved by his kindness to the needy, Hannah decided to open up about her faith. "The book of Ruth in the Bible tells how after the reapers went through a field, the poor were allowed to come in and glean what was left for their own use. I always loved that example of caring for the poor."

"I'm not a Bible reader, but I like that." He lifted the handles of a nearby wheelbarrow and pushed it into the row. "You work this side, and I'll be on the other side as before."

She knew a rebuff when she saw one. She reached for the top ear on the stalk next to her. If a man wasn't familiar with God's Word, he probably wasn't familiar with God in the way she and her family and Ted's family were." She relaxed. That should make it easier to not be attracted to him. After she'd removed the first two ears on the stalk, she paused. "Hey, Carl, I have an idea. Why don't we bring one of those bushel baskets over and start collecting the nubbins at the same time?"

She glanced at him. "Why the surprised look on your face? You don't like my idea?"

He chuckled. "I do like it if the ones in these rows are ready. I'm just surprised you called me Carl."

Heat rose to her face. "I guess I did. I'm sorry. We didn't give each other permission to use first names."

"I don't mind if you don't mind. Is it okay to call you Hannah?"

She was tempted to say it wasn't okay because theirs was a professional relationship, but she called her other male friends by their first names, and after this morning, they would only be friends. "I don't mind. Go ahead."

"Are you sure? It took you a while to decide."

"I'm sure. I probably would have asked you to after we stop working today since our work here is completed, and we'll be friends only."

He grinned. "I like that we'll be friends from now on." He hunched down and inspected the nubbins on some nearby stalks.. "They look good, Hannah. I'll grab a bushel basket and bring it over."

She thought it would be awkward to be on a first-name basis, but it turned out to be better as some of the tension she'd felt earlier was gone. Two friends working side by side to get the corn ready for the markets and also for the needy. It was turning out to be a good day.

After they'd cleared the rows, they returned to where they'd worked two days ago and quickly worked up and down the rows, filling the bushel baskets with the nubbins. Some stalks didn't have a nubbin, and that sped up the process.

Carl tossed the last nubbin into the bushel basket and grinned. "We're done. I couldn't do it without the WLA's help. I know it's last minute, but I'd like to invite you and Miss Morrison over tonight for a corn roast supper. We have sausages we've made from a pig we slaughtered. They taste delicious when they are cooked over an open fire."

She quirked her head. "What do you mean cooked over an open fire?"

My dad built a brick cook stove out back of the house, and we've done this every summer since I was a boy. It will be my mother and me only and you two ladies."

Chances were Bea would decline, which meant it would only be she, Carl, and his mother. He sincerely wanted to say thank you, and the meal sounded wonderful. As long as his mother was there too, it wouldn't be inappropriate. "I'd love to. I'll mention it to Be ... Miss Morrison, when I get back to the training farm."

His face brightened. "Good. I was afraid you'd say no. It was actually my mother's idea, and she plans to make an apple pie."

"Now, you know I'm coming. I love apple pie."

CHAPTER THIRTY-FIVE

Hannah stared across the kitchen table at Bea and scrambled for words, but none came.

"Why do you think I'd want to spend any more time with that man than I already have?" Bea crossed her arms.

"Please give him a second chance," she pleaded. "He's really nice. It's their way of saying thank you for our help. We don't have to stay for the whole evening. Just eat, make polite conversation, and leave."

Bea shook her head, the dark curls that framed her face bouncing. "The idea to invite us to a dinner party on the same day."

"It's not a dinner party. He calls it a corn roast. More like a picnic, I imagine."

Her friend raised her chin. "Doesn't matter. I've no one to stay with my mother. Best, you go alone. You don't get as tongue-tied with men as I do."

So that was it. "Okay. Maybe I can bring you back a piece of pie. That would make Mrs. Johnson happy. I'm sure she's using her scant supply of flour to make the crust."

"Stop trying to make me feel guilty. It's not going to work. If it bothers Mr. Johnson, he'll have to change his ways and plan ahead better."

Hannah shrugged. "Carl's not easily offended. He knows your mother is ill."

Bea's eyes widened. "Carl? You're on a first-name basis with a client?"

"The WLA job is done. That doesn't mean we can't be friends from now on. I call all my male friends by their first names."

Bea huffed a breath. "Friends you've known since you were a child."

"I've only known my friends from law school a short while."

"I guess that's different."

"Everything is different during wartime."

"If you say so." Bea turned toward the door. "We gave the trainees the afternoon off. I suggest we do the same and use the time to collect ourselves. Have a good time with Carl. I'll see you tomorrow."

A FEW MINUTES before five o'clock, wearing a casual summer skirt and low heels, Hannah made her way from the cottage to the big house. She'd already informed everyone she was joining Carl and his mother for a corn roast and wouldn't be at the evening meal, but she wanted to say goodbye.

She found Mama and her sisters in the kitchen as the girls were gathering up plates and silverware to set the table. "Hannah, you have a skirt on. Your legs have been in those overalls so long, I've forgotten how your legs look." Margie giggled as she passed by into the dining room.

Annie picked up a stack of plates. "I think you look pretty, Hannah."

Hannah chucked her little sister under her chin. "Thanks,

Annie." She went alongside her mother, who stood at the sink, washing fresh-picked lettuce. "I saw only three plates in Annie's hands. Where's Pop?"

"He had an emergency at the hospital and won't be home until Lord knows when."

"Such is the life of a doctor. I don't expect it to be a long evening for me. They're farm people and have to be up early, as do I."

The girls burst through the door. "The table is set. Can we go now?" Margie asked.

You may each have one cookie from the cookie jar and take it outside. I'll call you when dinner is ready."

A grin spread across the girl's face. "All right." Margie made a beeline for the cookie jar on the Hoosier cabinet shelf and pulled out two oatmeal cookies and handed one to Annie. "Let's go."

Annie made a face. "I don't want it after your dirty hands have been all over it."

Margie rolled her eyes and lifted the jar down and held it out to her sister. "Take your cookie yourself then." She stuck both the cookies she'd offered to Annie in her skirt pocket.

Hannah held out her hand palm up.

Margie stared at it. "What is that for?"

"Mama said only one cookie each. Hand one of them over."

The girl huffed a breath, pulled one of the cookies from her pocket, and slammed it onto Hannah's hand. "I liked you better when you were away at school."

Hannah waited until the girls were out of earshot before she released her giggle. "Was I as bad when I was her age?"

Mama laughed. "Worse, I think. You'll make a good mother someday, Hannie." She dried her hands on her apron. "I sent them away so we could talk." She ran her gaze over Hannah, starting at her head and working all the way down to her shoes. "Is this something more than a thank-you dinner?"

Hannah took a saucer from the cupboard and set the cookie she'd taken from Margie on it, using the time to form an answer. Not having one, she opted for indifference. "No. Why?"

"New summer outfit and shoes, shampooed hair, and I detect a whiff of rosewater. Not to mention I've not seen you glow like that since Ted left."

Hannah winced and blinked away the gathering moisture in her eyes. "I hoped it didn't show. I've been confused, Mama. I love Ted with all my heart." Her lower lip trembled. "To even feel an ounce of attraction to another man is wrong. Yet, I have to admit I do like Carl, and if I didn't have Ted, I'd want to know Carl better. I don't want it to be anything more than friendship, and he hasn't given me any indication he wants more than that. Of course, he wouldn't since I'm still wearing Ted's ring. Maybe I should change clothes."

Mama shook her head. "Don't change. But do ask God to protect your heart and help you to be strong until you know for sure if Ted has gone to be with the Lord. I do have one more question, though. Is Carl a man of faith?"

Hannah shrugged. "I don't think so. I mentioned the book of Ruth to him, and he had no idea what I was talking about. Yet he always has the needy in mind. He grows his crops for the local markets to sell and gives the smaller ears of corn to the local needy."

"People can be benevolent and compassionate for the less fortunate without knowing the Lord. You know the Bible cautions us to not be unequally yoked with unbelievers. If the situation changes and you are free to see someone, don't you think you should be sure of his standing with God now rather than later?"

Hannah nodded. "I know the scripture. But I sometimes wonder if that was written to someone else and not me. I am, or was, engaged to a believer, and God took him away from me. First across the sea and now quite possibly forever. It seems

God isn't as faithful to me as I've always believed Him to be. If I fall in love with a man who doesn't believe the same as me, is that so bad?"

Mama sighed. "The man is supposed to be the spiritual leader of the home. If he doesn't share the same faith, how can he guide you and your children in your faith?"

"Can't he learn and grow and become that leader over time?"

"Yes, but what if he doesn't and chooses another direction? You're in a vulnerable place right now, Hannah. Please guard your heart and don't react on your emotions concerning, Carl."

She fell into her mother's embrace. "I wish this limbo I'm in didn't hurt so much. This week I've actually been able to push away the pain."

"And spending time with a man who is kind and easy to be with has helped you to do that. But be careful, my dear daughter."

"Thank you for understanding. I love you, Mama." Hannah kissed her mother's scarred cheek and glanced at the clock. "I've got to leave now, or I'll be late." As she passed by the table, she grabbed the cookie off the plate. "I'll take this contraband off your hands. Don't worry about me. I am not losing my head. I promise."

CHAPTER THIRTY-SIX

Hannah turned her car into the Johnson farm and parked beside Carl's truck, which he must have picked up from the mechanic earlier. She climbed out of the vehicle, then glanced down at her flowing moss-green skirt and ecru colored top. It was the kind of ensemble that made her feel pretty. Mama wasn't far from the truth. She'd picked the outfit in the hopes Carl would see her as a woman and not merely a farmette. If anything, when she stood next to him in his bibs tonight, the effect would prove they weren't suited for each other. City and country did not mix well.

She climbed the steps to the door and knocked. The door swung open, and she swallowed a gasp. God had better answer her prayers for His protection and fast. If she thought Carl handsome in his bibs, seeing him now in his dark flannel trousers and crisp white and brown striped shirt, almost took her breath away.

He ran his hand over his damp blond hair and frowned. "I'm sorry, I was expecting a nice-looking lady in bib overalls. Are you sure you're in the right place?"

She laughed. "I was about to think I came to the wrong

house. I don't know what I expected you to wear away from the farm work."

He ran his thumb down one of his dark brown suspenders and grinned. "Normal clothes like everyone else. Come in and meet my mother." He grabbed a light tan jacket from a hook on the wall. "Best, I put this on before I tend to our dinner." He opened the door to the right. "Mom, Hannah is here."

Hannah stepped into a large kitchen that smelled of baking apples. An older woman, her gray hair caught in a bun at the top of her head, scurried across the worn wooden floor, wiping her hands on her bib apron as she walked. "I'm so pleased you could come, Miss Murphy. Carl has told me all about you WLA ladies, and how much you've helped with the corn harvest." She glanced over Hannah's shoulder. "I thought there were two of you coming."

"I'm pleased to meet you, Mrs. Johnson. My co-trainer, Bea Morrison, has to stay with her sick mother tonight, but sends her appreciation for the kind invitation."

Mrs. Johnson's face fell. "I'm sorry she can't make it. We'll have to send her a slice of apple pie. And you may call me Etta. Everyone else does. Would you care for a drink? I made something the Swedish call *saft*. It's a refreshing mixture of strawberries, cherries, and elderberries from our farm."

Hannah nodded. "That sounds wonderful. And please call me Hannah." She glanced around the cozy kitchen. "Can I help you with anything?"

"No. Carl has the cooking under control." She gave him a pointed look. "Isn't that right, son?"

Hannah faced him, startled to see him staring at her.

"Carl, did you hear me?"

He winced. "Yes, Mom, right. I'd better check on the food." He crossed the room and exited through a different door than the one they came in.

Etta grinned at Hannah. "I love it when the men cook and

we ladies can relax a bit. He works hard, and I'm happy to cook for him. His daddy died way too soon, but I have a fine son, giving up his college to keep the farm going."

It almost seemed as if Etta was doing a sales pitch for her son. Was she afraid because Carl was so busy running the farm, he'd never meet someone? She wanted to tell her the man will have no trouble finding somebody to spend his life with. "I've been very impressed with all Carl has done on your farm on behalf of the country and our troops."

Etta glanced at Hannah's engagement ring. "Carl told me about your fiancé. I'm very sorry. It must be horrible not knowing."

She nodded. "It is. But I sense the war won't last much longer. I've heard the German troops are weakening. I choose to believe he's still alive and will be coming home."

Etta turned and looked out the window over the sink. "It looks like we'll be eating soon. Carl is removing the corn and sausages from the grate now." She lifted a pitcher filled with juice the color of strawberries and poured some into three glasses. She picked up two of the drinks and carried them to the table. "Perhaps you can bring the third one over to the table for me."

"Of course." Hannah picked up the drink and placed it in front of the one place setting that lacked a beverage. "I can't wait to taste the corn and sausage. I've never had anything cooked outside over an open fire."

Etta's face brightened. "Oh, then you are going to love this meal. I plan on roasting marshmallows over the flame for dessert. Along with the apple pie, of course."

Hannah's eyes widened. "My little sisters enjoy marshmallows for a sweet snack once in a while, but I never thought about roasting them."

Etta's eyes twinkled. "You can even roast them over the

flame on your stove. You don't need to have an open fire. But outside is better."

The door to the outside opened, and Carl entered carrying a huge pan of charred corn on the cob and sizzling sausage. Hannah sniffed, and her mouth watered.

He set the large platter on an arrangement of potholders in the center of the table and grinned at Hannah, "I hope you brought your appetite. I made enough for four."

She laughed. "If it tastes as good as it smells, I'll be able to do my share." She sat in the chair Etta indicated.

After his mother sat, Carl took the chair to Hannah's right and looked from Etta to Hannah. "Ladies, shall we begin?"

"Yes, we shall," Etta said. "Hannah, you can start filling your plate whenever you are ready."

She did as Etta suggested. They would probably say grace after their plates were filled.

Carl filled his plate last and began buttering an ear of corn. "I'm so glad we worked out a deal with Farmer Dade. His butter for some of our field corn. I do believe we got the better end of the deal." He lifted his buttered ear, took a bite, then wiped the melted butter from his chin with his napkin. He stared at Hannah. "What are you waiting for? Eat while it's hot."

"I assumed ... never mind." Thankful she caught herself from saying she thought he'd say grace, she buttered an ear of corn and sunk her teeth into the cob, letting the feel of the melted butter and the taste of corn mingle on her tongue. She swallowed and grinned at Carl. "This is the best corn I've ever tasted."

Etta slapped the table, causing the juice to splash out of the glasses. "I knew you'd like it."

Resisting the temptation to blot up the juice around her glass, Hannah lifted it and took a sip, surprised the mixture of the fruit and something else she couldn't place was so refreshing. "This is delicious. What makes it tingle in my mouth?"

He forked a piece of sausage he'd cut into bite-sized pieces. "Selzer water. You've never had it before?"

"I don't know. Not this way, anyway. I love it."

Two helpings of sausages and three ears of corn later, Hannah pushed her chair back from the table. "I know we have pie for dessert, but right now, I can't eat another bite."

Etta nodded. "Don't forget we're going to roast marshmallows too. Why don't you two take a walk, and when you return we can have dessert?"

"No, Mom. When we get back, you'll have washed all the dishes. I don't want you working tonight. I'll wash up the dishes before we go anywhere."

His mother shook her head. "Nothing doing. You cooked after working in the fields. I can wash dishes. You young people get out of here and go enjoy yourselves."

There went the not-so-subtle matchmaker again. Hannah stifled a smile. So opposite from her own mother.

Carl stood and rested his hand on her chairback. "When my mom says go, she means to go. Come on, I'll take you on a walk that I guarantee won't dirty your pretty shoes."

Hannah chuckled. "I did put my galoshes in the car just in case."

"Not necessary."

Outside, she waited where he indicated by the walkway to where the vehicles were parked while he ran off behind the large barn. A couple minutes later, the shiny black Oakland appeared. Carl pulled up next to where Hannah waited and exited the car. He came around and opened her door. "I know the perfect place for a walk."

She took her seat, and a moment later, he slid behind the wheel, shifted the car into first gear, and drove to the road. "Have you ever been to Lake Lawn on Delavan Lake? It's a nice place to walk."

Hannah shook her head. "I've heard good things about it, but

I admit to having such a busy life on Geneva Lake and in town, I've never ventured far during the summer."

"Well then, you're in for a treat."

A few minutes later, he turned in between a pair of stone pillars and drove down a lane. Clusters of guest cottages appeared, and as they neared the lake, a rustic lodge came into view. He pulled into a parking place, and after he assisted her from her seat, he offered his elbow. The man wasn't lacking in manners, and that warmed her heart. She slid her hand through his bent arm. The summer weight fabric of his shirt did little to hide the size of his bicep muscle. Large from years of farming. A warning bell sounded in her brain, and she pushed it away. He was only acting a gentleman. She couldn't help it if he had large muscles. Ted's were probably larger now than when he left, thanks to all the exercises and weight lifting the military required of him.

They came to a bench that faced the water and sat. Making sure there were a few inches of real estate between them, she angled herself toward him and regarded his profile while he stared out at the water. His strong jaw, not covered by a beard like many farmers still wore, along with a perfectly formed nose —all traits that favored his Scandinavian ancestry. Were full lips a part of that too? She had no idea. What would it be like to ... She forced her gaze away and stared out at the calm water, praying for God's help. "Do you attend church, Carl?"

She felt him startle. "That wasn't a question I was expecting."

"I'm sorry. It's been on my mind. God has been a huge part of my life for as long as I can remember. He's provided me the strength to get through Ted's going missing. My faith is impor-tant to me. I noticed you didn't say grace before our dinner. I'm not saying it's wrong, but I'm so used to having that done ... "

"My dad used to say grace. But after he died, I never took it up. I also quit going to church. It was always Dad who said we needed to be in God's house on Sunday mornings. Mom and I just followed him. After he passed, we had no one to follow. Mom and I attend a church in Delavan on Easter most years. But no, I don't attend church regularly. I believe in God, but I'm my own man, and He's not that involved in my life."

Her heart fell. "You never pray?"

"Not really. It never occurred to me to say grace before a meal myself. That was my dad. Not me. I'm glad for you that He's helping you through Ted being MIA. Does it matter to you what I feel about God?"

She drew in a breath and let it out. She told Mama earlier what Carl believed didn't matter, but did she really mean it? "No. We can be friends no matter how we each believe. My best friend from law school doesn't believe the same as me, and we're tight friends just the same."

"Does Ted believe like you do?"

"Yes. And that brings me comfort because if he did die in the plane crash, I know he's in heaven."

"How can you know for sure?"

"Because the Bible tells me it's true."

He frowned and worked his pursed lips back and forth a few times. "Maybe I'll look for my father's Bible and start reading it."

She grinned. "Carl, that would be a good thing for you to do."

He stretched his arm across the back of the bench and gave her shoulder a squeeze.

Her stomach dipped. She needed to move farther away, but it was as if she was glued to the seat. Surely, he wouldn't do anything more than that.

"Thanks, Hannah, for telling me about the Bible. Sometimes I wonder about those things and wish my dad were still around to ask him."

"You could go to the pastor of the church you attend sometimes and talk to him."

"He probably has no idea who I am."

"It doesn't matter. The reverend should welcome you and your questions regardless of not having knowledge of you."

He pulled a gold watch from his pocket and held it out for her to see. "My dad's." He flicked the lid open and peered at it in the fading light. "We'd better get back. Mom's probably wondering about us."

CHAPTER THIRTY-SEVEN

Hannah followed her family into Faith Community Church on Sunday morning and settled into the family pew. As the organ music played softly, her thoughts drifted to Carl. If he didn't attend church on Sundays, what did he do these mornings? Of course, the farm chores never stopped, but other than that, she couldn't imagine Sundays without attending church.

Ted had even mentioned in one of his letters that whenever he was on duty and couldn't attend church, he felt strange. Since Ted left, she'd often dreamed of sitting next to him right there in the family pew. That dream could possibly be gone forever. Sitting in Sunday service alone, knowing your husband was at home tending to the farm was better than nothing.

The organist switched to a hymn, and the music became louder as the congregation was invited to stand. She pulled herself back into the present. Her daydreams should only contain Ted, and no one else.

MONDAY MORNING, as she arrived at the training office, the telephone rang. She picked up the receiver, "WLA Wisconsin Training Farm, this is Hannah Murphy."

"Hannah, this is Hilda."

"Hilda, how fortuitous. I was about to call you. I'm wondering if that set-up we used last week with Bea filling in mornings while I assisted in a corn harvest nearby could be done again. The same farmer is expecting to harvest his field corn in about a month or so, and I'd like to schedule it on the calendar."

"Before this morning, I would have approved the request, but now something has come up. I'm not usually the one to move the Wisconsin farmettes around, but Marion Schultz, who has been handling it, is also out of commission. One of the farmettes working on a dairy farm near Oregon, Wisconsin, has been called home due to a death in the family. I'd like you to take her place. I'm sorry to do this, but the assignment in Oregon isn't easy, and I have no one else to send. There's no fieldwork. Only tending and milking a large herd of dairy cows."

Hannah's stomach cramped, and she pressed her palm to it. "I'd prefer to not go. With word of Ted's status coming at any time … perhaps Bea could go."

Hilda sighed. "I already checked with Bea and, although her mother is on the mend, Bea needs to be home with her at night. You're one of our best farmettes, Hannah. I'm counting on you."

She swallowed the lump in her throat. What was wrong with her? She was acting like a schoolgirl with a crush on a boy. "Of course. Give me the man's telephone number, and I'll get instructions to the farm."

"Thank you. You'll report to Mr. Sam Amsler the day after tomorrow. He can be reached through the Oregon, Wisconsin central operator. Perhaps in a few weeks, the woman who was assigned there can return."

It wasn't until later in the afternoon she was able to get away and drive to Carl's farm to deliver the news. She found him in the sweet corn field, gathering the stalks.

She stood on the edge of the field until he noticed her and approached, his bib overalls covered with mud. "This is a surprise. You weren't scheduled for today, were you? The field corn needs a lot more time."

She shook her head. "I wanted to tell you in person that something has come up. I'm being sent to a dairy farm near Madison and will likely be there for several weeks. Miss Morrison is taking over as lead trainer while I'm gone. It's likely when your field corn is ready, you will have to work with her. I'll tell her to plan on it."

His face fell. "When do you leave?"

"Day after tomorrow."

He let out a long breath. "I guess I won't see you again for a while. By the way, I've been thinking about what you said about the Bible. I thought we had my dad's somewhere, but Mom said she tossed it after he died. I plan to buy one. Looks like I'll have to keep it out of sight."

She smiled. "Carl, that's wonderful you're willing to explore the Bible for yourself. It sounds like your father was a godly man. I have a feeling if he were still alive, he'd be giving you a thumbs up."

He frowned. "What do you mean by thumbs up?"

She demonstrated the gesture. "Like this. Ted wrote about it, saying the men in his unit would give a thumbs up to the pilots before they left on a mission. I remembered reading about it in a novel that came out last year. I like it and have been giving it to the trainees before they leave on assignment as if to say you did a good job here, now go serve."

"I like that. I can picture my dad giving me a thumbs up from heaven. I'm not sure where to buy a Bible."

"There's a little store in Lake Geneva that sells dry goods and other things, including some books. I've seen Bibles on the shelf there."

"I know the one, I've been there but wasn't looking for a Bible then."

She stepped back. "I still need to wrap up some things at the training farm and head home to pack. I'll see you when I'm reassigned back here."

He stared at his feet. "I shouldn't say this, but I'll miss not having you around. I've enjoyed our talks and time together."

"Me too." She turned and headed to her car, convinced the assignment may have come from Hilda, but it was God who determined her steps, as the Bible said. As she backed up and moved the shifter into first gear, she glanced across the barnyard. Carl raised his hand and gave her a thumbs up. She returned the gesture and drove out onto the road.

Later that evening, Hannah sat with Mama in the spring house, trying to not think about Carl's words that afternoon. They'd come there at Hannah's request to talk about her conflicted feelings.

"We're here, honey, now what is on your mind?"

She looked at Mama in the fading light. "I think God caused me to be transferred to the new farm."

"Why do you say that?"

"I know it sounds silly, but what else can it be? I've begun to have feelings for a man when my fiancé may still be alive. One who isn't a churchgoer and has no personal faith in God. The Lord must be trying to keep Carl and me apart."

Mama cleared her throat. "I don't think He'd go that far. Unless you're more involved with him than what you've told me."

Hannah shook her head. No. We're good friends is all and talk about a lot of things like the Bible. It seems his father was a Christian; his mother is not. She threw away her husband's Bible after he died, and God isn't talked about in the house anymore. He plans to buy a Bible and start reading it. But even if I didn't have Ted in my life, at this point, I would be conflicted because of his lack of faith."

"Then why the concern?"

"He told me today he's going to miss me and our talks. That he likes spending time with me."

Mama stared at her. "How did you feel when he said that?"

"A little sad I didn't have the opportunity to know him before I met Ted."

"I suppose that's to be expected."

"I did say I'd miss our time together too. Before I left."

"Perhaps the Lord is intervening. You two probably need time away from each other before your feelings escalate."

"Mama, you have no idea how it is to be in love with someone and have growing feelings for someone else."

"Child, I know exactly how it feels. At your age, I was so certain Preston Stevens was the man for me. We were both passionate about life and very drawn to each other." She chuckled. "He certainly knew how to kiss."

Hannah's mouth fell open. "Mama!"

"Well, it's true. I think that's one of the reasons I was so attracted to him. Mind you, we never did anything but kiss. It turned out he wasn't the right man for me after all, as I told you before. Go to that dairy farm. Getting away will help you put things into perspective more than could ever happen if you stayed here."

CHAPTER THIRTY-EIGHT

November 1, 1918

Hannah led the black and white cow she'd named Daisy into the stanchion, a chute-like structure that kept the cow steady while being milked. Knowing a tray full of hay was waiting for her, Daisy needed no urging to get into position. The first week she arrived at the Amsler farm, she began naming the cows, which amused Mr. Amsler. To him, they were just cows, but to her, they were part of the Lord's creation, and they deserved names.

She pulled a three-legged stool up to the stanchion. "Okay, Daisy, it's time to give me that sweet, warm milk you're carrying around." The large black and white Holstein paid no attention to Hannah as she nibbled on the hay in front of her.

After she washed the udder and teats, she positioned a large bucket under Daisy and massaged the udder to signal the cow to relax. Sensing Daisy was ready, she gripped two of the teats between her thumbs and forefingers and squeezed. Soon, she had a rhythm going, and a stream of warm white liquid flowed into the bucket. She had to admit she liked milking way more than she ever thought possible.

As she worked, her thoughts went to someday in the future when she'd be nursing her baby, which she imagined was a boy, giving him her own milk that he needed to grow strong and healthy. She'd look down at the baby's closed eyes and, as he finished feeding, his long lashes would flutter and begin to lift. Suddenly, the daydream would fade. If only, it would last long enough to see his eyes and know if they were like Ted's dark chocolate ones or piercing blue like Carl's. It was silly to expect a daydream to tell her the future. Especially when she and Carl were only friends, and they'd kept it within those boundaries.

It had been almost three months since she said goodbye to Carl. A few times, she'd been tempted to pick up the telephone and call him, but having to use someone else's phone complicated things.

There'd been no further word on Ted's status, and her resolve to remain positive that he was still alive diminished a bit with each casualty report that included some who were lost when their aircraft was shot down. She stopped reading the reports, and it helped some. She'd heard that the Germans were weakening, and one of these days, weeks, or months, they would surrender. She let out a sigh. "God, please let it be soon."

ONE WEEK LATER, having finished the milking, Hannah buttoned her jacket against the chilly November wind. Her stomach growled in anticipation of chicken noodle soup and warm-from-the-oven cornbread Mrs. Amsler was preparing for the noon meal. As ever, there would be another hand-written recipe next to her bowl. Her recipe collection was growing.

After her first dinner with the Amslers—a wonderful

chicken dinner with potatoes and carrots from their garden, all cooked in the same cast-iron skillet—Mrs. Amsler graciously offered her the recipe. "Someday, Miss Hannah, your young man will be home, and you'll want to keep him fed and happy." She would always laugh and tell the older women she needed her optimism. Mrs. Amsler would say, "I feel it in my bones, he will be coming home to you, and when he does, we want to be invited to the wedding."

Hearing the woman call her Miss Hannah always gave her a warm feeling. The couple wanted her to call them Sam and Frieda as the previous farmette had done, but she explained as a trainer, she couldn't so easily bend the rules. They agreed, but calling her Miss Murphy all the time sounded strange. Would it be okay to call her Miss Hannah? She loved the idea and agreed.

From then on, whenever Mrs. Amsler prepared a new dish, she'd always write out the recipe and leave it at Hanna's place at the table with her beautiful script at the top: For Miss Hannah.

She'd not mentioned Carl to the Amslers except to say that his farm was her last assignment. It was Ted she was engaged to, and he was the one missing in action. Besides, her friendship with Carl was none of their business. She finished up with Daisy and returned her to the stall where she'd stay for the night. She poured the milk into a tall silver can and set it next to the others she'd filled over the past hour. Mr. Amsler would place them with the ones he'd done in the milk house that was kept cool with a water reservoir. Like clockwork, a man from the local dairy would pick them up tomorrow morning.

After donning her jacket and wrapping a wool scarf around her neck, she pushed her shoulder against the barn's outside door and slid through the open gap, letting the wind push it back in place. Keeping her head down, she began her trek to the house. Bits of dust from the path blew into her mouth, and she spit it out. As much as she wanted to complain, knowing the men in the trenches at the front were putting up with far worse circumstances, she held her tongue.

"I think we might get some snow out of this system. I can smell it in the air." Mr. Amsler shouted over the wind as he walked up, wearing his wool hat pulled down over his ears.

She lifted her head and raised her voice. "I didn't see you coming. I hope it doesn't snow. It's too early."

"We've had real bad snow this early."

She laughed. "Don't remind me. I spent four years in Madison, don't forget." A blast hit her, and she teetered backward.

Mr. Amsler grabbed her by the arm. "Whoa, Miss Hannah. I almost lost you there."

Assured she had her balance, she eased out of his grip. "Thanks for catching me."

He held out his bent arm. "Grab hold of my elbow. We're almost there."

They reached the back porch and climbed the steps to the stoop.

The door to the kitchen flew open, and Mrs. Amsler stuck her head out. "Get in here! I have news."

They hustled inside, pushed the door closed, and stood in the warm kitchen, still wearing their thick coats. The older woman stared at them, her eyes wide, not saying a word.

Mr. Amsler pulled off his hat, the static electricity causing his gray hair to stick out haphazardly. "Well, Frieda, we're waiting. What is the news?"

Her eyes darted back and forth. "I'm sorry, but I'm too excited to talk. My friend at the *Capitol Times* called me. She said it came through the wires that an armistice is signed in France! I'm about to burst. The war is over, Miss Hannah. Your man will soon be home, and so will our nephew and farmhands." She grabbed Mr. Amsler's elbow, and the pair started whooping and dancing in a circle.

Hannah couldn't help but smile, watching the usually serious couple in a joyful mood. She wanted to join in, but her feet felt as if they were anchored to the floor. This was what she'd been praying for. But, not knowing if Ted were dead or alive felt better than finally knowing the truth, which would likely be what everyone expected. When she received the official word he'd been killed, there would be no more wondering, and the pain would be unbearable.

The shrill ring of the phone came from the hall that led to the front door, and the Amslers stopped dancing.

"Oh, maybe it's my friend with more news." Mrs. Amsler scurried to the hallway.

Hannah looked at Mr. Amsler. "I still can't believe it."

"Me, either." His grin dissolved. "I suppose you'll be wanting to pack up and head home now."

"I'll do no such thing. The cows still need milking, and it will be a while before your men are back, or I'll know anything about Ted."

His shoulders relaxed. "Thank you. I was a little worried."

"Miss Hannah, the phone is for you."

She startled. "Oh, it's probably my father calling about the news."

Mrs. Amsler shook her head. "It's a man, but not your father. Said his name is Carl."

Her breath hitched. She wanted to ask her to say she was in the barn, taking a nap, had left the state. Anything but that she was nearby. But she knew without asking, Mrs. Amsler had already told him she was right there. "He's a good friend. Thanks."

Hannah walked the dozen or so steps to the phone, praying for help to remain rational and calm. She gripped the earpiece from where it dangled from the wooden wall phone, stared at it a moment and put it to her ear. "Carl. This is a surprise."

"Hi, Hannah. It's good to hear your voice. Did you hear the

news?" His low, rich voice came through like smooth sweet molasses.

"It's good to hear your voice as well. A friend of Mrs. Amsler's who works for the Madison newspaper called. We've been celebrating in the kitchen. I still can't believe it's actually over."

"When do you think you'll be coming home?"

"Not for a few more weeks. Mr. Amsler still needs help with the milking, and his men won't be back for a while. He's finally decided to order a milking machine and will probably get that before the men get here. Either way that will be my signal to come home."

"I suppose you've not heard any more about Ted's status."

She didn't miss the hint of hope in his tone. "No, I haven't. It's been a comfort all these months to not know for sure because I've been able to think of him as living somewhere. But if I find out he was killed, that's the final word. No more hoping, only grieving."

"That makes sense. I'm still reading the Bible and read some passages about giving comfort to others."

"You're already good at that in how you provide food for the needy."

"I guess I am. I went to church last Sunday."

"Carl, that's wonderful. If you were with me, you'd see my big grin. Did you go to the one in Delavan that your dad attended?"

"No. The minister there changed, and the new one wouldn't have known my father or me. I went to your church in Lake Geneva, Faith Community. I liked it."

Her stomach clenched. That was her church, not his. What was wrong with her? She should be glad he went to a church where the sermon he heard would explain the scripture clearly.

"I saw a pew with the name Quinn on a plate at the aisle side. Is that your family pew?"

Yes, and the people you saw sitting there were likely my parents and little sisters."

"Do members have to buy a pew?"

"Oh, no. It's not like that at all. The church building you were in is not the original church. The previous one is the smaller wing they now use for children's Sunday school classes and meetings. I think it was during a drive to build the new church that if you pledged a large amount, your family was given a pew in the new sanctuary.

"I heard my grandfather, who was an Irish immigrant at the beginning of his life, hated having his name on the pew like he was someone special, but he was convinced to allow it. I think it's kind of nice that even though my last name is Murphy, I'm still half a Quinn, and the faith of the family that came before me is rooted in God's Word and in the church."

"That makes sense. I'm sure this Sunday everyone will be praising God for the war ending."

"I suppose they will. I wish I could be there to celebrate with them."

"I do too. I miss you, Hannah."

A warm feeling washed over her. Right then, she wanted in the worst way to be with him, but praise God they were apart. The war's end and the fear of finding out for sure about Ted had her way too vulnerable. What she needed now was a good cry. "I miss you too, but I have to go. I'll let you know when I arrive home."

"Um. Okay."

Silence fell between them until she finally spoke, "Bye for now."

"Bye, Hannah."

The line went dead. She let the earpiece dangle and leaned against the wall, covering her face with her hands. "Lord, please let me find out soon what's happened to Ted."

"Miss Hannah? Is everything okay?"

She took her hands away and looked up as Mrs. Amsler nestled the earpiece on the switch hook. "Yes. I'm fine. It's an emotional day." She pushed away from the wall and started toward the kitchen, then faced the woman. "No. I'm not okay. I'm confused. Scared. I want to go far away and never come back.

CHAPTER THIRTY-NINE

The shrill alarm jarred Hannah out of sleep, and she pulled the pillow over her head. Five-thirty a.m. came quickly when one didn't fall asleep until after three. Yesterday was a blur from noon on. News of the armistice, Carl's phone call and hearing his voice again, then unloading her sad tale on Mrs. Amsler—Frieda. During their talk yesterday, she'd insisted Hannah call her Frieda, which she did while they were talking as friends and celebrating, but not today when she would be back in her farmette role.

Later in the afternoon, Pop and Mama called to celebrate. They hadn't heard the news until a patient told Pop during his appointment. Word was spreading fast, and the morning papers were sure to be filled with descriptions of the celebrations and hopefully news of when the troops would be returning home. Would there be mention of the men listed as MIA and their status? She doubted that would happen for days, maybe even weeks.

She said her usual morning prayer, thanking God for the day and praying for His strength—especially since she'd had so little sleep. She climbed out of bed and wrapped her robe around herself. Mr. Amsler got up at five and by now would be out at the barn.

It was her turn to use the bathroom, which was in the back of the house on the first floor. Every morning she thanked God for the small washroom. Indoor plumbing was a rarity in rural areas, and she was told it was Mrs. Amsler's Christmas present last year so she wouldn't have to traipse to a freezing outhouse in winter.

After donning her bibs, a flannel shirt, and work boots, Hannah inhaled the aroma of freshly brewed coffee as she descended the stairs to the kitchen. For once, she'd appreciate Mr. Amsler's robust brew. If his wife made the coffee, she'd better have received a lot of sleep because the coffee would be significantly weaker.

Mr. Amsler looked up from reading a newspaper.

"The *State Journal* is here already?"

"Yup. Guess they decided to work all night and had the presses running early. I suspected as much and went down to the road, and there it was. They were dancing in the streets in New York City and Chicago. I bet you wish you were there."

She yawned. "I'm so tired right now, all I want is to be back in bed."

His eyes widened. "Are you too tired to milk?"

She walked to the stove where the coffee pot sat over a low flame and, using a potholder, gripped its handle. "Never. I've done it so many times by now, I can do it in my sleep." She lifted the pot and filled her cup.

The door to the hall flew open, and Mrs. Amsler burst into the room wearing a thick cardigan over one of her ever-present house dresses. "I'm sorry to be late. Too much excitement yesterday. I'll get breakfast going."

"Glad to see you, Frieda. I was afraid I was going to have to make the eggs this morning." Her husband chortled as he looked at Hannah. "You don't want to taste my eggs." He went back to the newspaper, then let out a low chuckle. "I'd better let that company I ordered the electric milker from know I'm going to need it soon. If that boy you're engaged to comes home, Miss Hannah, you're not going to want to be cooped up on a farm with a couple of old folks like us."

Her heart squeezed. "I love being with you and Mrs. Amsler. But I'm not going to pretend that I don't want to be home."

"I'll give them a call as soon as I think they're open. Maybe they can give me a delivery date."

She gulped down her coffee. "I'd better get to the barn. I'm sure the girls are waiting to be milked."

Mrs. Amsler finished tying on an apron. "Go on, Miss Hannah. I'll send Sam out to fetch you when your breakfast is ready, and he'll take over for you."

By the time Sam arrived in the barn, Hannah was ravenous.

She grinned. "You timed it well. I got Daisy milked and just finished Fiona here."

"You go ahead and eat. I'll get Fiona turned out and bring the next one up."

"I was going to do Annie next."

He laughed. "You and your names. But I do admit it's easier to sort them out and track them by names rather than by their numbers that I'm always forgetting."

He got Fiona backing out of her stall and led her away to the other end of the barn while Hannah headed to the house and sat at the table. Mrs. Amsler set a plate of fluffy eggs and a couple slices of bacon in front of her. She was going to miss farm breakfasts, both here and at the training farm. Not to mention working outdoors in the soil and caring for the animals. Funny, but she'd always fancied herself a city girl, but this sort of life appealed to her.

A sinking feeling came over her. She'd changed a lot since Ted left and after all he'd been through, he'd probably changed too. Would they even still love each other when he got home?

She set her fork on her empty plate and sipped the coffee. If he got home.

Later, after she finished milking the cows in her section of the barn and turned them back out to their pasture, she went upstairs to where Mr. Amsler was milking.

She found the farmer sitting on his milking stool, arms on his knees, staring at the ground. "Mr. Amsler, are you okay?"

He looked up and nodded. "I'm all right. Frieda heard from her friend at the paper that they are getting indications over the wires that the armistice never happened. Our boys are still fighting."

Hannah gasped. "Oh, no. How did that happen?"

"Someone over in France misunderstood something and jumped the gun. It's all a mistake. What an awful thing to do to people who have loved ones over there sacrificing so much. Guess that means you won't be knowing about your young man."

A sudden weight pressed against her shoulders, pushing away the euphoria and hope that had carried Hannah through the morning. She sat on a nearby milk stool and worked to gather herself. If she didn't get out of the chill, she might pass out. "I'm feeling weary. Do you mind if I go inside and lay down? Maybe after I have a nap, I can do my chores."

He flicked his hand as if to shoo her away. "Go. The cows are milked. The rest can wait."

Inside the house, she found Mrs. Amsler on the phone in the hall. "Here, she is now." She held out the phone. "It's your father."

She took the earpiece and pressed it to her ear. "Hi, Pop. I suppose you heard the latest."

"Yes, the president confirmed a few minutes ago there is no end yet, but he did say negotiations are going on. So, there's hope."

"I don't suppose Louise has heard anything new about Ted."

"That's why I'm calling. She heard this morning. A long silence filled the connection. Hannah's pulse raced, and her mouth went dry. "Pop, what did they tell her?"

"Oh, Hannah." His voice broke, and silence came over the connection.

A lump rose in her throat, and she braced herself.

"It's been confirmed that Ted perished in the crash. I'm so sorry, Hannie."

November 18, 1918

Hannah loaded the back of her car with the few things she'd brought with her four months earlier and bid Sam and Frieda goodbye. With her duties over, she felt comfortable calling them by their first names.

Despite the confirmation of Ted's passing, she'd managed to stay at the farm for the past four days, helping with the milking. Sam expected delivery of the milking machine in about a week, but Hilda had called last night to say that the woman Hannah replaced had agreed to return to the farm later that day. She planned to stay until the Amsler's nephew and farm helper returned. Hannah was now free to leave and grieve with her family surrounding her.

The news came a short time ago that the real armistice had finally been signed in the early morning hours in a railroad car in France. This time, the news was true, but how could she rejoice knowing for sure Ted was gone?

She pulled out onto the road, heading south. With the highway free of traffic, she pressed her foot on the gas and brought the speed up. As she gripped the steering wheel, Ted's engagement ring twinkled back at her from her left hand. She should take it off, but doing so was akin to accepting that Ted was never coming back.

As she approached the state road that by turning east would take her to home, on impulse, she turned west. What she was doing may look wrong to others, but it was something she couldn't ignore. She turned into Carl's farm and parked. She found him in the barn at a workbench pounding a nail into what looked like a frame for a chicken coup. She cleared her throat, and he turned.

A grin filled his face as he dropped the hammer to the ground. "Hannah. Why are you here?"

"Ted died in the crash." The sob she'd been working hard to throttle broke free, and suddenly she was in his strong embrace. She pressed her face against his chest and wrapped her arms around him.

"Oh, Hannah, I'm so sorry. What can I do to help?"

"Just hold me." He pulled her closer and rubbed a circle on her back with his palm. It had been so long since she'd been held this way.

"I've wanted to hold you in my arms for a long time."

He loosened his embrace and looked down at her and thumbed her tears from her cheeks. He searched her face with his gaze. "You're beautiful, even in sadness."

He brought his face closer to hers and paused. She raised up on tiptoe. His lips hungrily claimed hers, and she melted into the kiss as it deepened, and her pulse raced. Surprised at the passion that rose from somewhere within, she moaned. He lifted his lips then kissed her eyelids, her cheeks, and jaw before he claimed her mouth again, and the kiss intensified until they parted, breathless.

Hannah gulped in a deep breath and willed her pounding

heart to settle. She stepped out of his arms. "I need to go." She turned toward the barn door.

Carl gently gripped her arm. "I overstepped my bounds, I'm sorry."

She faced him, running her palm over his grizzled jaw. "In case you didn't notice, I kissed you back with equal fervor."

He drew her into his arms. "I noticed." He kissed her, this time gently, then stepped back and took her face in both hands. "You must know I'm in love with you, Hannah."

She winced and turned her head. "I can't love you back, Carl. I'm sorry."

She ran out of the barn, praying he didn't stop her before she reached her car. She drove to the road, then glanced at the forlorn man in the rearview mirror, and her heart ached for what could never be because she knew somehow Ted was still alive and the whole time she was kissing Carl, in her mind she was kissing Ted.

By the time she pulled into Safe Refuge's drive, the ache in her chest had mushroomed to fill her entire torso. All she wanted was a hot bath and her bed. She parked and climbed out of the car, not bothering to unload, and walked to the door. She was about to grip the door handle when the door swung open.

"Welcome home!"

Everyone—Mama, Pop, Louise, and her sisters—greeted her with both smiles and tears. Mama opened her arms, and Hannah fell into her embrace. "Oh, Mama, it's so good to be home." After a few moments, she stepped back and looked from one person to the other. "My goodness, I've never had such a welcome. You'd think I'd been off to war."

"In a way, you were." Pop hugged her to his side. "Look at you. I can even feel your muscles through your shirt. Are you ready to convince Katie and Jake they need a couple more cows now that you're an expert milker?"

She shook her head. "Absolutely not. I loved the cows but didn't love having to milk no matter what day it was or the weather. I'll gladly take my milk from the glass bottle it comes in."

He chuckled and hugged her again. "I've missed you, Hannie."

"Pop, you don't have to act like you're all happy. Not when we had such awful news about Ted."

Pop's smile dissolved. "It's not entirely an act. I'm thrilled the war is finally over, and this time it's not a false report. At the same time, all of us are very heartbroken about Ted." He stepped aside and tugged Louise over. "We'll give both of you all the time necessary to grieve and heal."

After a quick lunch, Hannah finally brought her suitcase upstairs and began sorting through the clothing, separating farm clothes from regular ones. Of course, the farm pile was higher. She wouldn't need them at least for a while.

A soft knock came at the door, and Mama stepped in, carrying a cup. "I thought you might like some hot tea."

She smiled. "You always know what's needed. I'd love some." She took the cup and sipped, letting the warm liquid sooth as it went down her throat.

Mama tilted her head and regarded her. "How are you really doing, Hannah?"

She set the tea on the nightstand and shrugged. "Okay, I guess."

"Have you seen Carl since you left?"

"I stopped by his farm on the way here for a few minutes. Just being with him, all the feelings I had before rose to the surface." She drew in a breath and let it out. "I'm still holding onto hope that there's been a mistake, and Ted is still alive. I have no more room in my heart for another man."

"Perhaps in time—"

"No. Mama. The extent of what I feel for Carl falls way short of the amount of love I have for Ted."

Mama drew her into a hug. "I'll leave you to a hot bath and a long nap. Don't worry about coming to the dinner table unless you want to be there."

"You don't think I'm wrong to keep believing Ted is alive?"

"No. You'll know when it's time to give up that hope."

Mama started to go but turned back. "Peter is coming tonight to be with his mother to help plan for Ted's arrangements. You'll want to be in on those discussions."

"Yes. Thanks, Mama, for being such a good mother."

Later that night, as Hannah crawled into her bed, her thoughts swirled with all they'd discussed regarding Ted's memorial service. Since his remains were buried with the multitudes of Allied casualties in France, there would be no funeral. Hannah planned a trip overseas after things settled down, to find his grave.

The trill of the doorbell sounded from downstairs. It was almost ten when she'd turned out the light. It wouldn't be the first time Pop had a patient's family member come to the door for help. Her dad's footfalls sounded through her door as he scrambled down the stairs. Followed by his loud voice, but she couldn't make out what he was saying. Mama's voice came as Pop ran back up the stairs. Her door opened and light flooded the room. Mama stood there in her mauve dressing gown, her lips twitching as if she were fighting a smile. "That was Western Union with a telegram addressed to you. It appears to be from Ted."

Hannah's breath hitched, and the room began to spin.

CHAPTER FORTY-ONE

Someone was shaking her shoulder. The strong odor of ammonia stung her nose. "Hannah! Wake up."

At Pop's command, she coughed and opened her eyes to stare into his troubled eyes. "I just dreamed Mama said Ted sent me a telegram."

He handed the smelling salts to Mama and eased her into a sitting position. "It wasn't a dream, Hannie." He grinned and held up a yellow envelope. "It's right here."

"What does it say?"

"We don't know because it's addressed to you."

She took the envelope and, with shaking hands, tried unsuccessfully to open it. "You do it, Pop."

He loosened the flap and pulled out the folded paper and handed it to her.

She forced her eyes to focus:

LONDON, ENGLAND. 12:05 A.M. NOVEMBER 18, 1918

MISS HANNAH MURPHY, LAKE GENEVA, WISCONSIN

HANNAH, I AM IN LONDON. I AM ALIVE. IN ST. MARY'S HOSPITAL

FOR REPAIRS TO INJURIES. WILL NOT BE IN U.S. FOR ANOTHER

MONTH. I LOVE YOU AND CAN'T WAIT TO BE WITH YOU SITTING IN
THE SPRING HOUSE AND LOOKING OUT AT GENEVA LAKE. ARMY IS
NOTIFYING MOTHER AT TP ADDRESS. LETTER FROM ME COMING.
ALL MY LOVE,
TED
CORPORAL THEODORE BAUER ROYAL AIR CORPS

Hannah's pulse finally slowed. "Someone has to tell Louise her telegram is at Tranquility Point. If one is there, I'll know this is for real."

"I'll go." Mama turned toward the door.

"No, you stay here, Mo. It's too late for you to be out driving around. I'll go."

Mama snickered. "At least put some trousers on over your nightshirt."

Hannah laughed. "Good idea."

Pop glanced down at his bare feet. "Right." He bolted for the hall, and a few minutes later, the front door slammed.

She looked at Mama. "Am I dreaming?"

"I don't think so, honey. Perhaps there's a way you can send him a wire to let him know you received his?"

She looked at the telegram. "Nothing is said here, but I would think if I sent one to St. Mary's hospital in London, it would get to him."

The outside door slammed, and Louise called out. "I'm here. Where is everyone?"

Mama stood. "I'll go down to be with Louise. Join us when you're ready."

A few minutes later, Hannah stepped into the kitchen, wearing a wrapper. Her mother turned from where she stood next to the stove. "I thought we could all use a strong cup of coffee after such a shock."

Hannah went to Louise, who sat at the table, wearing her wool coat over her flannel gown, her long hair gathered at the base of her neck with a clip. She leaned into Louise's arms. "I feel like I've just gotten off the longest roller coaster ride in history. How about you?"

Louise nodded and grinned. "Yes, but what a wonderful ending if this is true."

Hannah handed her Ted's telegram. "It appears to be. The way this is worded, it sounds like him."

Louise read the telegram and hugged it to her chest, "He mentions the lake and your spring house. I'm sure it's from Ted."

They were on their second cups of coffee when Pop arrived home with a yellow envelope in his hand. He handed it to Louise. She opened the envelope and scanned the contents then looked up, her eyes glistening. "My boy is alive. Hannah, please read it to everyone."

Hannah picked up the telegram. "I'm not sure I can. My tears are clogging my throat."

"Then, I will." Mama picked up the paper. "It was sent the same day as Ted's. We are pleased to inform you that Corporal Theodore Bauer of the Royal Air Corps has been located alive, having been kept protected by Belgian citizens for the past six months. He is now a patient at St. Mary's Hospital in London, England. His injuries are not life-threatening, but he will be in hospital for about a month before he'll be able to return to the United States. You will hear directly from him soon."

Mama looked up. "It's signed by an Adjunct General of the Royal Air Corps on behalf of the U.S. Army." She stood and pulled Hannah and Louise to their feet, and the three ladies hugged. Hannah broke away and looped her hand around Pop's elbow and got him dancing around the kitchen while Mama and Louise did the same.

"Why is everyone awake and dancing?"

They stopped and looked toward Annie, who stood in the door, rubbing her eyes with her fists.

Hannah bent down and hugged her sister. "Annie, our prayers were answered. Ted is alive and coming home soon."

The little girl blinked. "Really?"

Pop scooped her up and whirled her around. "Yes, really. Ted's coming home."

"Put me down, Pop. I want to wake up Margie and tell her."

"I am awake. Who can sleep with all this noise?" Margie came into the room. "Did I hear it right?"

Hanna grabbed her hands and twirled her in a circle. "Yes, my sweet sister, Ted is coming home. He's alive."

CHAPTER FORTY-TWO

The next afternoon, grateful for the unusually warm November weather, Hannah went to the spring house, the one place that always brought her peace and calm. She hadn't yet called Carl to tell him the news. She opened her Bible to the comforting words of Psalm 23 and bowed her head. "Oh, God, I need your strength. When I kissed Carl, I thought Ted was gone, but I still feel guilty. Please help me to understand that it wasn't wrong, but if it was, please forgive me. Thank you for the blessing you've given us—given me."

"Hannah, who are you thanking?" Annie walked up.

She smiled through her tears at her little sister. "God. He answered my prayer."

The child tilted her head. "I know, but that makes me happy, so I'm not crying."

She pulled Annie on her lap. "When you're older you'll understand that we cry when we're sad, and we cry when we're hurt, but we also cry tears of joy."

The child sighed. "I guess I need to be older to understand. She wrapped her arms around Hannah's neck. "I'm glad you're home. I missed you."

"And I missed you too, little sister. Now there go my tears again." She leaned back and tweaked Annie's nose. "Tears of joy. Now run and play. I have something I need to do."

Hannah gathered her Bible and notebook and headed inside, where she found her mother in the hall. "I'm going upstairs to finish my prayers, then I need to call Carl and tell him the news."

Mama nodded. "He's likely to be let down, so do it gently."

Later that afternoon, when she thought Carl would be done with the day's work, she called him, relieved he picked up the telephone.

"Hi, Carl, it's Hannah."

"I didn't expect to hear from you."

"I didn't expect to call, at least not this soon. I received a telegram last night. Ted is alive after all, and in a hospital in London."

Silence filled the connection for a few moments. "Wow. That's wonderful news." The lift in his voice seemed forced.

"It is beyond wonderful. We've all been walking around here with grins on our faces. Carl, I need to apologize for what happened yesterday. I should never have allowed the kiss."

"You said yourself we both allowed it. It was an emotional moment, and it happened."

"I know, but what you said afterward ... I had no idea you felt so strongly. I shouldn't have let it happen at all."

"Regardless, it did. The way you kissed me gave me hope."

"I'm so sorry. From the day I first met Ted, he's occupied a huge part of my heart. If the outcome had been different ... Well, there's no use thinking that way. Maybe I'll see you at church on Sunday."

"What's the use of my going to church?"

"Getting to know the God your father loved and honored. Seek God's will for your life, Carl. In due time, He may lead you to the right woman."

He sighed. "Maybe I'll be there on Sunday."

Mama was in the kitchen, making tea when Hanna found her. "May I join you?"

Mama took down another china cup and dropped in a teabag. "I was hoping you'd come in here. I was at the cottage with Louise. I think she finally settled down enough to take a nap. She barely slept after we all went to bed for the second time."

"Do you think I should sleep over there tonight?"

"Not unless you want to. You've been through a rough time yourself."

"Okay. At least for tonight, I'll stay here." Hannah settled at the table and waited until Mama brought the teas and sat across from her.

"How did your talk with Carl go?"

She shrugged. "I didn't want to hurt him, but I guess it couldn't be helped. I should never have let the business side of our relationship become personal. I'm more troubled that when I suggested we might see each other at church, he asked why bother. Was he only interested in the Bible because of me?"

"Probably. What did you say?'

"I reminded him of his father's faith in God. That in time, God might lead him to someone perfect for him. He said maybe I'd see him Sunday. That was the end of the conversation."

"Oh, Hannah, your life is so similar to mine before I married your father."

She scrunched her brow. "How so?"

"As I've told you, Preston Stevens and I were very attracted to each other, but that didn't mean he was the man for me. When I became sick, the new town doctor—your father—took care of me that whole month. He and Bea Ambrose were the only ones I saw the whole time."

Mama caught Hannah's gaze in her own. "That's when I fell in love with your dad, but I didn't realize it at first. After we had begun to court, Pres came here and all but demanded I break it off with your father and go with him to see the world. I declined, and he grabbed me and violently kissed me, right here in this room. I managed to wriggle away, and he left."

"That doesn't sound like Mr. Stevens. Even so, a romantic relationship with Carl never had a chance to develop."

"But the mutual attraction was there, and, whether you want to admit it or not, you were waiting to see if Ted was alive before giving in to the spark of attraction you felt for Carl."

She nodded. "I agree. Everything seems so upside down. Neither Ted nor I have finished law school. Will he even still want to be a lawyer? I'm not sure I do, but what that means I have no idea."

"God may redirect your goals, depending on the state of his injuries. I never dreamed of being a nurse until I helped take care of a young girl with smallpox. During the war, farming became your life, and you and Carl hit it off doing farming things together. When Ted gets home, you two will have to reevaluate your next steps. My best advice is to turn all of it over to the Lord. She threw up her hands. "I don't know if I'm helping you much at all."

"You are. I hate having to wait so long to see him."

"I think passenger travel to England is soon to be reinstated. Why don't you surprise him and go over there? Once you're in London, I'm sure a lot of the confusion will resolve itself."

Hannah smiled through her tears. "I need to wait and not try to make things happen. I seem to get in trouble whenever I do that."

CHAPTER FORTY-THREE

Three Weeks Later

Hannah sat at the kitchen table, staring at a letter from the law school. The school was reopening in February, and if she wanted to be reinstated as a first-year student for the second semester, she needed to fill out the enclosed form and return it within a week.

She'd hadn't yet received the promised letter from Ted, but had dashed off a letter to Clarice, telling her the wonderful news about Ted and that she couldn't wait for her to be back in the states. She set the school letter down and sighed. She doubted neither she nor Ted would be able to enroll for the second semester. They had plenty of time to figure things out before the fall semester.

The telephone rang from the hall, jarring her back to the present, and she went to answer it.

"Hannah, is that you, my love?"

At the sound of his voice, her heart melted and tears came to her eyes. "Oh, Ted, I've missed you so much. Where are you?"

"I'm in Washington D.C. at an Army hospital. They're

keeping me isolated because that nasty Spanish flu is overtaking the town, but I'm due to go into a ward. They didn't want me to travel by ship this soon, but I insisted I needed to get home, and here I am."

She grinned. "That's wonderful. How long before you can come here?" A long silence fell over the connection. "Ted, are you still there?"

"Yes. I was trying to calculate the time. Probably not for at least a month. I so ache to see you again, my love. Hold you in my arms."

Unbidden tears filled her eyes. "Oh, Ted, I want that too. Do we have time enough for you to tell me where you were those months you were missing? The telegram your mother received said you were protected by some Belgians."

"I was hidden in a farmhouse cellar by a brave Belgian farmer and his wife. When the allies found the plane months after the crash, the remains weren't recognizable, and my dog tag was on John, the guy in the front seat, God rest his soul. They thought he was me, and I was listed KIA. Now his poor family has the bad news John is gone. I can't shake the thought that he took a bullet for me being in the front position. The couple tended to my injuries as best they could, but I needed some work done before I can come home to you. Hannah, it's wonderful to hear your voice."

Her love for him washed over her. "And I'm loving hearing your voice. What hospital are you in that I can write to you?"

"Walter Reed. I'm not sure of the address. I'll send it to you."

"What kind of repairs do you still need?"

"Nothing to worry about. How's my mother doing? The last letter from you before my crash said she had appendicitis and was recuperating in the cottage."

"Mama left a short while ago to take her to Pop's office to have some tests done."

"She's still not well?"

"She's never been the same since her appendectomy. They're trying to find out why. Hearing you're alive has been the best tonic for her. She's had a spring in her step ever since the news came. I'll let you know what they find out."

"I'm grateful to your dad for taking care of her. Hannah, I have to go now. The nurse is here to take me to see a specialist. I love you."

They said a quick goodbye and she sat staring out the window as snow started to fall. What did he mean by a specialist?

A couple of hours later, Mama and Louise returned, and she assisted in getting Louise back in bed before she shared the news.

Louise rested against the mountain of pillows set up against the headboard. "I've been poked with so many needles I feel like a pincushion. Will they ever find out what's wrong with me?"

Hannah grinned and looked from Louise to Mama. "Ted called while you were gone. He's in the States now in D.C. at a hospital called Walter Reed. He should be home in about a month."

Louise's eyes widened. "Thank the Lord he's in the country again, but what is wrong with my boy that he keeps getting shuffled from one hospital to the next?"

"I don't know," Hannah said. "He became evasive when I asked and changed the subject. I've been thinking and praying ever since we hung up, and I've decided I'm going to Washington to find out for myself."

Mama clapped her hands. "That is the best news. I suggest you book your train soon. With Christmas coming and the war over, the railroads are going to be busy. Don't forget you still have a trust from your grandfather you've never touched. You can use some of it for your travel and hotel."

Hannah looked at her future mother-in-law. "Louise, are you

okay with me going to see Ted, even though you aren't well enough to travel?"

"Oh, yes. I'd be eternally grateful. He needs someone from home by his side, and I'm in no shape to go, nor will his father be when he arrives home."

"Then it's settled. I'm going to Washington D.C." She twirled around the small room. "I don't know if I'm more excited to find out what is wrong with him or to see him again. I think it's the latter."

"How soon do you plan to leave?" Mama asked.

"Is tomorrow too soon?"

CHAPTER FORTY-FOUR

December 18, 1918

Hannah stepped off the train and breathed in the chilly air. Washington was no warmer than Chicago. She scurried down the platform, suitcase in hand, to the depot then outside to the street. She hailed a cab that would take her to the trolley and eventually to Bethesda, Maryland, where the hospital was located, just across the Washington D.C. city limits.

Grateful because of her time in Chicago, she made the transfers with confidence. By her calculations, the trolley stop she wanted was only a block from the hotel. During the hour-long trolley ride, the soft murmurs of the other passengers and the gentle sway of the car acted as a lullaby of sorts to her weary body. Her head nodded downward until her chin hit the knot of her wool scarf, and she jerked awake. She couldn't chance missing her stop and wake up in another town. She had little time to make it to the hospital when visiting hours opened.

"Next stop, Bethesda. If you're going to Walter Reed, this is your stop!" The driver's shout snapped her out of another near nap. She looked out at the passing buildings. How interesting that while still in Washington, the streets were abuzz with activity, and many of the homes sat so close together they almost appeared attached. Here the clapboard homes were built farther apart.

They entered the town's business district, and the trolley slowed down. She gathered her suitcase and purse and prepared to stand.

"Bethesda, Walter Reed, Dunworth Hotel! Several others stood along with Hannah, and she eased into the aisle and followed a tall man to the exit. Out on the sidewalk, she looked one direction down the road, then the other. The hotel was around the corner, but which corner? The tall man and a woman, who had been in front of him earlier, began walking off to her right, a suitcase in his hand.

She scurried up to him. "Excuse me. Are you going to the Dunworth Hotel?"

They stopped, and he peered down at her. "Yes. Are you too?"

"Yes. I've not been here before. Would you mind if I walk with you?"

The woman smiled. "We're here to visit our son. We come every week, and will be glad to show you how to get to the hotel and the hospital."

Hannah offered a smile. "Thank you so much. I'm Hannah Murphy. I'm here to see my fiancé, who arrived recently from a hospital in London."

"Pleased to meet you, Miss Murphy," The woman said. "We're the Maguires."

By the time they arrived at the Dunworth, Hannah knew no more about the couple than she did when they agreed to take her to the hotel. It seemed Mr. Maguire was the unfriendly one and kept control on his wife. She hadn't missed the way he pinched her elbow after Hannah introduced herself, and Mrs. Maguire made their introduction.

They approached the registration desk, and the clerk greeted the couple with a huge smile. "Mr. and Mrs. Maguire, it's good to see you again. Your room is ready and waiting." He glanced at Hannah. "Oh, did you bring a friend this time?"

"No." Mr. Maguire said. "We met her when we got off the trolley. She's not with us." He faced Hannah. "Tell Joe here when you want a cab to go to the hospital, and he'll arrange it." He took the key Joe gave him and picked up their suitcase. "Let's go, Ethel." As they walked away, Ethel looked over her shoulder at Hannah and made a face that said she was sorry for her husband's abruptness.

Hannah shrugged and faced Joe. "I'm Hannah Murphy I have a room reserved for the next week. I wired a deposit to you as requested."

The man opened the registration book and ran his finger down a list of names. "Yes. Here it is. You are in Room 340. Right next door to the Maguires. Their cab is due here in half an hour. Do you want to share a ride with them? She shook her head. "I'd rather leave in fifteen minutes. Is it possible?"

"I think so. Perhaps the same driver could take you over then return for the Maguires." He picked up the phone and dialed a number, then turned his back and lowered his voice. "Okay. Thanks. I'll tell her." He hung up and faced her. "It's all set. Be in the lobby in ten minutes, and the cab will be here. The driver's name is Nate. You want me to write it down?"

She shook her head. "It's the same name as my father's. I'll remember."

He handed her the key. "The elevator is around the corner. If it's on an upper floor, it will take a minute or so to come down. You operate it yourself. You familiar with that?"

"Yes, I've been in one or two like it." She accepted the key and glanced around the lobby, noticing the worn chair and sofa cushions. She'd wanted the Harrington in Washington, but it was over twenty miles away. Seeing Ted was the reason she was here, she'd sleep in a tent if she had to.

To her delight, the elevator door opened as soon as she tapped on the up button. She pushed aside the accordion-like safety gate and stepped in, then pulled the gate in place and pressed the third-floor button.

The car jolted and began to rise at a slow pace. She shifted her weight from one foot to the other. At the rate it climbed, the cab would be there before she got to her room. Finally, it stopped on the third floor, and she exited into the corridor.

Hannah scurried down the hall, unlocked her room, and stepped inside. Small but tidy with hangers in the small closet. The bathroom appeared clean. She quickly unpacked her suitcase and hung her dresses.

With no time to change clothes, she stepped into the hall and spotted a "Stairs" sign above a door. She could take the stairs faster than the elevator. "Okay, Ted. Here I come."

At the first floor, she stepped outside as a cab pulled up. She opened the door to the back seat. "Nate?"

"Yeah. You Miss Murphy?"

"Yes." She climbed in and pulled the door shut. He got the car moving and she leaned back and closed her eyes.

Please, Lord, prepare me for whatever is wrong with Ted.

"Here you are, Miss."

She opened her eyes and stared at the large building. With its red brick exterior and white pillars, Walter Reed Hospital reminded her more of the Wadsworth estate back home than a hospital.

"Miss, you need to pay me so I can go back for the Maguires."

She startled. "Oh, sorry. She pulled a bill from her purse. The ride was fifty cents, right?"

"Yeah, that's right."

She handed him a dollar. "Keep the change."

His eyes widened. "Thanks. When you're ready to go back to the hotel, call Hawkins Cab Service and request me."

She smiled to herself as she climbed the steps to the front door. "A larger than normal tip might be to her advantage."

In the lobby, a gray-haired woman at the front desk greeted her with a smile. "How can I help you?"

"I'd like the room of a patient, Ted—Theodore—Bauer. He arrived here recently with a war injury, and I'm not sure where his room is."

The woman flipped through a book of records, looking one place and then another. "Here he is. In the orthopedic ward." She scribbled on a piece of paper and handed it to her. "Take the elevator to the third floor. His ward is off to the right at the end of the hall."

She thanked the woman. Orthopedic? She'd heard many of the soldiers were coming home without an arm or a leg.

She found the elevator and was relieved it was much newer and faster than the one at the hotel. She stepped off on the third floor and stopped a few steps from the ward entrance. It was a mistake to come without notice. What if he refuses to see her? Yet she'd spent her great-grandfather's money to get here, and Ted was in that room just ahead. She couldn't turn around. *Lord, give me strength.*

Hannah entered the ward and ran her gaze past the beds on either side of the room. Men, some in traction, lay in their beds, and a few of them—none Ted—occupied wheelchairs. On the second sweep, she spotted him sleeping in the last bed on the right No sign of traction. Both his arms were visible above the covers.

She started down the aisle between the beds, careful to not announce her arrival with her footfalls. As she came closer, love for him exploded within her. Fighting the urge to rush up and smother his face with kisses, she pulled her gaze away from his face and scanned the whole of him. The steady rise and fall of his chest assured he was very much alive, his arms, although not as muscular as before, appeared intact, then his torso and hips, … then the mound of his right leg.

She gasped.

Ted opened his eyes. He blinked and caught her gaze in his own. "Hannah? What are you doing here?"

"I've come to see you, my darling man." She leaned down and kissed him full on his mouth, relieved that he responded in kind, his kiss as delicious as always. She lifted her head. "You didn't think I was going to sit in Wisconsin with you only a train ride away, did you?"

He chuckled. "I was hoping you'd be okay with it. I've not yet come to terms with the new Ted. Maybe you didn't notice…"

She pulled over a straight back chair and looked him in his beautiful dark eyes. "I didn't fall in love with that left leg. I fell in love with the man who once owned it." This was where she belonged.

"We'll see. If I'm having a hard time, I can't imagine it will be easy for you. How long can you stay?"

"As long as you want. I have a week booked at the Dunworth in town."

His brows rose. "That sounds costly."

"It doesn't live up to its name, but it's the closest hotel to the hospital. I'm grateful to be there." She kissed him again. "My great-grandfather is footing the bill with a trust I didn't know about until recently."

"The one who built Safe Refuge. Right?"

"Yes."

"How is my mother? You said earlier she was getting medical tests."

"We don't know yet. With Christmas coming, it may take longer to find out. Knowing you're in the U.S. again lifted her spirits more than anything. She's staying in the cottage until someone can be with her at Tranquility Point. She refuses to live in the city. We're hoping your father will be able to join us for Christmas." She squeezed his hand. "And you too."

"That's doubtful. I hate spending it alone, but what else can I do?"

"You won't be alone, my darling, because I'm not going anywhere without you." She kissed him again and was surprised when she leaned back to see his mouth twist into a grimace.

"We need to talk. I can't marry you, Hannah."

What felt like a dagger sliced through her chest. "Why?"

He searched her face with his eyes, their earlier gleam replaced by dark sadness. "I'm not a whole man anymore. It's not fair to you to be saddled with me. About all I'm good for is getting a peg leg, and wearing a pirate suit to entertain children. The trainee that was flying with me took a bullet that should have been mine. It's not right that I only lost a leg when he lost his life. Losing my dream of being an attorney and marrying you is a fair tradeoff."

She swallowed forced-back tears. "Oh, Ted. That's not how God operates. It was John's time, not yours. I read the other day in Psalms that every day of our lives is written in God's book before any have happened. Your life hasn't reached the last chapter yet. You can still be an attorney, and we can still marry. I fell in love with you, the man, not one of your legs."

He rolled over. "I'm tired. I need to rest."

"Excuse me, but Mr. Bauer has an appointment with his doctor in a few minutes." Hannah turned. A nurse stood a few feet away. "It's going to be a long session. Are you his wife? We can make an exception and let you accompany him."

"Is it with his orthopedic doctor?"

The nurse shook her head. "No. It's with a counselor. It's part of the healing process."

She stood. "I'm his fiancé. Is it okay for me to come?"

"I'm afraid not. A spouse only; no exceptions."

Her heart sank. "I'll leave." She bent and kissed his cheek. "I love you, my darling Ted, and you are not getting rid of me. We'll deal with this together." He rolled over and looked at her through tear-filled eyes. "I don't deserve you, Hannah. I love you too." He raised his head and kissed her.

She straightened. She hadn't heard the wheelchair roll up behind her. A young man, his skin the color of hot chocolate, grinned at her from behind the chair. "Sorry to interrupt. I'm Corporal Bauer's transportation for today."

"There's my man." Ted pushed himself to a sitting position. "I'm ready, Edgar."

She smiled at the young man. "Thank you for taking good care of him." She slipped past the wheelchair and headed for the door.

Sometime later, at the hotel, she threw herself on the bed and released the tears she'd held at bay. She rolled on her back and stared at the ceiling. Ted wasn't thinking straight. At least he was getting counseling, but what kind? Yes, she was at first horrified at the sight of his missing a leg, but she came to her senses and realized it was him she loved, not the absent leg. He could still become a lawyer. Didn't they make false legs that looked like a foot and leg? Pop would still be at his office. She picked up the phone.

CHAPTER FORTY-FIVE

"I'd like to place a call to Doctor Nathan Murphy's office in Lake Geneva, Wisconsin." Hannah fluffed her pillow and placed it in front of the headboard and leaned against it.

A woman's voice came through the connection. "Doctor Murphy's office."

"Hi, Cathleen, this is Hannah. Is my father available?"

"Hannah, I heard you were traveling to Washington to see your fiancé. Is everything okay?"

"Yes, but I need to talk to my father for a few minutes."

"Okay. Hold on."

Static came through the connection as she visualized Cathleen switching the call into Pop's office. "Hannah, I'm surprised you called here. We were hoping to hear from you tonight at home."

"I know, but this can't wait. Pop, he's lost his left leg."

"I was afraid it was something like that."

"He's really down. Says he can't marry me because he's not a whole man and he can't go to law school or do anything. That he deserves to lose everything he dreamed of, including being married to me, because he should have been the one to die and not his trainee in the front seat of the plane. I wasn't there long, because he had an appointment with some kind of counselor. The nurse said I could go with him if I were his wife. I'm only a fiancé. You know about these things, depression after war. And, isn't there something other than a peg leg he can wear so he can walk and look normal?"

"The answer is yes, I do understand his mental state. It happens often during wartime with men who have lived through it. They feel guilty to still be alive when their comrades died. He needs you now more than ever, Hannie. And as for the question about what is called a prosthesis, I've been researching the latest developments since I suspected he might have returned an amputee. They've made some significant improvements in recent years. Do you know how much of the leg is gone?

"I'm not sure, from what I could tell, at least from just above the knee down."

When will you see him next?"

"Tomorrow. I have a crazy idea, Pop. If we get married right away, I'd have a lot more freedom to find out what the doctors are doing to help him."

"That might not be a bad idea. Maybe if he's released to my care, he can come home sooner. Explain to the doctors that your father is a physician and has worked with people who have symptoms of shell shock and post-war depression. I also have a knowledge of working with amputees as one of my patients has a prosthesis. Maybe as his wife, you can get him released to my care within a few days. We can have a late Christmas celebration."

Hannah couldn't help giggling. "You've convinced me, I hope Ted can be convinced too."

The next morning, unable to sleep, Hannah arrived at the hospital before visiting hours and approached the front desk.

A kindly middle-aged woman greeted her. "Visiting hours don't begin until ten."

She returned the woman's smile. "I know. I was hoping to speak to the hospital chaplain."

The woman frowned. "I think he should be in his office now. She picked up the phone. Can you please ring Chaplain Wells?" A few moments later, she nodded. "Chaplain, I have a young woman here, wanting to meet with you for a few minutes." She looked at Hannah. "What is this regarding?"

How much did she have to say? "It's about my fiancé who arrived recently from a London Hospital. He's in the orthopedic ward."

The woman repeated what Hannah said and nodded. "Okay. Thank you." She looked at Hannah and pointed off to her left. "Take an elevator to the second floor. Turn right, and you'll see Chaplain Wells standing in the hall waiting for you."

At the second floor, Hannah stepped off the elevator. Up ahead, a short, stocky man wearing a black suit with the turned around collar some preachers favored stood next to an open door. He waved at her.

She approached him. "Thank you for seeing me. I'm Hannah Murphy."

I'm Chaplain Wells. He gestured for her to step into his office. "Can I offer tea or coffee? Hannah shook her head. "No, thank you."

He let the door close. "Please sit." He took the visitor chair next to her. "I prefer to not have a desk between us. He reached for a pad of paper and a pencil.

"I'm here to ask if it's possible for my fiancé, Ted Bauer, who is in the third-floor orthopedic ward, and I to marry here at the hospital as soon as possible."

His brows rose. "The name sounds familiar, but I can't place him. We have so many men coming in now from the war. Is he terminally ill?"

"No, but he lost a leg when his plane was shot down. He's depressed and feeling guilty he survived the plane crash and his trainee didn't. He's lost all sense of purpose. We're from Wisconsin, and he has no family here. I was asked to leave yesterday because he was taken to see a counselor, and since we aren't married yet, I couldn't accompany him. If we can be married as soon as possible, I can be with him during some of his sessions. My father is a physician and has experience dealing with shell shock and amputees. I'm hoping we can convince the doctors here to release him to my father's care. I'm going to his ward now to see him, and I'd like to know how this might be arranged."

Tiny lines formed between his eyes. "Once you have a marriage license, there's a 24-hour-waiting period. I do have a license to perform marriages and have done a couple of them here in the chapel. I can have someone bring the license application form here and have you both sign it. It only costs two dollars."

She relaxed. "I didn't realize it would be that easy."

"During wartime, no one wants to make things more difficult than they already are. If we can start the procedure right away, I can take the license application with me when I leave at noon and drop it off. I can marry you tomorrow afternoon. We could have your fiancé wheeled to the chapel, and the ceremony can be done there."

Her heart felt like it was going to leap out of her chest. "Oh, my goodness. I'd better get upstairs and talk to him right away."

He handed her his pencil and tablet. "Before you go, I need both your names and birthdates. Write them here along with which ward he is in on the third floor. I'll come by in half an hour to talk to both of you."

He pulled out his pocket watch. "Visiting hours don't start for another half an hour. I'll call up there and ask them to let you see him now."

She picked up the pencil he handed her and wrote the requested information.

She didn't bother with the elevator but raced upstairs to the third floor, then all but flew down the hall to Ted's ward, praying the chaplain had already cleared her to stay. She spotted him right away and scurried up to him.

He flashed her the grin she'd been longing to see for months. "Hannah, I wasn't sure if I dreamed you were here yesterday or if it was true. How did you get in before visiting hours?"

She pulled the chair she used yesterday close to his bed and leaned down to kiss him. He turned his head. "I haven't cleaned my teeth yet."

She gently nudged his head back until they were face to face. "I don't care. I'll be waking up next to you for the rest of my life, and neither of us will have cleaned our teeth."

"No. I told you yesterday—"

"You told me nothing, you big oaf. Do you think John would want you to live a life without meaning because he died and you didn't? God must have something more for you to do before you leave this earth. We don't have much time, so listen. After the way I was excluded yesterday from your counseling appointment because I wasn't your wife, I decided to investigate. We can change the problem."

He frowned. "How?"

"By getting married tomorrow afternoon in the hospital chapel. I met with the chaplain a few minutes ago, and he can arrange the whole thing, even getting the marriage license application done right away."

His eyes grew larger. "You're okay with no wedding dress or church with your dad giving you away?"

"We can have that later at home if we want to. Right now, I only want to be your wife. I talked to Pop last night, and he suggests we fight for an early release since he can take over your care at home. He's already been looking up information on a prosthesis. You can get the style that's right for you, and it's not a peg leg. You can be walking around as if you still had that leg."

"Tomorrow, huh?"

She grinned and nodded.

"Some wedding night we'll have."

She kissed him. "We'll make up for it later."

"I have my uniform here. I could wear that. But what will you wear?"

She smiled. "You're not supposed to see me until the time, but I packed a nice dress."

"Excuse me. Am I too early?"

Hannah jumped and turned.

Chaplain Wells stood next to a tiny older woman holding a clipboard to her chest.

"You're right on time. Tomorrow afternoon is good."

The chaplain grinned and stuck out his hand to Ted. "Chaplain Wells, Corporal Bauer. Can you be ready to be wheeled to the chapel by two o'clock tomorrow afternoon?"

Ted laughed. "I've got nowhere else to be. He shook the chaplain's hand, then took hold of Hannah's hand and looked her in the eyes. "We don't even have wedding rings. Can you?"

She nodded. "I can, but how will I know the right size for you?"

He leaned over and opened the drawer in the bedside table and lifted out a box. "There's a ring in here I've been wearing. Take it."

She opened the box and gasped at the pins and medals. "You earned all these?"

"Yeah, but the only one that matters is the wedding ring you'll be buying."

The chaplain cleared his throat. "You two must fill out this form immediately to make the 24-hour deadline by tomorrow afternoon. I'll take care of getting them approved and will bring the license to the chapel tomorrow." He handed Hannah the clipboard with a form and a fountain pen under the clip.

Hannah skimmed the form and filled in her information, then signed it and handed it to Ted.

He studied the form as if it were a law school test.

"Ted, the chaplain is waiting."

"I'm still reading it. I want to know what I'm signing."

She sighed. "Two years of law school doesn't make you a lawyer yet. Please fill out your portion and sign it." He laughed and took the pen, "While I'm writing, there's money in an envelope in the drawer. Use some to pay for your wedding ring, the chaplain, and the license."

She pulled out a couple of one-dollar bills for the license and enough to cover her ring and a stipend for the chaplain. She knew better than to object.

After the chaplain and the woman left with the completed form, she leaned in and giggled. "Can you believe it?"

"No, but I'm loving it all and loving you." He kissed her. "I was foolish to think I couldn't marry you. I love you, Hannah Murphy. I'll see you tomorrow at two." He grabbed her hand and called out to the guy in the next bed. "Hey, Woodward. I'm getting married tomorrow."

The man gave a hearty laugh. "I know. I was here the whole time." He looked at Hannah. "How'd you get such a pretty lady?"

"Just blessed, my friend. Just blessed."

CHAPTER FORTY-SIX

At the hotel a short time later, Hannah called home. When Mama answered, she blurted out. "Ted and I are getting married tomorrow afternoon. Oh, Mama, I wish you and Pop were here."

"My sweet girl, we've been wondering what you decided. Your father and I both wish we could be there, and Louise too. But we understand, and we're praying this helps to get him home sooner and under your father's care. What time is the wedding?"

"Two o'clock, Eastern Time. I have to shop for our wedding bands now. I hope the one nice dress I brought is suitable."

"Which dress did you take?"

The moss green long-sleeved one that comes to several inches above my ankles. I have the black pumps with me. It's not the wedding I dreamed of, but I'm marrying the man I love with all my heart. Can you believe it? The next time you see me, I'll be married."

They said their goodbyes, and she took the dress out of the closet and slipped it on with the black shoes. Relieved she had until tomorrow and could have it pressed, she twirled around the room, the full skirt raising in the air, and sang out, "I'm getting married, I'm getting married."

The phone rang, and she scurried across the room and answered it.

"Is this Miss Murphy?"

"Yes."

"The lady who is getting married tomorrow in the hospital chapel?"

She giggled. "Yes, that's me."

"This is Elsa Gillespie, the chaplain's secretary. He asked me to tell you that the hospital has arranged for you and Corporal Bauer to spend the night in the Admiral's suite here at the hospital. Be sure to pack an overnight bag. Oh, and Chaplain Wells is sending a car to pick you up at your hotel at one-thirty tomorrow afternoon."

Hannah blinked away her tears. "Oh my, thank you so much. I'm overwhelmed with the kindness everyone is showing."

"With Christmas a few days away, we're all in the Christmas spirit. It's the lift we all needed with so many war injuries filling our beds. Do you have a lot to do yet?"

"I'm about to shop for both our wedding bands."

"Do you know what store you're going to?"

"Gelfand's Jewelry across the street from the Dunhurst where I'm staying."

"I'll give them a call and ask to have men's and women's wedding bands ready for you to look at."

As Hannah walked across the street, large snowflakes floated around her. She tilted her head back and let them melt on her face. A kiss from heaven on this beautiful day. She approached Gelfand's Jewelers and stepped inside.

A short, balding man with a gray mustache scurried up. "You must be Miss Murphy."

She stamped the snow off her boots. "Yes, I am."

"Sid Gelfand at your service. Please step over to the counter.

I've been waiting for you." He moved behind a glass counter where a tray of bands was already placed. "You want to see both men's and women's bands. Is that correct?"

"Yes." She took Ted's ring from her purse. "I have this ring of the groom's for sizing."

"That helps a lot. Do you want gold for him or white gold?"

She removed her ring and handed it to him. "Here's my engagement ring, and I'll be wanting a white gold band to match it. Let's make his the same."

"Ah, good choice. He lifted several white gold rings from the display and set them against a dark velvet background. "Anyone of these would be suitable."

She studied the rings and picked one up. "This one looks nice. How much is it?"

He told her the price. "It's the most expensive of the three. Is that okay?"

She slid it onto her thumb and visualized it on his ring finger. "Yes, it's fine." She handed it back to him.

He held it up against Ted's ring and smiled. "Perfect. It needs no resizing. Now, for your ring." He turned and lifted a similar tray from a counter behind him and set it in front of her. He chose a ring and held it against her ring. "This one complements your engagement ring nicely with the tiny baguettes across the top. Put it on, and see how it looks."

Hannah slid the ring onto her finger, then added the engagement ring. She held up her hand. "Oh. Mr. Gelfand, it's perfect. And it's the right size, too. What a blessing. How much is it?"

When she heard the price, her heart fell. "He gave me two hundred dollars for my ring. I'm sure he can bring the balance to you another day."

He frowned. "Your new husband, he was wounded in the war. Correct?"

"Yes. He lost his leg when his plane was shot down."

He smiled so wide a gold tooth gleamed back at her. "Tell

him Sid Gelfand paid for the ring. It's my thank you to him for sacrificing a leg for our freedom."

Her mouth fell open. "Oh no, he'll want to pay."

"Then tell him to give the money to someone less fortunate." He gathered the rings. "I'll be right back."

He stepped through a door, and Hannah whispered, "Thank you, Lord, Another blessing from you."

Mr. Gelfand returned carrying two ring boxes and a small black bag. He opened the lids to reveal the rings she'd chosen. "Okay?"

"Yes. Very okay."

He closed the boxes, then slipped them into the black velvet bag and closed it with a drawstring. He handed it to her. "I wish you God's blessing on your new married life."

December 20, 1918

Pleased to have Edgar, the orderly who'd been pushing his chair all week, to wheel him to the ceremony, Ted slid his arms into his uniform jacket Edgar held out, surprised at how much weight he'd lost since he last wore it. These past months had taken a toll. He'd lost all his muscle tone. At least he was able to get the jacket and pants pressed that morning.

His mother had called a couple of hours ago, and he couldn't wait to see Hannah's face when she saw her surprise. It would be a magnificent day.

He knotted his tie and stuffed the last of his overnight items in the knapsack someone loaned him, along with a pair of casual pants and an open-collared shirt. Since tomorrow was Saturday and his sessions only took place on weekdays, he wasn't due back in the ward tomorrow until noon and would change into his hospital garb a few minutes before someone came for him.

When he heard that in the spirit of Christmas, the hospital

was providing them with the Admiral's suite for the wedding night, he was dumbfounded. A whole night sleeping next to his bride. He chuckled. He doubted he'd get much sleep. He glanced at the wall clock. One-forty-five already. He looked up at Edgar. "Let's go. I don't want to be late for my own wedding."

"Then we'd better be on our way." Edgar grinned like a jack-o-lantern.

Ted laughed. "Where did you get that bow tie, Edgar. Bend down here and let me straighten it out."

The young man leaned down. "Someone loaned it to me."

Ted fiddled with the bow, tugging it one way and the other. "So, you're staying for the ceremony?"

"Yes, sir. Those are my orders. Then I'm to whisk you upstairs to that fancy suite."

Satisfied with his work, Ted grinned.

The orderly glanced around and made a face.

"What's wrong?"

"I was to bring your crutches, but they're not here. Maybe someone else took them." He began pushing him out of the ward as the men applauded and shouted out their best wishes, including one whose voice rose above the others. "Lucky you, Bauer, getting to be with your bride tonight instead of us."

Edgar brought the chair to a stop at the elevator and hit the down button. "I assume your bride is that pretty lady who visited the past couple of days."

"Yes, that's she." A thought popped into his mind. Not the usual way of doing things, but then nothing about this wedding was usual. "You're a good man, Edgar. I don't think I have a best man. How would you like to do the honors?"

The man's eyes widened. "I'd be happy to. What does a best man do?"

"He holds onto the ring until it's time to say my vows. I don't have the ring yet. Hannah is bringing it."

"Hannah?"

"Yes. My bride."

"Oh, that would be Miss Murphy."

"For a few more minutes, yes."

"And then she'll be Mrs. Bauer." Here's the elevator. "Let's get you down there."

HANNAH STOOD out of view of the chapel entrance.

Elsa, the chaplain's secretary, waited with her, peeking around the corner for the signal that Ted was inside the chapel. She turned and looked at Hannah. "Nothing yet, but it's not quite two o'clock."

The faint sound of heels tapping on the tile floor from down the hall filled the air. The taps became louder until a woman swept around the corner wearing one of the newer length dresses that stopped mid-calf in a soft cranberry color. A pretty lady of medium height with a straight blonde bob that gave her a striking appearance, she looked at Hannah. "I'd know you anywhere, Hannah. You're a near image of your mother. I'm Sophie Watson, your mother's friend from college. I live in D.C. now, and Mo called to tell me you were getting married today, and would I please stand-in for her. I'm sorry, I'm late. The snow has traffic snarled, and it was hard hiring a car." She took a breath, "I'm talking way too fast." She stepped back and looked at Hannah. "You look lovely. Your mother explained the circumstances, and I'm so grateful I could help."

Hannah took the woman's extended hand in her own. "Thank you so much, Mrs. Watson. Mama has mentioned you many times. You don't know how much this means to me. My best friend is still serving the Army in France as a telephone operator, and with it being such short notice …"

"Please call me, Sophie."

"I'd be honored to, Thank you."

Sophie handed her a gift that was wrapped in white paper and festooned with a large white and silver bow. "This is from your mother. She was concerned you only had your flannel nightgown with you. A woman wants something pretty to sleep in with her new husband beside her."

Hannah smiled. "I was bothered by that a little." She removed the bow and fancy paper and lifted the lid on the box. She separated the tissue paper and gasped. "It's beautiful." She slid her fingertips under the garment's dainty straps and lifted the pale blue satin gown up high. "Much better than my flannel."

"I'd say so," Elsa said. "Now, all you need is a bouquet."

"I almost forgot." Sophie reached for the shopping bag she'd set on the floor and pulled out a bouquet of red roses. "I stopped at a florist on the way here." She handed the blooms to Hannah. "Your mother said you love red roses."

She breathed in the scent and grinned. "They're perfect."

"I take it you have no maid of honor?"

Hannah shook her head. "I hadn't even thought of that. Don't tell me you have one in that bag."

"I don't, but I can be your matron of honor if you'll have me."

"Yes, of course." She handed the bouquet to Elsa, then pulled the velvet bag from her tote and handed it to Sophie. My ring is in the black box, and Ted's is in the maroon one. Can you give his to whoever is standing up for him?"

"Of course. I'll be right back. The sound of her heels faded as she scurried away.

Elsa looked at Hannah. "She's your mother and maid of honor all in one package. That gown is gorgeous,"

"I've never met her, but Mama mentions her often when she tells tales of her college days before she met my father."

Elsa ran her gaze over Hannah. "You're stunning in that dress."

"I hope so. I have several others at home that would have

been better suited. I never thought I'd be getting married on this trip."

Sophie came around the corner. "Hannah, the chaplain had something come up and the ceremony has been delayed about fifteen minutes."

Hannah let go of a sigh. "What's an extra fifteen minutes when you've been waiting to marry the man for over a year?"

Your groom looks very handsome in his uniform. He peeked at the ring he's to give you and said to give you this." She made a thumbs up gesture.

Hannah giggled. I guess he thinks I did a good job picking my ring out. Did he look at his ring too?"

"No, I gave it to the best man. He didn't see it."

She raised her brows. "I didn't know he had a best man."

"It's the hospital orderly who brought him down in the wheelchair."

Hannah's love for Ted grew even more. "I wonder if it's the same fellow he had yesterday."

Sophie crossed her arms and paced a circle.

"Why are you so antsy, Sophie? I'm the one who should be pacing."

Mama's friend stopped and shook her head. "Silly, isn't it? I get this way at all weddings."

Running footfalls sounded, coming closer.

Hannah looked at Elsa. "There must be an emergency."

The footfalls slowed, and Pop appeared carrying a large box. He caught his breath and grinned at Hannah. "Sorry I'm late. The snow—"

"Pop!" Hannah dropped her bouquet and fell into her father's open arms. "How did you get here so fast?"

"I caught the last train out of Chicago yesterday afternoon and arrived in D.C. a couple of hours ago. I hired a car to bring me here, but the snow is causing major traffic snarls. I couldn't let my daughter get married without my giving her away." He handed her the box. Your mother sent this dress. It was hers when we were married." He glanced at Sophie. "Sophie, thanks for helping me pull this off." He gave her a side hug. "Did you bring shoes?"

Sophie grinned. "Hi, Nate. I was getting a little nervous. She reached in her bag and pulled out a pair of white heels."

Hannah looked from her father to Sophie. "Wait, you knew my dad was coming?"

Sophie grinned. "Yes, and I loved every minute of it. Let's get into the restroom over there and get you changed."

A few minutes later, Hannah stared at her reflection in the ladies' room mirror and ran her fingertips over the lacy yoke. "I'm amazed at how well the dress looks after almost twenty-five years."

"And it's as beautiful as the day your mother got married. There's one more thing in here. She reached into her bag and lifted out a lacy veil. Your mother's didn't survive the years as well as her dress did. I brought you mine. She attached the flowing veil to the back of Hannah's head. I wish we had a photographer. You look gorgeous."

I'll let the chaplain know we're ready to start. He knew about it too, this was the real delay."

Hannah stepped out of the room, and Pop walked up, his eyes misting over. "I can't believe how much you look like your mother did on our wedding day. You are a vision." He tightened his tie and tugged at his suit jacket. Do I look like I've been on a train all night?"

She giggled. "Maybe a little, but you're here, and that's all that matters."

He kissed her on the cheek. "Are you ready?"

She took her bouquet from Elsa. "I think my heart has calmed enough that I can walk."

She slipped her hand around his bent elbow. "I'm ready if you are."

Elsa took a step into the hall, and Sophie walked behind her, followed by Hannah and Pop.

Hannah sniffed her bouquet and smiled up at Pop. "The scent is almost like it would have been if this were a summer wedding at Safe Refuge."

He grinned. "You are so right."

Sophie and Elsa stepped inside the chapel, and Hannah waited beside Pop. Only a few more minutes and she'd be married.

Elsie reappeared. "It's time. Don't keep your groom waiting."

Hannah and Pop stepped inside the door. Surprised at how many people filled the chairs, she spotted Ted immediately, his grin as wide as ever. And he was standing? Then she noticed the crutches he leaned on. His chair sat nearby. She didn't take her eyes from his face until she arrived beside him and he took her hand. "Hello, my beautiful bride, were you surprised to see your dad here?" He ran his gaze over her. "Where did you get that beautiful dress?"

"Pop brought it on the train. It was my mother's. I'm so happy. I love you, Ted."

He squeezed her hand. "I love you, too." He wobbled but regained his balance. "I'm still not used to these crutches," he whispered. Edgar pushed the wheelchair closer, and Ted waved him away.

The chaplain smiled at Ted. "Take your time. We can wait."

Ted nodded. "I'm fine."

The chaplain opened a little black book, then looked out past Hannah and Ted. "Dearly beloved, we are gathered here to witness the uniting of Theodore Bauer and Hannah Murphy in holy matrimony. Who gives this woman to be married to this man?"

"Her mother and I do." Pop placed Hannah's hand in Ted's and stepped back to an empty chair.

After a short meditation and prayer, Chaplain Wells asked

Ted to take Hannah's hand. Edgar handed him the band, and he slid the ring on her finger. He repeated the vows, never taking his dark eyes off Hannah. She felt as though her heart would burst. Then Sophie handed Hannah the ring for Ted. She slipped it onto his finger, and he winked as if to say he liked her choice. She repeated her vows their gazes intertwined the whole time.

The chaplain looked from Ted to Hannah. "Insofar as you have both vowed to love, honor, and cherish each other until death do you part, I now pronounce you husband and wife. Ted, you may kiss your bride."

Ted leaned toward her and kissed her softly then pressed his forehead against hers. "I love you, Hannah Murphy Bauer."

The chaplain motioned for them to face the people. With Edgar's help to keep Ted balanced they turned. She surveyed the smiling faces, most unfamiliar except for Pop, Sophie and Elsa.

"Special guests, please come forward to greet Corporal and Mrs. Ted Bauer." A dozen or so people stood and approached them. Ted knew a few, but the only people Hannah knew were the ones she'd met that day.

The nurse who told Hannah she had to leave yesterday came last. "I've already checked the suite, and everything looks good for Ted's stay there tonight." She looked at Hannah. "He's not been enthusiastic about using the crutches. Maybe you can get him on board. Edgar will take you to the suite when you're ready."

Ted looked at Hannah. "Is there anything else we need to do?"

"We need to sign the license along with our witnesses, and then we're on our own."

Pop came up and hugged Hannah and shook hands with Ted. "Ted, Maureen, and I are so pleased to have you as our son."

Ted nodded. "And I'm pleased to be a part of the family. I promise to take good care of Hannah."

"I know you will. I have an appointment with your doctors in an hour and hope to set the wheels in motion to get you released to my care. From what I understand, they think you'll be well enough to travel by Monday. If we can get on a train for Chicago that day, we can be home for Christmas."

"Maureen is readying the downstairs bedroom and bath in the big house for you two until we can prepare the cottage." He hugged Hannah again.

After they'd signed the license, Pop walked with them to the elevator with Edgar pushing Ted's chair. When they arrived, Pop kissed Hannah on the cheek. "I'll see you tomorrow."

At the suite door, Ted looked up at Hannah. "Aren't I supposed to carry you inside? I can't do that, but if you sit on my lap, I can wheel you through."

She handed Edgar the crutches she'd been carrying and lowered herself onto his lap. Making sure to put most of her weight on his right leg, she wrapped her arm around his neck.

"Okay, Edgar, give us a push," Ted said with a grin.

"Yes sir." Edgar pushed them over the threshold. "See you at noon tomorrow." He set the crutches against the wall and closed the door behind him as he left.

Hannah grinned. "Alone at last." She kissed him soundly, and they let the kiss linger awhile. Ted glanced around. "This is quite a room."

The telephone rang, and they both jumped. "It's probably a wrong number." Ted rolled both of them to the nightstand and answered it. "Yes, put her through." He looked at Hannah. "It's your mother. Hi, Mrs. Murphy. What's that? Oh. Okay. Maureen, it is from now on. Yes, Nate made it in time, and we're married. Hannah's right here. We've been riding my chair around this huge room. She's on my lap." He handed her the receiver.

"Hi Mama."

"Hi, Hannah. Are Louise and I interrupting anything?"

"We've only been here a few minutes. I'm glad you called. Pop really surprised us. It was wonderful having him here to give me away and wearing your dress made it so special. What a surprise you pulled off with Sophie's help. Pop's meeting now with Ted's doctors."

"I can't believe I'm old enough to have a married daughter. Just don't go making me a grandmother too fast."

Hannah laughed. "I've only been married for about two hours. If you don't want grandchildren too fast, you shouldn't have had Sophie give me that beautiful nightgown."

Ted's brows rose into perfect arches. She whispered, "I'll explain later."

Mama laughed, "You know I'm kidding. It's all in God's time."

"I know. I hope we can get Ted on a train by Monday."

"It's already decided we won't be having Christmas until we're all together. When does Ted have to be back in the ward?"

"He has an appointment with his counselor at noon, and I can go with him."

"Louise is about to wrestle this phone away from me."

She glanced at Ted. "Your mother is coming to the phone."

He nodded and kissed the tip of her nose.

A rustling sound came through the connection. "Hello, dear. Now I can really call you daughter. I'm so happy you two did this. Is your husband nearby?"

"Yes, my husband is right here." She grinned and handed him the phone. "Go ahead and hang up when you're through. I'll be in the other room."

She crossed to the bathroom, shut the door, and bowed her head. "Thank you, God, for blessing us so much. Please help me to be the best wife I can be for Ted. Help me to keep from making decisions on my own. I'm not alone anymore. You've given me a good man. He's to be the spiritual leader of our home, and his faith is strong."

A rap came at the door, and she jumped. "Hannah, is everything okay?"

She opened the door, surprised to see him standing with the crutches. "I thought you didn't want to use those."

"That was before I heard you talking."

"I was praying for our marriage and for me to be the best wife I can be for you."

He kissed her. "You are already doing that, my love. Now tell me about this nightgown you have and how it might lead us to giving your mother a grandchild."

EPILOGUE

Six Years Later

Hannah opened the door to T. H. Bauer Attorney at Law and tugged at her five-year-old daughter's hand. "Come on, Gracie. Daddy doesn't have a lot of time for us to dawdle." The curly-haired strawberry blond girl ran past her mother, then Hannah pushed the wicker stroller through the door.

Joan Bronson, the office receptionist and secretary, jumped up from her seat and came around the desk. She hunched down and looked the little girl in her eyes. "Hello, little Gracie, how are you today?"

Gracie grinned. "I'm doing well, how are you?"

Joan looked up at Hannah. "She sounds so grown up."

Hannah laughed. "Sounding and acting are two different things."

Joan stood and peered into the stroller. "And how is little Rory?" She chucked the almost one-year-old boy under his chin, and he giggled. "He's the spitting image of his dad."

"Who's the spitting image of me?" Ted came into the room,

305

and, as always, the sight of her husband sent Hannah's pulse racing. He went down on his right knee and held his arms open to his daughter. "Come here, sweet Gracie, and give your daddy a hug and kiss. I've missed you since I left home this morning."

The little girl stepped into his embrace. "I missed you too, Daddy." She wrapped her arms around his neck, and he gave her a big noisy smooch on her neck, sending her into a fit of giggles. He released her and used a corner of Joan's desk to push himself to his feet, putting all the weight on his right leg. He looked at Hannah. "Your mother isn't here yet. Did she say she was running late?"

Hannah shook her head. "She's probably in deep conversation with someone and lost track of time.

The door behind Hannah opened. Gracie ran to her grandmother and hugged her legs. "Hi, Granny."

Mama ran a hand over Gracie's hair. "Hi, yourself. Are you ready to come home with me for the rest of the day?"

"Can we go swimming?"

"No, but we can turn on the hose, and you can run through the water. Your granny isn't up to going down to the dock."

Hannah frowned. "Are you okay, Mama?"

Her mother waved a hand. "I'm doing okay for someone who's going to be fifty on her next birthday, Do I have to take the stroller too?"

"Leave it here," Ted said. "We'll bring it home later."

After they got the children settled in Mama's car. Hannah followed Ted into his office and shut the door. "I just came from Doctor Swanson's office."

His brows rose. "What were you doing there? Checking out your dad's competition?"

"I went as a patient a few days ago for some tests."

He gaped at her. "Tests? And you didn't tell me? Are you all right?"

"Nothing that won't be cured in about seven months." He stared at her. "Uh oh. How'd that happen?"

"Well, we already know how. As to the why let's put it this way. That old saying that when someone is nursing, they won't get pregnant is wrong. We can't blame it on the blue nightgown like we could Gracie or our delayed honeymoon like we can Rory."

His eyes twinkled. "Ah, and what a honeymoon that was." He pulled her into his arms and kissed her soundly.

"She leaned back and looked him in the eyes. We have one of each already. Do you want another son or another daughter to wrap you around her little finger?"

"All I want is a healthy baby that favors you and not me. You're the better looking one in our family."

"That is a matter of opinion. What do you think captured my heart when I first laid eyes on you?"

He grinned and kissed her. "It wasn't my scintillating personality?"

"Eventually, but before I was treated to that, you were a feast to behold."

"Me? A feast?" He frowned. "Why didn't you have the tests run at your dad's office?"

"Because I want him to be surprised at our announcement along with everyone else."

"What time is your appointment at the library?"

"In about fifteen minutes. I've decided to accept the appointment."

His brows rose. "Are you sure?"

"Yes. With our growing brood, being on the library board is enough to keep me sane and still make our family and home my top priority." She sighed. "Perhaps one of our children will attend law school and follow in your footsteps."

"Do you regret not finishing law school?"

"Not at all. One lawyer in the family is enough. I think

getting involved with the library is going to work out well for me. Who knows what will come of it in the future."

A knock came at the door, and Joan opened it. "Sorry to interrupt. Mr. Taylor is here."

Ted released Hannah from his embrace. "Thanks, Joan. We're done. Send him back."

She left, and Ted winked at Hannah. "Looks like we're fast outgrowing the cottage. Time to start looking for a new house."

Later that evening, they left the children in Margie's care at the cottage and Annie upstairs doing homework, then settled on Safe Refuge's veranda with apple pie left over from yesterday's Sunday dinner and coffee.

Hannah glanced at Ted. "Should I tell them, or do you want to?"

"I'll do it. Hannah has accepted a position on the Lake Geneva Library's board, and we're here to give notice that we'll be moving out of the cottage as soon as we find a new place to live."

Mama gasped. "Why? We love having you next door."

Hannah giggled. "It's going to be a bit crowded come seven months from now. Sorry, Mama, we're going to make you a grandmother again."

Pop held up a hand. "That's wonderful, but how is it I don't already know this? Did you get a test?"

"I was sneaky and went to Dr. Swanson, so you would be surprised at the same time as Mama. Don't worry, you'll still be our doctor."

Her father shook his head. "And surprise me, you did. Funny how things work out. The tenants in our house on Main Street gave notice yesterday they're moving in a month. The house would be perfect for you, and you could use the former doctor's office as your law office, Ted."

"Sounds good, Ted said. "How much is the rent?"

"You know we would prefer to not charge you anything. But

you need some equity built up, so let's negotiate a price, and you can pay monthly until it's paid for."

Ted took Hannah's hand. "What do you think, honey?"

She grinned. "I say yes. I love that house and would love to raise our family there. Besides that, it's across the street from the library. I won't have to go far to attend the board meetings."

Ted stuck out his hand to Pop. "Nate, you have a deal."

Later that night as Hannah snuggled up to Ted, spooning as they always did while falling asleep, she whispered. "Are you really okay buying the Main Street house from Pop?"

"Absolutely. It's a perfect solution. God is good."

"All the time." She answered as she slipped off to sleep.

THE END

When I decided to write the *Newport of the West* series, my main intent was to provide a picture of the rich history of my hometown, Lake Geneva, Wisconsin. What has emerged over the last three books is the secondary theme of strong women, who, through the decades, have shown their strengths in different ways. These characters weren't wholly products of my imagination but showed up as I read about the strong women of their generations. Hannah Murphy Bauer was no different in this book.

When I was in high school in Lake Geneva, I worked for the local telephone company as a telephone operator during the tourist season. When I first got the job, my grandfather—a lifelong employee of Ohio Bell—was excited I was to be a "hello girl." When switchboards and telephones first became common, telephone operators were often called "hello girls," because they would greet a caller who rang the switchboard with "hello." The nickname transcended to the operators working near the front in France and it stuck. I loved writing Clarice into the story, and it only seemed fitting she should become a "hello girl" given her background. I sometimes think she is interesting enough to garner her own story. But that will have to wait for another day.

As shown in my story, the U.S. Women's Land Army (WLA) had its roots in the U.K. When the U.S. declared war on Germany, the concept jumped the pond to New England where Hilda Loines spearheaded the idea. I took poetic license in this part of the story. Wisconsin and a number of other states never had the opportunity to establish a WLA because of the war's end. To the best of my knowledge, the Illinois WLA never sent farmettes to farms in Wisconsin as I portray in the story, but since the Lake Geneva area is very near to the Illinois state line I made it work.

One of the most unique facts I uncovered in my research was that on November 7, 1918, an announcement came that the war had ended. People danced in the streets, singing and blowing horns. The celebrations lasted well into the predawn hours and when people woke up a few hours later, news came that the announcement was a mistake and the fighting was not over. A summit meeting with the Germans had been planned to take place in France and a cease-fire for the local area where the German negotiators would have to cross the Western Front into France was arranged. Someone had misunderstood and thought it was a general ceasefire and announced the war was over. On November 11, 1918, the real armistice was signed and people celebrated all over again. Of course, I had to use that in the story. I found it amusing that a "fake news" story was a part of World War I.

The discrimination toward those of German descent shown in the story was very real. Unnaturalized Germans were sent to one of two internment camps and people with German last names bore a lot of bullying and mistreatment. My family name is really Meyer, not Meyers. My grandparents added the 's' to the name, hoping to make it sound less German. As I included in the book, my dad and his brother, who were children at the time, were dressed in WW I Army uniforms and told to walk around their neighborhood to show that the Meyer family was loyal to the U.S.

As in wars before World War I and since, war vets suffered a lot from PTSD (known then as shell shock). And many returned home as amputees. A few years ago, I wrote a novella about wounded warriors, and the things I learned then about PTSD and dealing with missing limbs helped me in writing about Ted's injuries. I love how research for one story has served in the writing of another.

I'll soon be delving into Book Four. I can't wait to write about the forties and home-front World War II.

Until then, God bless and happy reading!

Pam

Pamela has written most of her life, beginning with her first diary at age eight. Her novels include *Thyme For Love, Surprised by Love in Lake Geneva, Wisconsin (a reissue of Love Finds You in Lake Geneva, Wisconsin)*, a 1933 historical romance set in her hometown, and *Second Chance Love*, a contemporary romance set at a rodeo in rural Illinois. Her novella, *What Lies Ahead*, is included in *The Bucket List Dare* collection, and another novella, *If These Walls Could Talk*, was published in May 2017, in a collection called *Coming Home: A Tiny House Collection*. Future novels include *Whatever is True*, a sequel to Second Chance Love.

Safe Refuge

Newport of the West—Book One

In two days, wealthy Chicagoan, Anna Hartwell, will wed a man she loathes. She would refuse this arranged marriage to Lyman Millard, but the Bible clearly says she is to honor her parents, and Anna would do most anything to please her father–even leaving her teaching job at a mission school and marrying a man she doesn't love.

The Great Chicago Fire erupts, and Anna and her family escape with only the clothes on their backs and the wedding postponed. Father moves the family to Lake Geneva, Wisconsin, where Anna reconnects with Rory Quinn, a handsome immigrant who worked at the mission school. Realizing she is in love with Rory, Anna prepares to break the marriage arrangement with Lyman until she learns a dark family secret that changes her life forever.

Shelter Bay

Newport of the West—Book Two

Adventure girl, Maureen Quinn, isn't yet sure of her life's direction, but she knows she isn't cut out to be a bookkeeper for the town's undertaker. Wearing her stylish new bloomers, she suffers a bicycle accident in the middle of downtown and her long-time crush and fellow childhood mischief maker, Preston Stevens, comes to her rescue. He's back in the area and he couldn't have shown up at a better time. It isn't long before they become inseparable and she's sure he's the man God has for her.

Unlike his older brothers who are shackled to desk jobs at their father's financial services company, Preston yearns to see the world. What better person to do that with than Maureen? But after being expelled from Yale, because of a prank that brought embarrassment to the family, his dad has issued an ultimatum: Enlist in the military or join his brothers in the family business. He signs up with the U.S. Life Saving Service, a division of the Coast Guard, reasoning the time spent on the shores of Lake Michigan, keeping people safe, is far better than being stuck in a landlocked encampment. After his two-year stint, he intends to live out his dream of world travel before settling in Lake Geneva. But it isn't long before life-altering events occur affecting both his and Maureen's lives forever.

Returning to historic Lake Geneva for Book Two in the *Newport of the West* series, the Hartwell family saga continues through the life of Maureen Quinn, the daughter of Rory and Anna Quinn from *Safe Refuge*. Set mainly in beautiful Lake Geneva, *Shelter Bay* also carries the reader to the northern shore of Michigan and to the 1893 World's Fair in Chicago, also known as the Columbian Exposition.

Coming from Pamela S. Meyers in May 2021:

Rose Harbor

Book Four of the Newport of the West series.

Stay up-to-date on your favorite books and authors with our free e-newsletters.

ScriveningsPress.com